Shahrukh Husain, born and brought up in Pakistan, has studied myth and folklore from around the world for many years. She is the editor of *The Virago Book of Witches*, author of *Women Who Wear the Breeches*, several children's books and a play for children. She also works on film scripts and screenplays for various film companies. A practising psychotherapist, she is married with two children and lives in London.

Acknowledgments

As always, I want to thank my publisher, Lennie Goodings, for being so lovely about my work – also, in this instance, for being wonderfully patient when my technological aberration made me lose (irretrievably) 45 per cent of my manuscript, causing a long delay. Also to Sarah White – always good-natured and helpful. My brother, Aamer, for his comments on the finished manuscript, my dear friend, Mary Ann Hushlak, for the timely prods and large doses of care and comfort. To Christopher for all the bibliographical titbits he put my way and to Samira for always being prepared to listen and comment with her prodigious erudition about all things associated with writing and storytelling. All of you made the task lighter, more fun and truly worthwhile. I hope the result will be as enjoyable for you as the process was for me.

Temptresses

The Virago Book of Evil Women

SHAHRUKH HUSAIN

A *Virago* Book

Published by Virago Press 2000
First published by Virago Press 1998

Copyright © Shahrukh Husain

The moral right of the author has been asserted

All rights reserved.
No part of this publication may be reproduced, stored in
a retrieval system, or transmitted in any form or by any
means, without the prior permission in writing of the
publisher, nor be otherwise circulated in any form of
binding or cover other than that in which it is published
and without a similar condition including this condition
being imposed on the subsequent purchaser.

A CIP catalogue record for this book is
available from the British Library

ISBN 1 86049 563 X

Typeset in Horley by M Rules
Printed and bound in Great Britain by
Clays Ltd, St Ives plc

Virago Press
A Division of
Little, Brown and Company (UK)
Brettenham House
Lancaster Place
London WC2E 7EN

Contents

For Safinaz
. . . need I say more?

Introduction

Wicked women have featured in stories since the beginning of recorded history. Every culture has them. They are terrifying and fascinating. The source of their power is the dark ruthlessness which connects them irrevocably to the Female Omnipotent. Religions have frequently branded them witches and temptresses.

Who were these women? What were their origins? Were they really as fiendish as we have come to believe? Perhaps they are the vessels of our own inner darkness, our personal potential for evil. And it is precisely because the illusion of their evil comes from ourselves that they acquire the immediacy and power that has survived through the centuries. Today when society is attempting to reassess its general attitudes, it is appropriate to look afresh at stories of demonic women.

In order to free them from centuries of exile we need to look at them in the context of the other story in which they are wound up; a long, varied and multicultural narrative which generates and frames their tales. It is the story of the power struggle between the genders. When certain men such as the Indo-Europeans and Semites of ancient worlds found their universe dominated by powerful women who were both uncontrollable and unpredictable, they invented alternative theologies which were best served if these forceful females could be made to 'be fruitful and multiply' – that is, to concentrate on motherhood and stay well away from all else which was now male territory. The fantasy was that, harnessed to men, wilful women would learn to defer to them and procreate for the survival of their kind. Thus female potential would be reduced to the single function of motherhood and all desire, sexual and personal, would gradually be relegated to the dominion of husband and son. A woman would participate in sex to pleasure the one and incubate the other, while her personal ambition would consist of sustaining and serving them both and preparing them for the world. The fantasy was close to being fulfilled but for the occasional wilful woman who flouted the rules and thumbed her nose at authority, subverting the establishment in the process.

I make no secret of my fascination with these subversive women. The ones in this book have been at my elbow for years, urging me to tell their stories. Four qualities loom large in their make-up: disobedience; ambition; independence; sexuality. They are the daunting, intriguing temptresses of myth, legend and religious literature. Denizens of the Bible, Romance and European fairytales, they have goaded me persistently to bring them out of their dark corners and into the limelight.

Their close link with evil is entirely illogical, apparently resting on the fact that each woman in some way makes the choice to transgress a social taboo, either because she selected, like Lamia and Granya, an inappropriate partner, or like Sheba, Medea and Morgan an unsuitable occupation, activity or alliance, or then again like Eve, Lilith or Melusine, an unbecoming course of action. By disregarding the basic precepts of society, such women often brought about destruction and in so doing bonded with death. This engendered the twofold image of mother and demon, the creative and destructive sources, in one body. Perhaps it was to escape the potency and apparent ruthlessness of such women that men like Gilgamesh, hero of the first surviving epic, set out in quest of immortality. This continual preoccupation of Man with finding a means to elude death may in turn have given rise to the concept of the soul as an eternal entity of divine or parthenogenic conception which minimised the role of woman to the mere container of the child.

Here lies the anomaly at the heart of male psychology. Men are simultaneously petrified and enthralled by woman's dual capacity for ruthlessness and nurturing. When, in the process of confining women to motherhood, men infantilise themselves, they are left with two alternatives: they can control women by belittling them or demonise them to justify their fear. And so another set of stories is written depicting women as progressively more evil, then repeated to perpetuate their notoriety down the generations. It is time now to write them again with the benefit of hindsight and the reams of research, theory and argument that have proliferated through the centuries.

In this book I have taken the threads from various, pre-existing traditions and extended, dramatised and emphasised some of them. Others I have quarrelled with or queried. Largely I have resisted invention, except in the case of Lamia where the mythos is lost and I have had to create a scenario almost from scratch. Let us take a brief look at the 'facts' of the individual cases. When the viewpoint changes, so do the perspectives on reality and truth.

Lilith possessed me more than almost any of the others. Her history is a long and complex one. An ecclesiastic battle was waged against her and in defence of God, which continued for centuries. She not only disobeyed his laws by demanding equality in Eden, but actually tricked him into letting her live free on earth. And like the most savage of defenders in a rape case, the holy fathers subjected her to the worst kind of defamation over the years. But, to my mind, they failed to prove their worst accusation – child-killing. During my research I discovered some folktales in which Lilith appears to be a threat to children. However, here she has obviously become cognate with local nature-witch figures since the stories have a distinctly regional, folksy flavour cut off from the richly mythic biblical one in which she originates and thrives.

Melusine has always haunted me. Even more than some of the other women in this book she seems an 'outsider' trapped between mortal and fairy worlds. It struck me as so unfair, when I first read her tale all those years ago, that her mother should punish her so severely and for so long simply for trying to help. I tried to imagine the impact of her mother's ambivalence on Melusine; other than that I have followed the fairytale quite faithfully.

Sheba is portrayed in tradition as perhaps the greatest *femme fatale* of all time. Looking at the various accounts of her tale, it appears that she is mainly at fault for enjoying her sovereignty, for questioning Solomon's reputation as a wise man and for being a pagan. Her testing of Solomon implies that she wanted to assert her own supremacy. That was probably what stuck in the patriarchal gullet.

Medea's name instantly evokes the archetypal image of evil even though most of us remember her from our schooldays as Jason's helper in his quest for the Golden Fleece. This could be because she betrayed her father and killer her brother (though most children's versions are sanitised and do not mention the fratricide). But it is more likely because she is a skilled magician, a witch. Here I have picked up the thread when her marriage to Jason ends. Medea is another 'outsider' – dark, enigmatic, outlandish, she has travelled from Colchos (today's Georgia) to the Hellenic lands of blond, blue-eyed Greeks and her ways have never quite been accepted.

Granya breaks two of the strongest social taboos when she chooses the occasion of her betrothal feast to coerce the groom's close friend to elope with her. And once she has succeeded in sinking in the proverbial claws, she never lets go. Is it ego or stubbornness – or does she enjoy the havoc triggered by her act? She has been described as the Celtic Eve because of her lust for Forbidden Fruit – and she audaciously indulges every temptation to the very end.

Lamia was clearly a pre-Hellenic figure who won her place in Greek mythology because, like many other goddesses of conquered nations, she had somehow to be co-opted into the pantheon of the current rulers. Thus her own mythos was supplanted by the surviving fragment pertaining to her relationship with Zeus. All we know about her apart from her slightly confused genealogy, is that she incurred Hera's wifely wrath because Zeus kept trying to impregnate her. I have tried to imagine what her life was like after she became entangled with warring divinities.

Morgan Le Fay posed a problem for most of the early chroniclers of Arthurian romance. She was originally a Celtic sovereignty goddess whose function was to keep the divinely ordained king on his toes. Sir Thomas Malory construes this as hostility and makes her a witch in his fragmentary, episodic and unsatisfying account, *Le Morte D'Arthur*. But he never explains the reason for either her hostility or her subsequent support. I have tried to return coherence to Morgan's role in Arthur's life by weaving together the strands from various traditional narratives. I hope I have succeeded in relocating her in the authentic context.

Eve in Eden always makes me think of a non-conformist living in a smug, conventional suburb. She needs a subversive friend – or a therapist – to encourage her to make the choices that will free her from her prison. The serpent was the ideal choice. It is present in many of the tales of creation and is often seen with the Goddesses of Creation at the beginning of the world. Since Eve comes from the same mould as the ancient Creatrix it seemed an appropriate confidante.

In each of these stories, the bad reputation of the woman far overshadows the extend of her deeds. But even though she is outrageous rather than truly wicked, there is no doubt that she upends the safe little patriarchal set-up. Common themes of the tales are power and defeminisation; female monarchy; challenge to male supremacy; regicide, patricide and child-killing; well-defined sexual appetites and the demand for sexual equality linked with deformity of the lower regions – bird talons, hooves and snake-tails; theriomorphism.

Wilful, in the case of such a woman, comes to mean wicked. She is believed to have lost the ability to love and nurture in her lust for sex and power. Her appearance alters to expose her inner, bestial nature, frequently that of a nocturnal creature (Lilith the screech-owl; Lamia and Melusine the snake-women). She acquires a demonic ancestry (Sheba's mother was a jinn). Her fondness for riddling conveys her underhand character and the desire to trap and humiliate. She mothers monsters.

Her qualities and actions strike at the very core of patriarchal religion and its commitment to the survival of certain beliefs. Consequently, the traditional device of the patriarch has been to demonise and degrade such women by continuously associating them with evil. Such a woman must at all costs be disempowered, or she could, like the wild and ruthless ancient goddesses and queens, destroy the patriarchal system altogether. Degraded to a demon, she is deprived of the power to corrupt the women of subsequent generations.

But even the sustained effort of centuries could not suppress her magnetism. When we were susceptible to the propaganda we were tantalised by her: the illicit pleasure of her way of being enthralled and terrified us. Now, when we disregard the old agenda, we are profoundly inspired: she entices us to rise above preset boundaries, lures us to what we can find of her qualities within ourselves. For me, every one of these women, in her unique way, is the quintessential temptress – she draws us irresistibly.

Shahrukh Husain

Lilith

Bring out the cups — you see this spell on them? It'll keep Lilith away. Keep Lilith away! Keep Lilith away! The chant resonates, echoes, begins again. Lilith will be hovering, ready to take the child as it slips, wrenched from its mother's womb, into the world. Beware the screech-owl condemned by Isaiah. Is she an owl, then, who carries away little creatures in the deep of night, in claws like a vice? But look she's there again, in a picture this time — etched into the cortex of a bowl — all stick legs and scratched cheeks, hair scraggy, eyes baggy, waiting to suck you into her vortex. And here she's twining around the Tree of Knowledge wearing Satan's face, nudging Eve's arm into that last little thrust that caused the sweet, plump flesh of the apple to explode against Man's teeth and release its bud-bursting juices. Screech-owl, serpent, demon, devil-woman, bitch — which is she?

Oh, how the books confuse you, like the pictures and scriptures and tales, like birds at war, chattering and wittering and chirruping without telling anything. But through the confusions about who she really was, what she actually did, one message resounds loud and clear: she is the embodiment of humankind's fear. Lilith is lethal. Lilith corrupts. Keep away the serpent woman. Let the child live. Keep out Lilith.

Some say that she is evil as the night. The one who visits children after dark. She tickles them and jokes and makes them laugh. Is she Lilith the secret friend? Lilith who banishes the terrifying, devouring monsters which parents create for their babes: bogeymen, night-fiends, harpies. Lilith of the Night, all naked and gold and tawny with the light from her flaming hair. She catches the wasted howls of the tormented babes in her widespread arms, weaves them into gossamer memories for the future. She comforts them and orders away the monsters, whispering that these creatures only come to fill the empty corners and stand guard over their fears. Fears, she says, are man-made – unreal: if you know that, they vanish.

In the morning when mothers come in and soothe the nape of their infants' necks, feeling for the tangled tufts that Lilith is said to leave, they murmur: 'It's smooth, Lilith wasn't here.' And they smile smugly and pat the talisman on the baby's cradle. 'It kept away Lilith,' they say. But the speechless babes know better: they crow and wink and their parents smile indulgently, putting their toothless grins down to 'wind'.

Lilith's laughter fills the minds of the babies. And the tone and twist and curve of the laugh becomes set in their minds so that some part of their laughter sings and harmonises with hers ever after. It says: *I like Lilith. I'll be like Lilith. I'll summon her when they tell me to be ashamed. I'll do as she did, up there in Eden, when the Powerful One would not give way to her. I will. And the next time Father raises his hand to me because I've upset my little brother, I'll bring Lilith into me and I'll bite his hand. Lilith wouldn't let anyone strike her.*

Lilith is the scourge of the honourable. Lilith rides men at night. Lilith is corruption. Lilith is evil incarnate. Lilith? She's shameless.

And does her depravity disturb her? No, not Lilith – she denies she's depraved, blames Divinity for death, exults in her banishment. She refuses, she says, to carry the darkness of others. The darkness of others! All that is eclipsed and evil and corrupt is in Lilith herself. Once, may the Devil's ears be deaf, she even dared to outmanoeuvre the Powerful One . . .

It was how it had to be. But the aeons have garbled the events. Or the truth is mixed with the thoughts of the tellers: there have been so many, these prophets – each with his own view, an imagined shame to hide, a presumed crime to be punished. They pile misapprehension on misunderstanding and the misguided desire to draw attention away from a truth that might disgrace their deity. Instead of clarifying, they obfuscate, try to redirect blame. They vilify and demonise and make ineffectual efforts to transform the truth. But what do they really know of the Powerful One? Or of the beginning of his world?

They say no one can recall the exact moment of birth but Lilith remembers. She sighs, sending a sinuous movement through the trees and clouds outside.

It was a long time ago, so very long ago. On the fifth day of Creation. She was Spirit. If the substance of the Powerful One was a sea of wine then she was its ridge of waves; if he was the mighty blaze, then she its ring of flames. He was the ground, she its manifestation. He was life, she the life force. As he was the mighty androgyne, so she contained male and female within her. She detached from the Powerful One to become incarnate in all that lived and breathed and grew and moved. And in those first moments of separation she yearned for company. It was she who infused the swarms that inhabited the seas and moved about on earth. But that was not enough. She longed for other beings in her own image – differentiated like herself – who did not look to her for their lives.

Longingly, she flew to heaven and circled around, gazing into the blaze of light which surrounded the Powerful One. Slowly, she looked into the glow and distinguished around him a ring of little faces, innocent and fresh, mirrors of her own.

'Let me live with them,' she begged. 'Let me stay with my own kind. I love them like myself.'

But the Powerful One told Lilith she did not know her place. 'You were not meant for Paradise. Man, my newest creation, needs you. He is lonely and I'm not sure I like the things he's getting up to, in Eden.'

And Lilith was forced to go down where she did not want to go. Man was no better than the animals around him. But Lilith came to see that he was very beautiful. So she decided she would do her best to obey the Powerful One's decree.

Lilith did not know her place. She romped with Man, always as an equal. In fact, she had the attitude of a superior. Man shared sexual acts with the beasts and plants of Eden before Lilith came; she showed him how all species were created in duality, male for female, to have sex together. And when Lilith lay down in the grass and called Man to her he abandoned the animals and the bushes and pounced on her with such vigour and eagerness that he would not let her alone ever after. He ambushed her in the bushes and he mounted her in the mountains and he rushed her in the rushes that whispered and whooshed at the waterside. They were good days, those romping days, spent companionably and erotically and ecstatically. Then Man changed.

After an enjoyable morning spent wandering through trees, bathing in the cool steams of Eden, she racing, he chasing, until he caught up with her and they lay caressing and kissing, Man had one of his erections.

'Aha!' cried Lilith, full of fun and so quick that she spotted the change even before Man himself. Like a flame freed from the flint, she straddled Man, her rounded form a column rising from his waist. Man watched, dumbfounded, as she reared and fell, stretching her body in a taut arch, arms preceding trunk, legs folded beneath, performing an ecstatic, writhing dance of union. What was Lilith up to? What did she think she was doing?

Lilith's being stood still inside her twisting body as she felt the surge of energy build, ready for release. Man saw her absorbed, lost. He struck, hurling his body sideways so that she was thrown askew. He grabbed her roughly by the shoulders, pinning her to the ground as he heaved his hips astride hers. He released her shoulders, held her by the hair at her temples.

'This is how it is to be,' he ground out. 'This is how it was always meant to be. I will be on top. You lie below me.'

Lilith screamed with rage. 'We're made of the same dust, the same hand, the same urge. Without me you're nothing. We're equals – why should I lie beneath you? Sex is a game for two, unifying and pure. Each one has a turn. Pleasure is all.'

But would Man agree?

'Equality!' he stormed. 'You are not my equal and you will always lie below me, just as you always have.' And he thrust into her, the first thrust of debasement – handed down to mankind from that moment on.

Lilith let out another shriek, torn apart but unwilling to let Man's act degrade her even if it was inflicted on her body. Her scream was shaped into 'the Powerful One' and it demanded arbitration.

But arbitration failed to come.

'You,' rasped Man, encouraged by the Powerful One's reticence, 'were made from the filth and impure sediments of my body. You are my inferior, made from my waste. You will never be my equal.'

In that moment, Lilith forgot her divine origins. In that instant she felt as repulsive as Man's excrement. Humiliation and self-loathing overwhelmed her. It was as if lying below Man was as great an honour as she could expect. But then the little faces swam before her eyes; the cherubim, reflecting her beauty and perfection. And clearly, boldly, she flew up to Heaven and asked again if she could stay with them, the cherubim, whom she adored. But, as before, the Powerful One refused.

Lilith became still, drawing her considerable power into her body, preparing to commit an act of such volition that its impact would stretch from then on into the eternal evermore.

Slowly, absolutely, her power filled her body and she chan-nelled it into her mind and focused on the one word that must never be spoken – the inexpressible name of God. It was an act of such enormity, of such consequence that no creature had ever committed it ever before, nor ever would again. But Lilith knew she had to do it – for the sake of all her sex for ever after, in the name of freedom, for the sake of life itself.

And when the whole of her power was concentrated into her mind, Lilith recognised 'The Name' – the unmentionable name of the Powerful One – and she let her thoughts formu-late it and speak it so that the Powerful One could hear.

'Give me wings and let me go my own way. I'll leave Paradise and Eden and live in the caves of the Red Sea.'

The Powerful One had heard his most secret name spoken. He understood the power of Lilith and knew he had to let her go.

'Go!' he thundered, disguising his surrender as a command, 'to the sea from which you came.'

And so it was that Lilith left the supernal realm and went to live on earth. And how she revelled in her surroundings! On one side of her, the Red Sea surged and heaved, frilled with rocks and caves, redolent of jewels and living creatures, stud-ded with shells and vegetation. On the other, dunes, shimmering silver-gold, rolled into the distance. Don't you believe the books that describe them as blood-soaked bad-lands, filled with malign vegetation and vicious creatures. It's all in the telling: ostriches are magnificent birds, hedgehogs appealing creatures and pelicans colourful to watch – owls are useful guardians and the wisdom and protection of ravens is undisputed in the history of powerful women. Aren't we all killers when we have to survive, scavengers when we have to eat? These creatures, hyenas or wildcats, wolves, satyrs or ostriches, they were the same. Very soon she met Taniniver, the Blind Dragon, and other demons. They knew the meaning of fun, the meaning of the joy of being. No, for all the decla-rations of history's chroniclers, the truth was different.

Lilith understood, then, that Eden was not particularly

better than anywhere else. In fact, where she was, restrictions, pretensions, status were all inconsequential. She knew now that the beauty or ugliness of an unseen place depended on the voice and the words of the storyteller. If he chose, he could toss the words up into the air so that they sparkled and pranced like the foam on the waves even though they described the hardest terrain, the harshest weather. If he decided, he could pitch his voice to make the most glorious surroundings terrifying, the warmest sunshine pallid and the gentlest moonshine dismal and painful. But though the voice of the Powerful One's storytellers may be fire and brimstone when they tell you that the Red Sea is harsh and cruel, that Lilith's sea caves are wet and hard and bleak, to her they were a delight.

No experience in Eden matched the joy of immersing herself in the endless ocean, sharing its infinity. Nothing matched the satisfaction of feeling the muscles in her feet, toes, arches, the totality gripping on the slippery rock surfaces as she withdrew into the protective crevasses formed by earth in her labour throes, of playing games with the creatures that crawled and crept on the ground. Lilith loved the dark and quiet of the caves with only the distant, consistent sighing of the ocean, heaving and falling, as it breathed in, breathed out, stabilising the world.

Here on earth, Lilith was part of something, not the parthenogenic creation of an uncreate being, made for aimless play. Here she felt herself: free, full and complete. Here her sexual activity brought forth creation. Oh, they might well look down at her from above, all those heavenly beings, and condemn her and hers as lowly and undesirable and evil. But what after all was a demon, except a creature who lived and breathed and did what it was created to do?

Lilith knew, deep inside, that every created thing had its own purpose. Creation, destruction, life, death – they had no innate values. It was the mischief of those chroniclers again, those troublemakers who chose to skew the truth by transforming their fears into taboos and their desires into virtues.

Yes, her demons were better by far than those pious creatures above who obeyed and bowed, never challenging the supreme will, happy to sit in judgment on its behalf. Creatures made all of rules and nods and constraint and not a scrap of initiative among them. It was no wonder then, was it, that they bitched and judged and sought to threaten and avenge at the slightest provocation. Well it was she, Lilith, who was getting her way, had acquired her will and had chosen her destiny. She was the first of the Powerful One's little coterie to break away and, in fairness, he had not tried to stop her. Lilith chortled: how could he, once she had spoken his most secret name?

So, he was angry and that was what motivated these hangers-on of his to decree that disobedience was demonic and demons were sex-crazed, and sex was despicable. Ridiculous! Sex had been fine underneath the bushes and trees of Eden – underneath Man – and with no progeny. She hadn't heard a word against sex, then. Now, suddenly, it was a terrible thing.

Well, it was simply a storytelling matter, this good and bad labelling. They even depicted her babies, the Lilim, sweet, fluffy little creatures with their large eyes looking through swathes of fur, as 'hideous, hairy, fiends'. It was, she knew, a matter of opinion – and very jaundiced opinion at that. Jaundiced, jaded and jealous. Maybe that was the heart of it. Apparently, procreation had been no part of the Powerful One's original plan. All he wanted was to add to his little group of selfless devotees – he'd be the Maker and they his puppets. But Lilith had made waves instead of playing his game. She had forced him to take sides. Now she was on the other side – the side the preachers called the 'left side' – the bad side.

Not that it bothered Lilith what they thought. And she was merry! Oh, how she frolicked and cavorted and gambolled on the waves and in the dunes, carefree and colourful. She cared not a jot that those up there condemned fun as they condemned sex as they condemned her.

Lilith loved the night and as the day dawned, her red hair flared into its deepest reds. She loved the artifices and mirages of Earth. Best of all was the cosmic night theatre with its domed blackness and its cavalcade of stars: heavenly bodies, their vast masses creating the illusion of tiny twinkles and flashing flares. There but not there, like the spray from the sea, intangible yet exploding into sight, sound, sensation, authentic and physical. But could you grasp it? No, though the wetness of your hand was proof positive of its existence. Like a beam of light, undeniably visible yet impossible to clench between finger and thumb, its reality branded across the clenched fist, defying definition.

Yes, Lilith loved it – but most of all she loved the wanderings of her mind, the workings of her will, the knowledge that comes from these things. Among her new friends and mates she loved Taniniver the best. Taniniver, Blind Dragon – the primordial beast who could see the invisible, hear the soundless, redeem the condemned. Sometimes he and the others spoke of Samael, the Devil, the Magnetic One. Then Taniniver would laugh his deep, rumbling laugh and say: 'One day, Lilith, you'll meet him. And he will light your fires so that they blaze up to the sky.'

Meetings happened when they fall due. Meanwhile solitude, when she could find it amid the frequent couplings with the demons of the sea and caves, was never as painful as it had been in those first moments of detachment from the divine matrix – the substance of the Powerful One. She welcomed the moments to think and feel and sense herself grow and be.

Man, too, found a new mate and Lilith was happy for him. He had complained bitterly and sorely to the Powerful One, who immediately supplied him with a wife – Eve, the new helpmeet, drawn from Man's side where she had been buried unable to see the light of day. Meanwhile, the Powerful One made sure Man had the right kind of partner this time. Obedient.

'You shall be eager for your husband,' he pronounced, 'and he shall be your master.'

For a while Man and Woman were very happy and frolicked in complete harmony. Then trouble came to Eden in the form of a serpent. Many said it was Lilith herself, or her emissary, or Samael, the Devil. But who's to know? There are those who guess and those who choose answers and pluck from the Tree of Knowledge the ones that best fit their philosophy. We only know this: whoever the serpent – male, female, demon or Messiah – it certainly pointed the way to a new question, and suddenly creation resounded with it. *Why?* And it was followed by another: *why not?* And so began the eternal questions which continue to be asked to this day.

The truth was, Lilith had no regrets. She was the free spirit of the earth. She could ask and answer the two questions and act accordingly. She had no reason or desire to return to Eden and take her revenge on the Powerful One. What, after all, had she to avenge?

But the surmise made her more enigmatic, more powerful, and she revelled in her title: Mystery of Mysteries.

'I'm here, am I not?' bubbles Lilith. Youthful and exquisite. 'What harm has calumny ever done me?'

Lilith tosses her hair. A smile of mysterious amusement plays on her lips as those prophets knock their heads together. Oh, how they puzzle and muddle and fumble and stumble, solve, dissolve, construct, deconstruct, reconstruct – all to put a gloss on the Powerful One's complicity in Man's rapacious behaviour. But what does it matter? They only broadcast a jumbled, confused message. In the end, the truth is simpler. Lilith was expelled from Eden. Eve came from Man's rib, turned renegade and tempted him to eat the apple. They fell to Earth, and very soon afterwards they forgot their shame and continued their revelling and fun-making. But now their coupling had a very different result. They were suddenly fertile and their intercourse brought forth infants. Little, pink, downy bundles, with their eyes scrunched and their faces bunched, who rolled their fists and pummelled the air and yelped and squawked like pups and birds. This meant that Man and Eve were sinful, decided those prophets who came later. For they should have hung their heads in shame and shown contrition instead of producing more of their own kind. Soon those infants grew into beings like Man and

Woman and aroused each other and copulated. But along with sexual passion came the need to feed and warm themselves, which led to rivalry and tension.

When the Powerful One preferred Abel's offering of meat over Cain's gift of grain, Cain became jealous of his brother. The first murder was committed and there was a macabre irony to it. Cain, seeing that the Powerful One favoured the sacrifice of life over grain, may have assumed that human sacrifice would please him even more.

After Cain killed Abel, Eve and Man were finally riven with guilt and felt compelled to do penance. They decided to be celibate and live apart for one hundred and thirty years. Eve consorted with the creatures of the air at that time, we are told. But we know for certain that Lilith visited Man and found him resigned and sad but as beautiful as ever. Mortality had not affected him. How exquisite he is, thought Lilith watching him as he lay alone, clutching himself, worrying about his sins, wakeful, fearful, anxious.

Quietly, she slipped in beside him. She held out her arms, embraced him, stroked and caressed him. Adam turned to her, mirroring her actions and soon he had a massive erection. This time when she mounted him, he succumbed, lying back unresisting, as she infused his body with her joyous energy. And he felt a surge of vitality he had all but forgotten.

In those years, Man understood that Lilith was the kind of woman who planted an undying passion in the thoughts of men. Lilith, flaming through the mind into the body, irresistible, unconquerable. The fear of losing her was never far from Man for she had a wildness about her which made her soar above rule, above reason, above duty. And that was the splendour of her. The only way Man could feel secure about her would be to clip her wings, beat out some of that wilfulness, that unruliness: he would rather half the woman, bonded and secure, than the whole, impulsive, whimsical, poised for flight.

'But,' Man admitted, resigned, 'that woman would not be Lilith. No man can clip her wings or hold her down. Lilith thinks for herself, she's true to herself. Less than that is not Lilith.'

And so Man conceded that Lilith would never abide domination. But though he accepted this, his talk was all of command and possession.

'You left me, Lilith,' he chided. 'Just flew off into the world and left me alone.'

Lilith was saddened. Man still did not know what he had done wrong. How he had made it impossible for Lilith to remain in Eden. How she might have stayed if the Powerful One had intervened and taught Man that he was culpable. But she could not countenance a situation where she was eternally vulnerable, with two males and their cohorts banked against her. She could never let that happen again.

'Oh, I left you, Man, I know. But I had to choose in the face of impossible odds. In those days, the anger for my loss was like a fire in me. But time transformed loss into gain, remoteness into sovereignty. I've lost intimacy with one and gained it with many. I'm free.'

So Lilith tumbled and rollicked with Man many times during those one hundred and thirty years and she bore thousands of children and they married the children of Eve by Samael, the Satanic angel. Suddenly the world was filled with millions of people full of the weakness of Man and Eve combined with those of their demon lovers. When the agreed period of a hundred and thirty years was over and Man and Eve were together again, Man, stricken with guilt, laid the blame for his progeny on Lilith's promiscuity. She was responsible for his night erections, she must have crept in when he was sleeping alone, ridden him without his knowledge. She made his dreams turn wet. The blame for those couplings which produced the plagues of mankind lay with her.

Truth or lies, Lilith's life did not alter much. Man had only been a minute part of it. Mostly, she frolicked in the waves and caves of the Red Sea, played with her children and rested and warmed in the wisdom of Taniniver, Blind Dragon, her oldest, dearest friend on earth. The trouble with Man was that he was too dependent and . . . would he ever grow out of his naivety?

Then once, as Taniniver plunged deep into the centre of the ocean, and Lilith drifted slowly back towards the shore, rocked back and forth, back and forth, on her undulating cradle of waves, she saw an iridescence break through the peaceful nightveil. Lilith's hand flew to her eyes, shielding them as she peered into the shine. She could discern three figures in the light.

Hypostases, she thought, her heart lurching. The Powerful One wants to talk.

'Lilith,' they chorused, as she recognised them. 'We have come with a message from the Master.'

'And who are you?' asked Lilith. 'Tell me your names, messengers.'

The angels said they were Sanvai, Sansanvai and Semangelof.

Three jesters from the heavenly court, thought Lilith. She smiled as the angels squared their shoulders, sensing her derision. An unspoken slight is the best kind of slight, noted Lilith, They can't defend if I don't attack. Aloud she said, 'What is your message?'

'The Master would like you to return to Heaven. He has a task for you.'

'A task for me? In Heaven?'

The angels nodded.

What could the Powerful One want from her? Lilith grew curious. And she was seduced by her longing to see the cherubim again, her beloved little faces. Still, she did not agree immediately.

'Why should I go?' she demanded. 'What have I to say to the Powerful One?'

The angels were outraged. They threatened to take her by the hair and hold her head under the ocean waves until she was asphyxiated.

The creatures have teeth, Lilith laughed inwardly. 'You'll have a job,' she baited them. 'I won't be easy to drown.'

Then, without waiting for them to respond, she spread her wings and soared deep into infinity, stopping only when she reached Heaven. She could see the little faces in her mind, the mirrors of her innocent days, still pure, still changeless, surrounded by the Powerful One's blaze. She felt a twinge of sorrow that they were denied the ecstatic experiences of earth; and for herself because she could no longer see them or be with them or know the newness and the thrill of fresh experience.

Lilith drew nearer. But what was this? Eden was surrounded by a gate and outside it sat the little faces.

'Why have you been moved from the throne of glory?' Lilith asked, gentleness spilling from every part of her. But they only smiled.

Lilith walked to the gate, bracing herself before entering her old stamping ground. But the gates were barred by a tall sword made all of flames. Sometimes it stood still and at other times it swivelled and revolved. Lilith watched, enthralled, walking round it, her head cocked, reaching out and touching it. It was of her essence. Yet intuitively she found it repulsive.

She called to the Powerful One to allow her into Paradise – to enlighten her. But the Powerful One's words struck horror into her heart.

'The cherubim guard Eden from the creatures of the world. Things have changed, you know, since you were last here. The earth is filled with people, many of them full of sin and evil. And there is work for you to do. You must be my sword of righteousness. You must snatch the children who are born of the sins of their fathers and you must destroy them.'

Lilith gaped, dumbfounded. 'But I love the little faces,' she demurred.

'Lilith, do not try to disobey me again. These earthly children must be destroyed if righteousness is to prevail. They are the progeny of the plagues of mankind, they are weak and prone to sin. If they aren't destroyed, their weaknesses will be perpetuated.'

'What makes a newborn babe evil?' Lilith protested.

'Many things,' replied the Powerful One. 'Lustful sex, for

example, even between man and wife, draws the evil spirit into a woman's womb.'

'By evil spirit,' mused Lilith, 'you mean me, of course. But once, I was the Mystery of Mysteries, the soul incarnate in all living things. How whimsical you can be. How you change your mind!'

The Powerful One frowned. Thunder barked. The clouds darkened, drew close. Lightning sparked. 'You sinned. You received your punishment.'

Lilith's laugh tinkled like ice on glass. 'Why can't you accept that righteousness won't – can't – prevail? It failed here in Eden right under your nose. And even in Paradise, when the Disobedient One – an angel, no less – refused to bow to Man. Now that proves something. Well, doesn't it? Man seems to be the common impediment. He causes disobedience. I won't kill the little faces. Your rules are impossible. You gave your creatures free will; why, if you wanted absolute obedience?'

'Obedience is of no use unless it comes of free will,' the Powerful One thundered.

'Or fear,' barked Lilith.

'You will not disobey me again, Lilith.'

'You love playing games, but you've got to win every time and woe betide the creature who won't let you. Well, Man and Eve and their descendants can play it your way. I won't, I never have. Besides, I love little children. You won't get me to hurt them.'

'They are evil, born of evil.'

'What, you mean, like my own children? Am I to kill them too?'

The Powerful One's reply chilled her.

'Yes. And if you fail to do as I command, they will still die. You must do as you are told, Lilith, evil one. Bitch-monster. You will not disobey a second time.'

'Watch me,' Lilith flared. 'Just watch me. I won't be your sword of vengeance. You are Master of Life and Death. Do your own killing. I have no quarrel with anyone.'

And as the sword jerked and turned again, flashing, flashing,

Lilith screamed involuntarily, in pain, in triumph, and flew away from Paradise a second time.

Lilith kept her word. Not one child did she kill. Nor did she know which ones were marked out to be killed, because she never went near that flaming sword as it revolved and flashed to indicate which children were condemned to death for the sexual enjoyment of their parents.

They were labelled monsters, plagues of mankind – but they were all born of the primal couple. Weren't these simply personifications of humankind's beast nature? They would never go away, surely? The threat of death dangling over their heads would merely force a part of their nature into some deep, shadowy recess of their being. And was she, Lilith, to be the enforcer and the vessel of the collective darkness of the human race so that the Powerful One and his hypostases could remain light and bright and good and gracious? Lilith would not be used in that way.

Still, the encounter had a profound effect on her. It was as if the Powerful One had put her into a category all her own, as he had done with Satan. That was where it began, the campaign of calumny. His spokesmen painted her evil, and everything she was – by virtue of being herself – became dangerous, treacherous and threatening.

Lilith watched her reflection in the clear pools, flanked by the tall rocks that reared up and ripped the air around her. They ripped because the Powerful One had made them so. Generations on she would be thought evil and malign, because he had decided that should be so. She would have to stay away from the birth of babes, fresh and newly made and warm with innocence and need. The smiles she brought them would be denied – put down to noxious bodily gases. And when they died suddenly, inexplicably, through the will of the Powerful One, she, Lilith, would be blamed.

She saw her reflection, her head drooping, the flames of her hair dancing around it, and she wanted to immolate herself in its fire. But she was deathless – essence of fire, essence of the Almighty, substance of eternity. What good would it do, anyhow, her dying? She'd just make way for another like herself. The mould was indestructibly made.

She could see far into the future how mankind would always need a Lilith, a woman of darkness to carry its guilt and its fear as it echoed down the memory chambers of each newly birthed babe in each generation. How womankind would be burdened with an ingrained terror of becoming her Lilith-self. How all her pleasures would come to personify the 'Do-Nots' that define womanly perfection. No, she would not destroy herself, even if she could. She would grasp the suffering, tame it, manipulate it, use it, and so pass on to womankind the capacity for pleasure, untrammelled by guilt, undefined by prescription. And her legacy would continue into the remote future, so far away that she herself would be an almost forgotten glimmer, her tale all but lost.

For now, she threw back her head and she howled. 'Ooohhh!' How she howled, then whimpered, then sobbed, then howled again. Wailing, clutching herself, weeping, weeping, weeping for all the humiliation and frustration that had gone before and that was still to come. 'Why?' she keened. Why did it have to be like this? Why was free will to be punished? What was wrong with disobedience? Why was copulation a disgrace? What was so terrible about wanting to be sovereign over her body, her actions, her desires? And the animals screeched with Lilith – the owl, the hyena, the raven, the wildcat. And her most beloved animals, the wolves and dogs. In the distance, Blind Dragon sensed Lilith's pain and did his best to sustain her.

For a long time Lilith wandered in the darkest caves, the most hidden holes, the most deserted spaces, wild with thorns, treacherous with swamps, accompanied only by a small pack of bitches who echoed her wailing and watched her every move. Then one day she looked up from her grief and saw around her an army. In the front, the bitches; behind them other creatures – an army of monsters, dragons, animals, demons. As Lilith gazed at them, they bowed before her. They knew her pain – rejected, cast out, condemned at the instant of creation, they shared her suffering.

'Where am I?' demanded Lilith.

'Sheba!' they told her.

'And where is the trail of my grief?'

'Through Zemargad.'

'Then this is my domain,' declared Lilith, feeling that old surge of exultation. 'I am the Queen of Zemargad and Sheba – and you are my army.'

Amidst the cheering of the dispossessed, now suddenly finding themselves bonded to the rest of creation, Lilith looked up at the heavens.

'Here's another one for you,' she gloated. 'Add it to your list – ambition. How long before ambition is proscribed as a sin among women?'

Lilith did not remain a lone queen for long. It was about now that she met Samael – distant, dark Samael, mysterious Samael – and she remembered Man: how they had held and caressed each other, how they had laughed together, how their limbs had intertwined. Man was beautiful. Lilith would not deny that even now, even after knowing that his beauty concealed such weakness and treachery.

Here stood Samael, like a sinuous shadow, veiled by the vast reflection of the rocks. The sun was so strong against her that she could only see his silhouette.

'Who are you?' she asked, and her voice was tremulous, not from fear but from passionate longing.

He did not answer but she saw a movement. She tossed her fiery mane, manoeuvred her shoulders so that the movement resonated down her curving body. But the creature stood motionless.

Lilith wondered what to do next. Sex had been simple enough with Man – he wanted her as much as she wanted him. But here Lilith sensed something different: a complex game, a ritual even, whose rules and stages infused the whole with power and mystery – and even a hint of fear. Her mind and body thrilled to the expectation. But how? What should she do? The stranger just stood there, unmoving, inscrutable.

So mesmerised was Lilith that she did not even hear the

gigantic splash in the background as the waters parted and Taniniver, Blind Dragon, raised his mighty head from the ocean depth.

'You need do nothing, Lilith,' he chortled. 'This is my job. I will introduce you to Samael. I will join you in marriage.'

'How do you know my thoughts?'

'Instinct is all to me,' Blind Dragon's laughter rumbled. 'You should know that by now. Primordial urges I feel and effect best of all.'

So saying, he raised his massive body and held Lilith aloft, moving her forward until she stood beside Samael, so close that there was no space between them. Her body, shimmering from the gold sands, clung to his which was dark from night and the ashes of hellfire.

'I'll burn you,' she whispered, drawing away. But his substance moved with hers, as if they were one.

'No flame burns me,' he whispered back. 'I am a creature of fire, just like you. We are a perfect pair.'

Lilith looked into his face, discerned the laughter in his eyes. Her mouth curved, stretched, lifted at the corners.

'Both disobedient,' they said together. 'Both devoted to pleasure.'

Samael was a wonderful companion. Lilith soon forgot the heavenly hosts and got on with enjoying her freedom to the full. How they played and made music and scattered joy and ecstasy among the people. If there's a body, they agreed, and it is capable of bliss, then why neglect it?

But the holy fathers disagreed violently. They berated those who enjoyed their bodies, they condemned sexual pleasure even within marriage, they insisted that the body was created for mortification, that it was, by its nature, an evil instrument, the punishment for Original Sin; that spiritual redemption lay in the loathing of the body. Lilith did not agree, nor did Samael, her partner in all things. They enjoyed baiting those angry preachers and rabid ecclesiasts. Who, they would ask slyly, offers the greatest temptation? Why if humankind must procreate should the process not be enjoyable? Why should they reject the bodies which house their pleasures? And most importantly, who could offer the most reasonable, the most attractive, the most pleasurable option?

'But,' laughed Lilith, when they admonished her and compared her censoriously with Gabriel. 'Wasn't there a poet who stated the Devil's case? "It is I who obsess the Almighty, goading, like a thorn in his side, while all you do, Gabriel, is chant, He Is, He Is, He Is," Well, I am the thorn – the thorn that prickles the Powerful One's conscience. The threat that shows up his weakness.'

But plots proliferated on Earth in defence of Paradise and the Powerful One. Preachers worked together and separately to destroy Lilith and her work and among them was a certain rabbi who went beyond himself.

'I'll not stop at the effect of their actions. I'll destroy them – I'll wipe them from the face of the earth. I'll obliterate them so that all that's left is the sorry tale of their pathetic defeat. I'll do it,' declared the Rabbi.

Other, wiser, men and women tried to restrain the Rabbi. 'If the Powerful One had intended them to be destroyed, then he would have told us. They are deathless beings. Our fight must take place on the battleground of the human conscience. We are here to protect and redeem humankind. It is not our place to interfere with the source of temptation – only with temptation itself.'

But the Rabbi would not listen. He discovered that Samael and Lilith loved to transform themselves into dog and bitch and frolic and cavort amongst humankind, spreading pleasure and inducements. And he learned slowly how to recognise them. Then he chose the top of a certain hill as their place of execution and one dark night, he lured them there.

'Don't feed them,' the others had warned him when he outlined his plan. 'For you'll surely die if you do.'

The Rabbi was careful to observe this safeguard when finally he had both dog and bitch under his control.

'Now you have me,' growled Samael, 'all I ask is a whiff of your frankincense.'

'Well now,' chortled the inflated Rabbi, 'I'll give you that since I need to light it for my own rituals.' And he held out the frankincense.

Samael snorted. Sparks showered from his fire-being. They lit the frankincense. He breathed in the fumes, devoured them, ate them.

All at once, the Rabbi fell to the ground as if dragged down by iron thongs. Towering over the prostrate Rabbi, in place of the dog, was a giant figure. Black and sinuous, glowing like embers.

'You cannot destroy the Devil,' he sneered. 'It wasn't meant to be. The divine will doesn't permit it.'

And from that day on, the Rabbi was rejected by his own for his hubris and destined to be a servant of Samael for the rest of his days.

People say he married Lilith but that is hardly likely, since the object of dog and bitch was to punish and not reward the Rabbi. And so the impious couple continued to cavort, putting the case for pleasure against mortification. And they found at least as many, if not more, advocates than the preachers.

But it annoyed the Powerful One. He may not have set the rules for them but he decided it was right to intervene on behalf of those who spoke up for him. He would put an end to that which his spokesmen believed was Samael's ultimate pleasure. All those pages written about the size of his phallus and those words spoken in condemnation of his virile use of it on mortal women – and if it wasn't him it was one of his penis-centred demon-children – monsters, imps, devils . . . That was it! He would deprive Samael of his most precious possession. As soon as the idea struck the divine will, it came to pass!

Samael was castrated and went howling his loss to Lilith.

'I never did have sex with mortal women,' he protested. 'Only opened their minds and made them see how receptive their bodies can be. That was not such a terrible thing, was it?'

Of course, he was right. Samael was made of fire, sustained by hellfire, product of the original, ethereal angel-substance. If he had lain with a mortal, touched a human body, he would have consumed it with his fire and flame and not merely passion.

'But,' said Lilith, 'has the castration happened to your body or your mind?'

And she opened his mind as he opened those of others, flinging wide door after door, window after window on to those alternative perceptions locked away behind a screen of secrecy and fear. Samael and his penis survived the castration and went on to be written about centuries down the line in the treatises of priests and kings. But that's a story to be told elsewhere.

Here, Lilith continued her capers with and without Samael and her army of friends and her guardians grew apace with her foe.

'And now,' she told her confidante, the great demoness Naamah. 'Now that I'm unattached again, they think no man is safe from me. So many ways to ban me from the beds of men! Divorce papers? Spells? The chantings of fear-filled people? Their invocations might make them feel a little more powerful – a little less fearful. They have no effect on me.

'The same holy men who chant spells in public – you should see them when they're alone. They lay out fresh white sheets for me, bathe and anoint themselves with scent of rose and essence of spring flowers. Then they meditate and bring me into their thoughts. And their fantasies filter from brain to skin and make it tingle. Their hearts beat my name and their loins burn with the fire that is Lilith's essence.

'They need me, Naamah, so I go to them. These men with their secret longings and their suppressed desires, I applaud their daring and I pity their secrecy and I go to them. They lie alone in their beds while their wives are away, dreaming dreams of my body entwining with theirs. They pray as they have never prayed to the Powerful One. Desire saps their strength and they close their eyes. Then I take pity on them and I visit them.

'Oh how they hand themselves to me, sweet and childlike and full of longing! How we play and romp and do mock-battle during the night hours. How we love and kiss and caress.

'But in the morning, when they awaken covered in sweat and shame and find their guilt smeared on their bodies and their sheets, they rush to cleanse themselves, wrap protective prayers around their bodies, explain their actions with terrible lies. Like Man.

"Lilith came in the night. Lilith stood at the crossroads, covered from top to toe in jewels and bewitching ornaments. She gripped me in a vice-like grip. She kissed me with a poisoned kiss, she forced the wine of enchantment down my throat. And when I was unconscious, she rode me, rode me, whipped me and drove me on. Then she left me and flew away, condemned me as if I was responsible for my actions. She lacerated me with a tongue like a sword – see, here are my wounds. She made fun of me, inviting me one moment, then, as I approached her, hypnotised, she grew enormous and burst into flames, menacing, terrifying and yet magnetic. But all I could see was the rose-red beauty of her hair, her lips, the gleam of her jewels, and taste the sweetness of the world from her mouth, still on mine. Then she tried to consume me in her flame as she had so many innocent fools before. But I remembered myself. I chanted my prayers and I was safe."

'How many times I've heard this twisted account. It is the weakness passed down from Man, this urge to revile sexual passion. Part of the conspiracy to squash the natural impulses, to enslave them inside, to spit their poison emissions on to a scapegoat so that they can escape. Lilith has deceived them. Lilith bewitches them. Lilith has raped them. Those soiled clothes, those spent, emptied loins – they were Lilith's doing. Those night emissions that happened all by themselves as they lay innocently alone – they were caused by Lilith. But why?'

Because Lilith, you know Lilith, she takes those ejaculations from men and she impregnates herself with them and she produces monsters. More monsters?

The fabrications were so naive, Lilith found them almost endearing. How she titters when she reads the restrictions placed on men and women even in their marital beds.

'Look here Naamah, how they restrict themselves. Man

and wife must not lie naked together – or for that matter alone.
Or the child of that coupling will come from the evil side. And
every man, when he has an erection, must say these words
before he gets on with it:

> *"In the name of the Powerful One, Lilith of the velvet veil*
> *You are present.*
> *Unbind. Unbind. Do not move.*
> *This kernel is not for you*
> *You have no right to it*
> *Return. Return.*
> *The ocean roars for you*
> *Its waves summon you*
> *I cling fast to the Pure One*
> *Cloak myself in the mantle of his sovereignty."*

'Then, Naamah, he has to cover himself from head to toe,
conceal his wife beneath him and perform his act.'

'I'm surprised he can,' cackles Naamah. 'It's enough to
dampen any man's virility. I wouldn't wait around for the end
of the performance if I was his wife.'

And so Lilith continued doing her part by the human race,
enjoying its quirks and trying to spread her message.

Then one day, as she retired to her cave, she heard a flutter
of wings and the clatter of rocks and felt a menace in the
atmosphere. She looked in wonder at the tall shadows cast on
all sides and a shudder shook her body as she realised the
heavenly hosts were here to haunt her. Not that she was frightened, but only they could say what the Powerful One wanted
from her now.

The past is such a thing, she thought, frustrated. It pursues
you wherever you go. Then she rose to a sitting position and
spoke loud and clear. 'I know you're there, what's the point of
hiding? Just tell me what you want and let's get it over with.'

Three hypostases detached themselves from the grey-black
sheen of the water-smoothed rocks.

'We have come to teach you a lesson.'

It was meant to be the wrathful thunder of the righteous but the voice quavered like a tremulous whine. What strength it contained, expired in the swishing sighs of the waves and the sportive spurts of spray.

'You terrify me,' yawned Lilith, stretching and bending her arm to make a pillow. 'Tell me more before I swoon away.'

'You're not to kill any more children,' blurted Sanvai.

'I don't kill children,' she retorted, 'I produce them. Two hundred and fifty a day, or hadn't your gossiping friends told you.'

'They're not children, they're demons,' Sansanvai protested.

'Demons, children, what's the difference? They're someone's young. They serve a purpose. It's the Powerful One who slaughters them in their hundreds, not I.'

'Your demons bring death,' accused Semangelof.

There was a game being played here, but Lilith was not sure that the three angels realised it. What was the Powerful One after? She shrugged, turned on her side, folded her hands beneath her cheek. Angels don't feel sexually aroused, but Lilith knew instinctively that this one was grappling to understand the prickling, surging sensation that ran through his incorporeal form, and she wondered if they had the wherewithal to satisfy erotic urges.

'You cause death. What do you say to that?' demanded Sansanvai, attempting with his aggression to camouflage his reaction.

'Death's not a punishment when it is natural. It has to be. That's all there is to it.'

'All right for you to say,' ventured one of the other angels. 'You females – you hold the secrets to eternity. You live on through your infants.'

'That bothers you!' Lilith's shrieks of hilarity cut through the angels, fragmenting them.

'What's more, you don't just reproduce yourselves – you spawn males too.'

'And you'd prefer the male of the species to die out, would you?'

'Well . . . it's just – you know, men feel excluded. You should tell them how.'

'Shouldn't you take that up with the Powerful One?'

Lilith stopped. What was this delicate clinking noise? A chain of sparkling light trailed to the rock floor, formed a glowing pool. Lilith's hands flew to her lips.

'So it's true!' she exclaimed. 'Angels do cry diamond tears.'

And her heart was filled with pity for these strange, wishless creatures who had the world convinced of their power and glory.

'Really,' she breathed, filling with tenderness, 'the Powerful One does ride roughshod over you. He could, just occasionally, let his servants relax and have a good time. What they think is a good time, that is. But no, he's always laying down the law.'

'It's not like that,' muttered Semangelof, attempting to recover his dignity. 'That's how we want it.'

'Now look here,' added Sansanvai. 'We won't have you criticising our Lord and Master. If it weren't for him you wouldn't be here.'

'You look here,' Lilith returned, stoutly. 'If it wasn't for *me* I wouldn't be here. It was only because I mentioned the unmentionable . . .'

'Yes, yes, we know,' the angels broke in hastily. You never could tell with Lilith: she just might have enough devilment in her to say it again.

Lilith smiled and stretched. She had the measure of them now. They were the pawns in the power games that the Powerful One was playing with her. She'd tease a little, play a little, then she'd give them their way. They were hardly more than infants themselves for all their great many years. She did not have the heart to send them back to their Master empty-handed failures.

'We meant, of course, that you would not have existed at all.'

Lilith rolled her eyes heavenwards. 'Maybe, maybe not. But you know, you really ought to realise there was spirit before the Powerful One.'

The creatures flung their hands over their ears.

'Silly,' giggled Lilith. 'You don't have bodies – well, not flesh. You don't hear with your ears, do you? Or speak with your mouths? You just sort of, well, absorb, don't you? Funny, I never really thought about it before.'

The angels mustered the shreds of their dignity.

'We are here to convey the Powerful One's command. He wants you to stop killing little children . . .'

'He really ought to make up his mind.' Could it be that even the hypostases believed that Lilith killed human children? She was bored with the game – it was leading nowhere. But she went along with the farce because she knew that the Powerful One never made any moves without an aim in mind. 'He asked me to kill in the first place "Those of them that will grow to do bad deeds," he said, clear as ever. I haven't forgotten.'

'He wants you to stop.'

'Are you saying he's changed his mind?'

'You must stop.'

'Do you mean I'm no longer his "sword of vengeance"? That's what he called me, you know? I'm not sure I want to give that up.'

'You must. He commands you.'

They were turning to jelly again. Lilith's heart went out to them. The time had come to stop mocking and make them feel strong and special. Oh, what it was to be fearless! To let another succeed, when you held the winning hand – that was true power, true autonomy. She knew now that the Powerful One was after a sign that would brand Lilith for evermore as a killer of innocent babes. Well, let him have it. Lilith felt generous. After all, nothing would change. What harm in promising to curtail a crime she never committed? A little ranting, some pointing of fingers. But she was above that now. She would reward the angels: their visit had brought home to her how strong she had become.

How different this was from her last encounter with the Powerful One. How devastating that had been. And here she was now, giving away – yes making a free gift of something he so desperately wanted. She tingled and shivered with joy. This was true freedom. Lilith was now truly on top.

'I'll tell you what. I'll promise faithfully to stay away from children who wear amulets and charms bearing your names. That should earn you some rewards from the Powerful One.'

'And there's the matter of the sleeping men . . .'

Lilith cackled. 'Well now, that's altogether different. I mean, are you really sure their "ups" are down to me? And if they are, do you think it fair to ask me to give that up, rampant bitch that I am?'

She flapped her arms and their shadow fell in great heaving wings on the rock face and the angels fled before she withdrew the generous promise she had made. The Powerful One would be pleased. He would honour them. But the greatest reward was from Lilith. She had ensured that their names would be known to the human race from then on. They would be exalted to a status they had never known before – that no angel had ever known before. Well, with the exception of Gabriel who had performed a good few major tasks but even he didn't have his name inscribed on amulets and cups and bowls and over doorways and on belts and frescos and ohhhhhhh – they had better return to Heaven and tell the Powerful One the good news. The children were safe. And so it is that they say:

Bring out the cups! Read out the divorce papers! Banish Lilith! Banish her from our homes! Put out the charm – pin it over your door so that she can never enter again!

But a few strangely phrased words, chanted in strange rhythms, make not the slightest difference to Lilith. She'll still tickle the babes and teach them to smile. She'll sing songs to lift their mind and enhance their will. Just you watch for the tangled bunch of hair at the nape of your infant's neck, the next time you lift her from her cot in the morning. And if you find it, you'll know that Lilith has visited and ruffled her hair and passed on her indomitable spirit. And so it is that Lilith lives on – in you, in me, in all our little faces.

Melusine

'That is the place where I was born.'

Melusine must have suffered that thought a thousand times as she sat at the window, gazing with her sisters through the misty veil of chance which separates Cephalonia from the world of humans, at the palace of Albion. She could just discern the pale shape of the castle. King Elinas of Albion. Her father. What did he look like? How did he speak? Was he a terrible man? What was it that had commended him, a mortal, to their mother, Pressina?

But did it all matter now? Elinas had broken his promise. And that was why Melusine and her sisters had been condemned to a fatherless childhood. Worse still – the tears still flowed from Pressina's eyes as she sat with her daughters staring across from the Land of Chance, hidden from mortals by veils of doubt and disbelief, at Albion Castle where she had once been queen.

'Fairies don't cry, Mother,' Melusine said when she was a child. 'Fairies never cry. We're happy.' And Pressina would clutch the little Melusine to her heart and hold back her tears and try to smile. Ah! How much there was to smile about if only she could go back before the end of the story and remember the past. But there, that's the lot of fairy creatures who give up their own kind and go to live with mortals. They learn mortal ways and forget their own. Pressina was never able to tell her daughters about the glad times because she could no longer inhabit the happy part of her life with Elinas; but the broken promise, the rancorous departure – they were still vivid, they scrubbed the rest from her mind. And she couldn't speak about them even when Melusine drew out her memories.

'I was so happy, Melusine, my darling!' she wanted to say as she slid her fingers through her daughter's raven tresses. Melusine's face was the mirror of her youth. Oh, she remembered well enough but the memories grew chill in her mind, froze on her lips, and she could not tell Melusine how she and Elinas had fallen instantly in love.

He had gone to the woods, alone, hoping to beguile his mind for a while to chase away the spectre of his recently dead wife. After some hours of hard hunting, he decided to stop for a rest and directed his horse to a fountain about a mile or so away. He rode steadily, his limbs as heavy as his heart, until a sound made him stop.

It was an exquisite sound. As if the flowing waters of the fountain had somehow turned into melody. As if the golden sunshine had tinged the waters and added a melting warmth to the melody and the strange, magical words. Oh how they eddied and swirled and pulsed before running smooth and clear and sparkling for a while.

Elinas could never pin-point when he looked back, how long he sat motionless on his horse, listening. A fairy instant, they say, is a hundred human moments, a fairy year a hundred human years. And one thing Elinas knew for sure – he was transported from mortality into an age beyond space, beyond time, a place where there was no memory of grief, sorrow, illness, fear. No past, no future, only the present and every nerve so alive, so responsive to its beauty that it exploded with the experience of intense joy.

Then Elinas was gripped with the desire to see the singer with the voice of cool, flowing waters tempered with golden sunshine. He leapt off his horse and ran lithely along towards the sound, each note striking his ears, his whole body, before descending into his heart. He was filled with gladness, a sense that nothing could be better, more satisfying, more enjoyable than this moment.

And there was Pressina! She sat on the fountain ledge, singing as she watched the water, sparkling with the kiss of the sun, dancing, frolicking down the stones. And each blended with the other like an ensemble.

Pressina saw him too. She was not startled or disdainful and continued to sing her song. It was as if she was expecting him, as if his presence was as normal as that of the birds and small animals going about their business in the woods. Elinas perched on a rock, watching, listening, never saying a word until Pressina finished her song. Then, without preamble, he asked her to marry him. Pressina agreed, on one condition.

'I won't keep any secrets from you,' she said. 'Nor will I withhold any part of myself. But I want complete privacy when I give birth to our children. And when I have completed a short period of lying-in, I will welcome you again with open arms and all my love.'

Elinas agreed immediately. It did not seem an unreasonable wish. He had heard that bearing children was exhausting, that women needed to rest afterwards. Well, it was right and proper that his bride should be allowed to recover properly. Of course he would give Pressina her wish.

In the days that followed Albion was a happier kingdom than it had ever been before. Pressina was an excellent wife and a gentle and loving mother to Elinas' little son. And when they announced that she was soon to add to the small family, there was great joy in the kingdom. Well, when the time came to deliver, Elinas paced up and down his chamber, waiting for news, torn with anxiety about Pressina's welfare.

'Mother has given birth!' cried his son hurtling in, face flushed and panting with excitement. 'We have three princesses, Father. Not one but three.' He held up three little fingers, reiterating. 'Three. They are to be called Melusine,

Melior and Palatina. Right now, Mother is bathing them so that they will be fresh and clean for you to admire.'

Elinas could not stay away a moment longer. Excitedly, he hurried to the birth chamber and rushed in, calling Pressina's name and muttering endearments and congratulations and thanks. But Pressina was bowed over the baby girls who bobbed and cooed in a shallow bath. At the sound of the king's voice, she whirled around, her face a picture of grief and anger. Too late, Elinas remembered – he had broken his promise.

'Elinas,' whispered Pressina, barely able to speak. 'You've broken the taboo. Now I must leave.'

And before the devastated king could open his mouth, Pressina disappeared, taking her daughters with her.

From that day on, she lived in Cephalonia, the invisible land, the land beyond intention, accessible to mortals only by happy chance. Here it was that Pressina sat each evening, gazing from her palace across to her husband's home, grieving over her lost life, berating her husband for his faithlessness.

The man who could not keep his word. That was the only way Melusine and her sisters knew Elinas. They could answer none of the questions that came up in their minds year after year but this was one thing they knew. So when the questions became too much for Melusine and no amount of probing, begging and argument would elicit a word more from Pressina, she decided that the damage Elinas had done her mother was so irreparable, and her experience of him so distressing, that she would stop talking about him.

Instead, she decided to avenge the wrong against Pressina.

'Come with me,' she urged Melior and Palatina. 'You've suffered like me, I know you have. This man destroyed our mother. He hurt her so much, she can neither forget him nor forgive him. Do you remember even one occasion when she took pleasure in anything? Is it right for a man to destroy a life like this? Come with me. If we punish him, we can lay our sadness to rest and release Mother from his strange power.'

Melusine's sisters agreed. Slowly, carefully, they got together a battery of enchantments and when at last they were ready to launch their attack, they stormed like a tempest through the veil of chance and lighted on Elinas' palace.

It was all over within moments. Elinas' soldiers were no match for the fairy magic of the three princesses. They captured Elinas of Albion and imprisoned him in Mount Brandelois. Then, triumphantly, they returned home to Cephalonia.

'Mother,' said Melusine, her face glowing with victory, her stature prouder and statelier than ever. 'We've come to take you back to Albion where you have every right to be.'

Pressina stood up, drew herself to a formidable height. Her face was pale, her expression stricken.

'Melusine! What have you done?' She held Melusine by her arms and shook her. 'Tell me what you've done.'

'We've done what we – or you – should have done a long time ago. My sisters and I waged war on Elinas and defeated him. We've locked him up in Mount Brandelois with all his wealth. Albion is yours. Oh Mother, we've watched you suffer for so many years. All our lives we've seen you looking out at Albion, day after day, night after night. Now Albion is yours.'

'Where is Elinas' son? What have you done with him?'

'Our brother is safe. He's waiting for you.'

'You evil woman!' spat Pressina. 'Who gave you the right to take things into your own hands? You've destroyed your father's life. How dare you interfere in matters that don't concern you?'

'Don't concern me? You're my mother. Elinas—'

'Don't ever mention his name again,' commanded Pressina, bitterly. 'You're not fit to mention his name. Your father didn't deserve this. He was anxious to see me that day, he longed to see his daughters. He was a father, a loving husband. He never understood the pledge properly. How could a human understand the importance of the taboos that govern us? He broke his pledge, true, but he broke it out of love.'

Melusine gaped at her mother, incredulous. 'You never said these things before, Mother. I saw you grieving, pallid, heavy. You made us believe he was worthless. You never told us about him. I longed to know more, to get a sense of the man whose blood runs in my veins. You couldn't bear to talk about him. I assumed—'

'You assumed wrong!' stormed Pressina. The frozen memories of the past decades thawed and flooded her, sweeping Melusine up in the ensuing chaos. 'And now you'll pay for it. I curse you, Melusine! I curse you for your unnatural act against your father. Instead of legs, you'll have a serpent's tail. And this affliction will affect you every seventh day. See if you can find a better mortal than your father. If your husband can leave you alone on the seventh day, you will eventually regain your legs. If he breaks the taboo, you will be banished from the worlds of humans and immortals. You'll haunt the air and drift in the clouds, alone and unloved for ten thousand years or more.'

Melusine was shattered. Her skin was white as snow and her dark eyes pools of horror as she looked incredulously at Pressina's spitting, snarling countenance. She had never seen her mother like this. She tried to gather her thoughts and senses together to speak, to justify herself. But she felt her legs buckle. She flung out her arms trying to break her fall but no one moved forward to save her. Not Pressina nor Palatina nor Melior.

They watched as she fell to the floor, crawling, slithering, unable to raise herself up until she realised to her horror that the curse had taken effect. She was half snake. In place of her legs was a bulky, white, serpentine coil. Without thinking, she reached for her legs but her fingers fell on the thick, numb, column twisting from side to side. It unbalanced her so that her upper half teetered and she had to place her hands firmly on the ground to stop herself falling this way and that.

'Do I deserve this,' she asked Pressina, 'for trying to avenge the wrong done to you?'

'You claim you did this terrible thing for me. But wasn't it really for yourself? Wasn't it because you wanted to see your father and to know him?'

'Is it so bad to want those things?' demanded Melusine.

'You never told us. I spent my life trying to find out about Elinas. You wouldn't even tell us his name.'

'At least you admit it was to satisfy your own curiosity . . .'

'If I'd been doing it for myself, I would have visited him with gifts and smiles and an open heart. I would have tried to win his affections and decide for myself why you mourned him. No, Mother, it was for you. You yearned so much and so long for Albion, for the home from which he forced you to go. You talked day in day out, year after year, about his broken promise, about how he let you down, how he destroyed your life. I thought he could at least be made to pay for making you suffer, for depriving you of your home. I hardened my heart when I saw my father and I refused to let myself feel the pleasure of seeing him for the first time. It was you who deceived me, Mother – deceived all of us. And now, when the damage is done, you tell us what we should have known long ago – that our father was good and kind and his mistake was to love us all too much – a mistake you always described as the violation of a sacred pledge.'

Pressina was dispassionate. 'You can make all the accusations you like Melusine. What you have done, and coerced your sisters into, is an unnatural thing. And you have to pay for it. The curse is set and it will take its course.'

Melusine knew her mother's heart was cold and vengeful. Her fairy nature had returned. She wanted to see her suffering mirrored in someone else, and who better than Melusine with her self-sufficient streak and her determined ways. Wasn't she the one who had badgered her with questions about Elinas? Demanded to know the reason for the abandonment? Asked if a reconciliation was possible? So, now, she too had acquired a taboo. What, she wondered, did my mother do to get her taboo? But she would never know.

Well, if a mortal fell in love with her she would simply tell him about the curse before she allowed herself to reciprocate. Then everything would be in the open and she would risk nothing by observing the taboo on the seventh day.

'Your snake form must remain a secret,' shrilled Pressina,

reading her daughter's mind. 'If your husband finds out about it, the taboo will be broken and you'll be condemned.'

Melusine looked at her sisters for help. But their blanched faces and trembling lips told her that they were too terrified to intervene on her behalf. Sadly, she turned to her mother for the last time. There was no future for her in Cephalonia. She could not stay in a place filled with resentment and bitterness and fear. And she could not bear to see her mother's heart paralysed with hatred. If she had known how Pressina would change, would she still have attacked Elinas?

Melusine set off immediately, travelling through woods and forests, air and water, deserts and gardens, and on the seventh day she always stopped to nestle behind a bush or sink to the bottom of a pond or crawl under a rock, coil around her white, scaly body and hide her disgrace.

Shame! Now there was a sensation Melusine had never felt before. But her mother had forced it on her – ten thousand years of isolation. It didn't bear thinking about. So she wandered on through France until she came to Poitou. There, she decided to rest by the Fountain of Thirst.

She drank deep and long from the fountain. Its waters refreshed and soothed her and she fell into a deep sleep. When she awoke, she was full of hope. She reached into her bag and drew out her dulcimer. She stroked it and caressed it, dear, faithful friend whom she had not touched for so long. Then she struck up a tune and began to sing.

The next moment she was surrounded by fairies. There were little ones and big ones, goblins and elves, trolls and brownies, bogeys and boggarts, giants and ogres. They all crowded round her, entranced by her singing. Some cried, they were so moved. Others smiled with pleasure and the rest nodded, swayed or danced. And when – all too soon – Melusine finished her song, they cheered so long and loud that the birds in the trees shuddered with fear that the earth would explode. Then one fairy came forward, her gown diaphanous with the sun's rays seeping through the branches, her movements light and airy, her voice tinkling like a bell.

'We are looking for a queen, Melusine, and after hearing your song, we've decided that you are the one we all want. I hope you will accept our offer.'

Melusine thought for a moment. Did she want to belong in this way to anyone? To become responsible for their concerns, to uphold their rules and laws, enforce them if need be? Did she want to put herself in a position where she could no longer bend and manipulate the rules? Where she would no longer be self-sufficient, or put her own needs first. But true autonomy, she decided, was a fallacy now. It had gone out of her life when the taboo came in. And becoming queen would tether her to reality. She would have as much autonomy as was good for anyone.

'I accept,' she said, after only a few moments' thought. 'But I have a secret which I must keep at all costs. On the seventh day of each week I must be left entirely alone. This rule is immutable. No matter what the circumstances. How it came about, what its nature is, that is for me alone to know. If you agree to observe this taboo, every one of you, I will be honoured to become your queen.'

And so it was that Melusine came to be the queen of the fairies of France. And as queen, she felt new feelings about herself. She danced and sang with the others. She revelled until deep in the night and she wandered carefree and curious in the air and the mist, watching and enjoying the antics of the human world.

She often returned to the Fountain of Thirst. Its waters invigorated her and she found many safe places here, to hide and bide the time when her hips and legs changed into hideous, colourless serpent coils. Then she would think of Pressina and reflect on her actions. But try as she might, she could not understand her mother's curse. Pressina must have become as twisted as the coils of a serpent and as venomous as its fangs to visit such a terrible curse on her own daughter. Did Pressina regret her action when she thought back to it now? Did she understand why Melusine had acted as she had? Melusine would never know. All she knew, with leaden certainty, was that Pressina had condemned her and, having delivered the sentence, she refused to consider a reprieve. Melusine, like Elinas, had acted out of love for Pressina and both had been rewarded with rejection.

It was on each seventh day when she was in her snake form that these thoughts pressed on Melusine the most. When at last the day was over and the dawn broke to release the new one, she regained her proper form and walked immediately to the Fountain of Thirst, bathed herself in its healing waters and drank deeply. And as she drank, all anger and despair were flushed out of her mind and replaced with the love of life. In a strange way, the curse had worked in her favour. Here, as fairy queen, she was her own mistress. This would never have happened if she had remained beside Pressina, always weeping, always wondering.

It was on one such day as she sat drying her hair in the sun that Raymond of Poitou first saw Melusine. Terrified that she would disappear as fairies do when they are surprised by an uninvited visitor, he hid behind a large, flowering bush and watched her.

How delicate her hands were as they separated the long strands of hair! How she held them to the light and the air, drawing her fingers through as if they were so many strings of an invisible harp. Raymond of Poitou was entranced. Never in his life had he seen such grace, such perfection.

When Melusine reached out and lifted her dulcimer on to her lap, Raymond saw a heavenly comet light the skies. When her fingers touched the delicate strings he heard music being born. And when Melusine added her voice to the music, he thought his time must surely have come. This was the heavenly music that people heard as they died. The music of the planets as they turned, the voice of the heavenly angels as they arrived to take him away. Raymond was transported. He knew that he could not live without this fairy being. If he could not persuade Melusine to marry him he would remain celibate for ever. That is, if he lived at all.

Melusine finished singing, put aside her dulcimer, rose and

looked around. And there, standing before her, was the hand-somest knight she had ever seen.

'I am Raymond of Poitou,' he said, bowing low. 'I have just had the honour of hearing you sing. I hope you'll forgive the intrusion but I wouldn't have had the power, much less the will, to walk away from you. I've never heard such music, such singing. But you must know that already. And here I am now – I place myself in you hands and at your mercy. Please, please take pity on me. Marry me or put me out of my misery with this sword.' With a flourish he handed her his sword and swooped down in a deep bow, his head at her feet. 'I love you with all my heart. If you refuse me, my life will not be worth living.'

Melusine smiled. Then she giggled. She touched the bouncing black curls on Raymond of Poitou's head. Then she laughed with pure joy. Loud and long and clear as a bell. And the sound of it was so frank and open and pretty that Raymond could not be offended. Instead, he began to laugh too until he could no longer maintain his stooping position and had to stand up beside Melusine.

Raymond of Poitou was a beautiful man. Melusine liked his courteous words and his honest manner. He was brave but not too bold as to be challenging. His open declaration of love was outspoken but by no means disrespectful. His proposal of marriage was direct but not importunate. And he made her happy.

She looked him up and down and she imagined what a bliss he would be in bed. She let her eyes wander over his thighs and his hips and then his hands and up to his lips before finally bringing them to rest on his face. Yes, this man would be worth having.

'Do you mean to say,' she asked, 'your life won't be worth living?'

'I do, with all my heart,' replied Raymond, shining, ardent.

'You know I'm not a mortal like other women you meet?'

Raymond bowed his head. 'I know.'

'And do you know fairy ways?'

She watched Raymond carefully but she could read no sign of awkwardness on his face, in his eyes, from his gestures.

'I freely admit, I do not. But I will be an eager student.'

'And,' said Melusine, relishing the moment, 'would you accept me as I am?'

'Accept you?' gasped Raymond. 'I would welcome you with the most magnificent reception my country has ever seen. You would be the glow that lights my life, you would be—'

Melusine held up her hand, laughing merrily. 'Stop!' she cried. 'There are rules we fairies have that we can never tell mortals about. Could you accept my secrets?'

'What kind of secrets?' asked Raymond, anxious.

'Perhaps I can't tell you.'

'Can you tell me the nature of the secrets?'

Melusine reflected. Her instincts told her she could trust this man. His response to her question had been neither swift nor glib. He was expressing his reservations. This was the moment that mattered. If he agreed to the taboo now, they had a chance of a long and happy life together. He would not forget his promise out of love or excitement or resentment.

The magnitude of the moment made her nervous but she preserved an air of nonchalance.

'Perhaps its nature is secret too.'

Raymond's eyes grew cloudy with disappointment. His voice was unsteady as he spoke. 'Then I can't promise.'

He would not give his word in the passion of the moment, on a promise he could not keep. He had passed another test. Now, Melusine braced herself for the answer that would matter.

'I will marry you if you agree to leave me in complete privacy on the seventh day of each week. You mustn't break your word even if it is a matter of life or death, fire or flood. Other than that we can live as man and wife without any restrictions between us. I'm sure you'll find me a suitable partner.'

Raymond persisted in his questions. 'What would you do on that day?'

Melusine looked troubled. 'I can't tell you.'

'Would you be alone?' he asked, desperate.

'I would.' Melusine felt the tension in her limbs as Raymond stroked his chin for an instant.

'Then I'll accept your condition. And I promise to stand by my word.'

Relief was an elixir coursing through Melusine's veins. Raymond had proved himself strong, and even fairy women liked to know that their men were a good match for them. Suddenly, she could look back at her exile from Cephalonia with a different eye. Her invasion of Albion had been a boon, though she hadn't known at the time. It had changed her life as she had expected it would. It might not have happened in the way she'd expected but all the same it had released her from the turgid past where Pressina had kept her tethered. And how, she wondered, were her sisters? Were they enjoying the release in some way, too?

But Melusine had no time for wistfulness and worry. The next days were filled with preparations and arrangements and a new queen had to be found for the fairies.

'We can see why you want to marry this man,' said the fairy council, their eyes lustful and their lips wet at the thought of Raymond. 'Many a fairy would pucker up her mouth for his kiss or slip into his bed for a night of pleasure. But why abandon the fairy world? Won't it be much easier to bring him here? Mortals have lived happily among the fairies before. Why not again?'

But Melusine did not want to pluck Raymond from his world. Besides, she yearned to savour the treats of human life. And since Raymond wanted to marry immediately, the fairies agreed to release Melusine. They had known when Melusine became their queen that she was half human and they understood her attraction for Raymond of Poitou. But they would watch over her and visit her and be vigilant of her welfare.

The marriage of Melusine and Raymond was celebrated with feasting and the revels, which continued for weeks, had hardly finished before Melusine announced to Raymond that their first child was on the way. To seal their love, she built

Raymond a castle called Lusignan. When the first flush of passion and excitement subsided it was replaced by a love they were convinced would last for ever. Often, as Melusine sat with Raymond in silence by the fireside, as they walked in their gardens, or as they lay in bed after making love, she wondered if her mother had felt this way about her father. But if she had, she concluded, she would not have let one broken pledge wipe it all from her mind.

She shuddered, vowing to herself that she would never be like Pressina – the fay with the frozen heart whose frosty fingers reached out to devastate the happiness of others. She prayed fervently that Raymond would continue to have the strength to honour his vow so that they could live together for the rest of their lives.

The birth of the baby was the first test of their love. Geoffroi was born with a tusk protruding from one cheek. But Raymond and Melusine comforted each other and showered so much love on the infant that he was not even aware of his deformity for the first years of his life. Then there was a second child, and a third and a fourth. The only normal child of the four was Freimond, whose pure, kind nature won him the title of Freimond the Gentle.

'Why is this happening to us?' Raymond agonised, looking at his beautiful wife. 'You're perfect, so it must be something to do with me. Perhaps an old family weakness, some blemish in our line . . .?'

Melusine put her hand to his mouth in an anguish of guilt. If ever she had come close to betraying her secret, this was the moment. Surely, surely, this was part of Pressina's curse. But damnation didn't frighten her as much as the memory of leaving Cephalonia, reviled and rejected. If she told Raymond the truth, he too might abandon her. Instead she said: 'It is neither your fault nor mine. These are questions of fate and we have no control over them. At least we have Freimond.'

And that was how they continued to comfort each other so that their love withstood the cruel test for many years. But friends and family and well-wishers and ill-wishers had all begun to talk and to surmise. Many blamed Melusine for the deformities of their children. It was she, after all, who was only half mortal. And wasn't it a well-known fact that fairy children were malformed and weak? Was that not why fairies frequently exchanged their own babies for healthy human ones, leaving behind changelings with staring, beady eyes and wrinkled leathery skins and fearful appetites that devoured an elephant's portion of food? Only the fairies knew the truth: Pressina had violated fairy ethics, for once a taboo is set, it must not be changed. But Pressina, resentful that Melusine had found a husband who would stand by his word, had added to her curse. She wanted to make life harder for Melusine, the test more stringent for Raymond. She wanted Raymond to abandon Melusine as Elinas had abandoned her. After all why should Melusine, her image, her daughter – a demi-mortal – fare better than she had?

But Raymond's people didn't know all this and they continued to believe that Melusine was somehow to blame for the imperfections of her children. Yes, there was no doubt that Raymond had fallen under the enchantment of a fairy and she was using him to some perverse end of her own. True, they appeared to love each other with a deep and profound caring, but wasn't it a speciality of fairy women to convince a man that his love fantasies were as real as life itself? She was deceiving him in some dreadful way and he was paying for it with the twisted faces of his infants, changelings one and all. So what was she doing with the real infants? they wondered in horror. Were their little spirits to burn in hellfire when the fairies had finished with them and cast away their bodies?

The physical blemishes counted for little in the eyes of those with open minds. But what of the children like Geoffroi of the Tusk who had a violent temper and who picked fights with all and sundry, and gathered together all the villains in the city to join him in his raids – plundering, marauding, fighting, not merely amongst each other but all over Poitou. And the others were no better. They bickered and fought until

Castle Lusignan resounded with their hideous bellows. And Freimond spent more and more time with the monks at the monastery in order to escape from the disruption.

'These are no kin of yours,' grumbled Raymond's cousin, Gérard. 'These are the children of some monster.'

'Then I must be that monster,' Raymond replied, his head stooping. It was how he seemed to be most of the time nowadays, bowed with shame for some terrible thing one or another of his children had done. Still, he and Melusine grew closer, clinging to each other for comfort and strength, trying desperately to find a way to understand and redeem their children.

But Gérard was determined to make Raymond see that Melusine's fairy nature was to blame. And Gérard would not be silenced. He whispered in Raymond's ear in company and ranted at him in private. He swore he would set spies on Melusine and he cursed her for the depravities of her children. Eventually he made allegations which shook Raymond to the core.

'Do you not know what fairies are, man?' he grumbled. 'They were discredited at the time of the Fall. When God denounced Satan and commanded all the creatures present to decide who was right, all the angels upheld God's word. But there were other creatures, wicked creatures, wilful enough to avoid committing themselves one way or another. They, no doubt, saw some merit in Satan's behaviour. And after Satan was cast down, God cast these creatures down after him. Then as they screamed for mercy, he took pity and halted their fall. Now they inhabit the air and the spaces below ground – wells and caves and other hiding-places where they live accursed and concealed from the eyes of man. These are the creatures called fairies.'

'I'll admit Melusine is half fairy but there's nothing demonic about her. She is the gentlest, most loving wife you could hope to find anywhere.'

'Have you never wondered what she does on these Saturdays which she keeps sacrosanct?'

'Not unduly,' replied Raymond. 'It's a taboo she must observe. Fairies are often subject to them – particularly when they marry mortals.'

'Well I think she's making a fool of you. I'm sure she sets aside these Saturdays for some demonic lover. One with horns and tusks and monstrous limbs who gives her the kind of sexual satisfaction no human ever could. Did you never hear about the researches of the Dominican friars from Germany? Their findings show that these evil creatures have phalluses so large and tumescent, so enduring and strong, that the members of ordinary men are like cat-droppings in comparison. Once a woman has congress with an imp, a mortal man is no good to her.'

'Well,' smiled Raymond. 'We have been together for twenty years now, man and wife, but I don't think Melusine has any complaints there.'

'She dupes you. Fairy women can make you see what you want to see. That's their power. Melusine is a witch. What's more, she is condemned in the eyes of God.'

Raymond put his fingers in his ears and shook his head. 'I won't let you malign Melusine any more. She is my wife and we love each other dearly. There's nothing evil about her. She's been a perfect wife. She has loved and nurtured me and our children. It's not she who needs me, Gérard – I am the one who needs her.'

'Perfect wife? Need? Nurturing! You're bewitched, man. Only a priest of God can exorcise the demon power this woman holds over you.'

'There is nothing demonic about Melusine. She married me in church, in the presence of God and his holy accou-trements.'

But Gérard continued his accusations until, at last, his words started to drip through Raymond's ears, into his thoughts. He began to wonder what it was that Melusine did every Saturday without fail. Once planted, the thought nagged at his brain uncontrollably and continually and he had to know for sure that he was right about Melusine and Gérard was wrong. He had promised Melusine he would never ask. And he knew something of Melusine's terror of violating the taboo. Perhaps he could ask her indirectly? But what would he ask? Do you have a lover, Melusine, are you unfaithful to me? It was useless. He would never risk losing Melusine. She was his succour, his equilibrium, his bliss. The one, precious, steady thing in his life.

But the suspicion continued to grow in his mind. What *did* Melusine do each Saturday? Her skin was soft and fragrant when she came back to him. Her body was pliant and responsive. Her hair was silken and her eyes glowed from the rest and relaxation. Could it be that she was copulating with a demon lover? Raymond would have to find out for himself. There was no other way. So he concealed himself behind a large iron screen which had not been moved from the bath-chamber for years.

—Look at her as she floats in, her skin transparent with the light from the casement. Her hair flows like a mountain spring, darkened by night, flaring outwards to the ground. She walks swiftly to the bath, tests the water and climbs in. She starts singing now, as she washes her hair, massages her body. But though her voice is light and her face sweet with the sweetness only contentment can bring, the words of the song tell of terrible times. Of a lost father, of a weeping mother, of a curse and a home lost.

—Raymond feels his manly juices flow as they did in his youth. Melusine, my beloved, he wants to call out. Does a man ever grow old when he loves a woman as he loved her on the day they first met?

—Melusine stops singing and raises herself slightly in the water, looking around. Her face wears an expression of concern. Raymond tenses. Lord, please don't let her see me. Don't let me lose her, please.

—Melusine's face contorts with pain, she flips to one side of the bath and he sees a huge, serpent body heave and thrash below her. Oh my Lord! Poor Melusine. That's the curse.

That's the secret. There is no demon or any other kind of lover.

Raymond sank back, weak with relief. It was nearly night and Melusine had spent the day immersed in her bath, reviving the memory of past unhappiness, wondering sadly and resignedly about the plight of her children. He knew that Melusine was faithful to him. She had no other lover. No fairy man with a virile member and sexual tricks to outshine Raymond's manhood. He did not doubt that there were such men in the fairy world – and perhaps the human one – but they would never be a threat to him. Melusine loved him. That was enough. But Melusine must never, never know that he had broken his word.

That night their reunion was sweeter and more passionate than ever before. And from that day on their bond grew stronger, though the rift between Geoffroi and Freimond grew deeper and more serious.

Raymond and Melusine did all they could to stabilise the discord between the brothers and for a while things remained under control. Then one day as Freimond visited the monastery to pay his respects to the monks, Geoffroi followed. Swiftly, silently, he summoned his men and laid siege to the monastery.

'Your Grace,' stuttered a messenger, 'Geoffroi of the Tusk has done a terrible thing. He has trapped Freimond in a monastery along with a hundred monks and razed the place to the ground. They are all dead.'

Melusine's eyes were flares of anger. 'Geoffroi will be punished. He will be banished for ever from Lusignan, to roam without name or fortune . . .'

'Enough!' commanded Raymond, sick at heart. 'Let's put an end to curses and taboos. Yes, Geoffroi must be punished. But it is from your snake nature that he has inherited his evil streak. And the dreadful deformities of the others must also come from you, Melusine.'

Melusine froze, a column of ice, white, tall and chilly. Only her eyes moved as the world's grief writhed and thrashed inside them. Raymond could not see their tragic message. He had lost the only child who could continue his bloodline unblemished. All reason and sanity was driven out of him, releasing the suppressed resentment of the past.

'Leave me and my children alone, you evil creature, you deadly snake. You polluted my children. I never want to see you again.'

No one knows how long Melusine stood rooted to the spot. But when movement finally returned to her limbs, she spoke to Raymond quietly and with dignity.

'The curse is on me, Raymond, and I must go. You'll never see me again. But I'll appear once in a lifetime to every man, woman or child who lives in Castle Lusignan. I will be their messenger of doom, come to announce each death as it looms.'

Melusine jumped lithely on to the windowsill and hurled herself into the air. And when we hear the wind howling around our roofs and windows in fury and in pain, we may *think* it is Melusine, mourning and bewailing her betrayal at the hands of Raymond. And we may imagine Melusine's face, malicious with death, appearing faint and pallid through the glass. But we would be wrong. Because, you see, the fairies were waiting for Melusine when she left Castle Lusignan. They expected that one day she would return to the freedom and eternal feasting of their world. And they knew that when Pressina broke the rules of her fairy taboo, she broke the final part of her own spell; Melusine was no longer bound to suffer eternal damnation.

So Melusine returned to the fairies, and from then on she kept away from humans and the strife and malice that they like to gather around them.

Sheba

What a swan-like neck! And that slender waist – a branch
bent over with the weight of its own fruit. That was Bilqis,
Queen of Sheba – a lithe and lissom sapling, holding up the
entire kingdom of Sheba and the vast load of the tradition and
culture behind it. She was not really to the manner born. Six
years, that was all. She had been brought to Maarib, the capital of Sheba, to be queen six short years earlier when she
became twelve and the blood came.

Bilqis lingered in the pool that filled the mouth of the
temple, letting her limbs float free, as if with a will of their
own. The weight of the crown lifted from her shoulders as the
water closed firmly around the crevices and curves of her
neck, cradling, supporting, massaging. The demands of the
throne eased away from her waist, the small of her back. She
stroked her stomach, let her hand slide down to where the tension was building as her cycle reached its peak. On the other
side of the pond, inside the temple, were ointments and oils
that would help ease the pain. As the ovulatory process ran
down, the cells lining her womb would crumble and prepare to
leave her body.

For an instant she felt the heaviness of the seven days – some

inner sense of opportunities lost. Then she shook herself out
of it. If a woman allowed herself to become impregnated
every time her body signalled the possibility, she'd spend more
than half her life carrying babies. Women were made for
better things than that. In any case, they were far too sophis-
ticated, too urbane, too scientifically aware in this day and age
in Sheba, to let themselves undergo such drudgery. With the
Great Mother Moon watching over them, they were only too
well aware of the ebbs and tides, of the whole microcosm that
was the female body. No woman in Sheba would allow hers to
be exploited or misused.

The Temple of the Moon was the sanctuary of Bilqis, ruler
of Eden on Earth, negotiator of peace treaties and safe routes,
merchant-in-chief of her nation's magnificent goods – the
most glorious gems, the most exquisite scents. She rose now
out of the moon-silvered water and walked into the ante-
room. The down on her legs was smooth as satin and here, of
all places, she felt completely unselfconscious about her dis-
figured foot.

Other women awaited her, most of them at the same stage
of their cycle. Maha moved forward, swooped fleetingly
before her, face bursting with mischief.

'Blessings, Maha. Are you well?' Sheba knew what the
answer would be almost before she'd spoken. Sure enough,
Maha let out a deep, resonant growl, her eyes glowing, her lips
glistening, her plump body iridescent with drops lit up by the
full moon. 'I want a man, Bilqis – and I'm going to get one,
two, three, maybe more.'

A cackle went up around them. 'One – the right one – is
often better than too many,' someone countered, amid chortles
and shrieks.

'I agree. You can show him what you want. How many can
you teach in forty-eight hours?'

For the forty-eight hours when the passion of woman is at
its peak, these women were as one. They had been since
infancy; born together, bred together. And because they lived
in consonance, their bodies acted in concert. Many of them

already had babies, born within minutes of each other, and they knew each others' moods and needs and husbands and lovers as if they had a manuscript before them that told them everything.

Maha was not to be outdone. 'They may not need teaching. It could be that I've already taught them.'

In a corner, Ninlil yawned, stoked her midriff as she stretched. 'Training, shmaining – it's all a lot of rot. It's the size that matters.'

'It's not the size that matters,' protested one. 'It's what they do with it.'

There were nods and head-shakes and murmurs and giggles.

'So your Assab has a little one, then?'

Ninlil wasn't daunted. 'Wouldn't you like to know?'

'Maybe I know already.'

'Maybe.'

'How odd it must be to have one,' someone chimed in. More laughter as she stood up and staggered around with a fist between her thighs. 'So awkward – there's nowhere to put it.'

'And it must feel so clumsy dangling around.'

'What if they want to scratch it?'

'It's disgusting when they do.'

'Handy to piss with, though.' Maha moulded her hands into a fist and placed them one in front of the other, whirling and hissing like a water-hose.

'I wouldn't have one, however convenient.'

'Size does matter.' Someone picked up the earlier remark: 'Not just the size but the shape too.'

Cackles and guffaws. 'There's only one shape – long with a blob on the end.'

'Not so! Not so!' Laughter followed amid a recitation of possible shapes.

'Listen,' persisted Maha. 'There was this man who flashed his phallus at me last moon-festival. My eyes were so wide, I thought they'd fall out – it was such a size. But when we got down to it, I noticed it was crooked.'

A shriek of amusement. 'How'd you notice that?'

'It crooked in the wrong direction. It didn't work for me. Mind you, if someone's ecstasy spot is at the right angle for it . . .'

Ninlil was nearly in tears with laughter. 'You should've sent him to a wizard.'

'Or done your own magic.' Sheba was thoughtful. 'It's only a muscle. A ligament pulling down in the wrong direction, do you think? Surgery or manipulation –' She was interrupted by hoots of laughter '– that could do the trick, perhaps.'

'Magic!' they all screamed. 'Magic would be best. Manipulation would be an investment without return.'

'There would *be* a return,' Sheba insisted, still serious.

'Here speaks a virgin,' shrieked Maha. 'A royal virgin. Perhaps *The* Virgin – but a virgin, nevertheless. Do you realise how desperate the need is for repayment at this time of the month?'

Bilqis, Queen of Sheba, smiled slowly. She felt the yearning too. The needs of her body rose and fell with the tides of the mighty sea that bounded her fabulous kingdom. But she was the royal virgin, the widow-queen, the promised of the Sun God. She it was, whose sexual rhythms regulated the equanimity of the wonderful land of Sheba. She would not give in to her cravings until the moment when desire was at its peak and her wisdom in full flower and her power at its height. And this would only happen when she had the perfect partner standing before her, who reciprocated her yearning with his mind and body and soul. Then, her passion would yield greater glory for the world. Bilqis knew this deep inside, so these monthly meetings with her friends did not disturb her. She had as much fun as the others, who had all lost their virginity years ago.

The hoopoes escorted Bilqis back to her palace, chattering and singing, swooping and hooping, entertaining her with sky formations and bird dances. She loved them as they loved her. She had found them as fledglings some years ago and adopted them as her own. Now they had grown into the most exquisite, crowned, plumed creatures. But did she sense some distress among them today?

'Is all well?' she asked.

'Well, since you ask, Majesty,' began the chief of the birds. 'We've had a message. And it sounds a little alarming. Solomon, King of Israel, has summoned us to his kingdom. We think he might be angry with us.'

Bilqis frowned. 'Angry? Why? Who brought you the message?'

'The west wind,' replied the hoopoe. 'You know, he can be misleading.'

'Hmm. Blustery, bombastic. It's his way. But could you not get him to clarify the message?'

'He says it's all he knows. Solomon missed us at an inspection of all his war troops – and he wants to see us.'

Bilqis' eyebrows made thunderclouds. She hated the thought of war. It was worse than a plague or a blight because it was made of intention not circumstance and could be avoided.

'I keep hearing about this Solomon and his temple and his kingdom – and his wretched wars. Why does he always make war?'

The hoopoes bowed their heads and were still. They knew very well that it was not worth questioning Solomon's ways. He was set in them and he was always determined to win.

'Go to him,' Bilqis commanded. 'The only way you'll find out what he wants is to ask. How long will it take you?'

'It takes a man seven years, a bird with powerful wings no less than a month. But if we ride the west wind, we'll be there in a twinkling.'

'Then go, and may the moon guide you at night and the sun guard you by day. And don't let this Solomon bully you.'

Bilqis watched the birds fly away. How easy it was for them – no routes to keep to, no boundaries to negotiate, no merchandise to carry, no predators, no pirates, no problems. True, she had worked things out satisfactorily with neighbouring kings at Ausan and the Arabian desert on one boundary, Erythraea, Danakil and Tigrai on the other, as well as the prelates and emperors so far afield as China, Rome and Persia. Her merchants took gemstones and incense to the furthest corners of the East and returned weighed down with gold – gold which lined the corridors and gilded the streets of Sheba, so much of it that it was hardly worth more than the stones and the sand. But Bilqis had never had truck with Solomon – this King of Israel – this man who was obsessed with war but also known for his love of his God. What kind of a god was he, Bilqis wondered, who constantly wanted him to fight and kill and then fight some more?

She had heard of him just recently when Tamrin, a merchant of Sheba, had sought an audience with her. Any day now, he would return from Israel where he had been received at Solomon's court. He would certainly have stories to tell about the strange, angry king.

And Tamrin did have stories about Solomon; he described a man with qualities that Bilqis could not have imagined.

'I met Solomon after he sent messages far and wide to the merchants on various routes. It was a generous invitation. We were to visit the king and show him the finest of our goods. If he chose anything, we were free to name our price. Solomon is constructing a house – no ordinary house, but a house for his God, a tabernacle for the worship of his deity – and he would not sully it or undermine its spirit by haggling about the price of necessities.

'I felt that he welcomed me in a special way. He found my potent and enduring fragrances could not be surpassed. He bought my entire stock of cypress wood because he could tell by touching that it came from trees that have existed since the beginning of time. He made me important and I felt puffed and inflated that a king could give me so much personal attention. But as the days passed, I noticed that Solomon gave the same importance to all his guests. If he found my goods so valuable and my country so fascinating, then he found the same degree of merit in someone else's language, another's livestock or a particular ability.'

'A hypocrite, then!' Bilqis exclaimed.

treating my wards, my hoopoes. I want to know about him.

Suddenly, there appears before Sheba a vast, echoing hall. Solomon's court, perhaps? It is permeated with a sense of justice, a certain relentlessness that makes Bilqis uncomfortable. And here are her hoopoes in exquisite formation. Like a massive, breathing jardinière They twitter a moment, then fall silent.

Now, in a blur of golden light, Bilqis can see limbs moulded to a throne. Arms lifted in welcome. No rebuke, no raised voice. Bilqis' tension increases instead of reducing as a voice of dark, deep velvet caresses her ears.

'I want to hear your story,' it says. 'Where were you when I commanded all the living creatures of earth, air and water to present themselves for inspection and to offer me their services?'

Altogether, the birds twitter. Bilqis wills them to organise themselves. Chaos will serve nothing. She reaches them and they fall silent. Then the chief bird differentiates himself from the fluttering mass. Bilqis' heart swells. How majestic he looks, how strong. And how honest the light that shines from his eyes.

'We did not know about your command. For some months now, we have been in Sheba, the land of peace and plenty, where we were reared. Since Sheba knows no war, we received no message from you.'

'No war?' She senses Solomon's interest; her breast quickens. 'A country where there's no war? Where is this country?'

'It is the kingdom of Sheba. It is a land situated in what was once a barren wilderness. Today, you'll see it green and lush. Its monarchs have placed tanks and ponds at strategic points on its mountain tops to catch the rain. And they have dug deep channels throughout Sheba for the water to flow in and irrigate the land.

'The trees of Sheba are as old as creation. Their sap is rich with precious resins – amber, myrrh and frankincense. Its men and women are highly skilled in the arts and sciences. But their special expertise is in husbandry and the cultivation of the land. The elders of Sheba are deeply spiritual. Every man there is a king, every woman a queen. They live together in peace and plenty. For six years now, it has been known as Eden on Earth and sometimes as the Blessed Land.

'Its ruler is Queen Bilqis, High Priestess of all Sheba.'

Solomon's entire being reverberates with the shock of the last statement. His voice shakes as he verifies it.

'Are you telling me this Sheba, this earthy paradise, is ruled by a woman?'

'It is,' replied the chief hoopoe.

'But what has happened to its men? Are they eunuchs, incapable of war? Has your queen emasculated them? When a man puts down his weapons he puts down his manhood. Are they only capable of . . .? What are they capable of . . .?'

The hoopoes are flabbergasted. They honour the men of Sheba more than any others in the world. Solomon quivers.

So it's true, thinks Bilqis. He can read their minds.

'They are honourable men – and peaceful. Forbearance makes them stronger than those who survive by reducing others. They plough the fields, they travel far and wide with Sheba's merchandise and they always return safe. They are not plundered or robbed or murdered by the brigands and pirates that beset the dangerous routes between Sheba and Mecca or Aden – or further still in the Persian Gulf and the Indian Ocean.'

Solomon throws back his head. His laughter is dark. 'You can't expect me to believe that. There is a pirate on every wave of the Red Sea. Are you telling me they don't molest Sheba's ships? Or that her camels get safe conduct through Samarkand and Bukhara when the rest of us pay mightily with the lives of our merchants and princes? I fight wars to save lives. How can a mere woman achieve what you claim? It's a fantasy! A fabrication! A glamour to deceive and enchant us.'

'I only speak the truth.' The hoopoe's voice is quiet, dignified. 'Sheba negotiates for her safety. The lives of her people are more important to our queen than possessions and territory. That has always been the way in Sheba but more so under Bilqis than ever before.'

'Why so?' Solomon is intrigued. Bilqis shudders. Her cry resounds in the ears of the hoopoes – a million miles away. 'No! Don't tell him! Not yet.'

'No!' they echo. 'It is not for us to say.'

The hoopoes clear their minds. When Solomon gropes for causes, he finds only blank spaces. The power of Bilqis' will has exhausted her energies and she slumps, in a faint.

Solomon questions his advisers. What do they know of Sheba and its queen? Nothing they say impresses him. He turns back to the hoopoes.

'Wake up! wake up!' The faces of the women formed a vault like a floral arch above Bilqis. As she opened her eyes, the flower-faces of the women retreated, making space for her to rise. 'It's noon. You should get up.'

Bilqis rose, recovered.

'It must have been a mighty spell,' Maha giggled.

'It was,' Bilqis replied. 'But it's whetted my appetite. And now I can feel the hunger gnawing inside me. I'm late for my prayers.'

She plunged into the water, the women behind her as they left the temple. Outside, the sun's chariot had reached its assigned position in the heavens. It was noon and the desert was a sea of molten gold. Bilqis shaded her eyes with her arm.

I wonder, she thought, what he's hiding behind that blaze. One day, I'll find out. Then an unbidden thought: One day, I'll meet Solomon.

The thought must have shocked the sun as much as Sheba for the next moment, the sky turned black.

Bilqis' women fell to their knees. The men in the fields craned their necks upwards. Was this a calamity? They'd not seen a single indication of rain clouds. Bilqis peered into the darkness. It was full of motion, energy, intent. As she continued to stare she began to distinguish the movement – it was like a hundred pairs of wings, fluttering, jostling, making a formation.

'The hoopoes!' she exclaimed, and immediately rays of light began to filter through the formation. 'You're back.' Bilqis flung open her arms.

Swooping and hooping, the hoopoes pirouetted down to Bilqis and handed her a letter bearing a large, six-point star.

'Solomon's seal,' said the chief hoopoe. 'He wants you to come and see him.'

Even before Bilqis opened the letter, she read Solomon's first combative signal. 'My God,' he was saying, by making the hoopoes obscure the light of the sun, 'is greater than yours.'

Bilqis paced up and down her chamber.

'Explain this, Tamrin,' she insisted. 'Explain this insult. You know Solomon. You told me he was gracious and diplomatic. How dare he speak to me like this?'

Tamrin said not a word but sat with his head bowed low until Bilqis dismissed him.

When he had left, she snatched up Solomon's letter and read it again. As she read, she began to remember his incredulous reaction when the chief hoopoe had told him about his queen. Solomon was challenging her. He was playing games. He was a gambler. Well, who better to play games with than Bilqis, Queen of Sheba, daughter of that greatest of all gameplayers and heir to the longest games-playing tradition in existence?

For hadn't the former King of Sheba been addicted to games? Games of chance and games of skill, but best of all, word-games? He could riddle you this and riddle you that and riddle you into the palm of his hand. And his stakes were high — oh so very high that those who sat atop them tumbled into a deep, dark abyss if they lost. He was unrelenting as he watched his opponents crash from kingship to worse than slavery. For yes, that was what he demanded of them. Their kingdom for a riddle. And what man thinks that can ever happen to him? Especially a king whose birthright is wisdom touched by divinity, whose legacy is insight, whose reach can command the most profound knowledge — whose habit, too, too often, is risk.

All those kings came to Sheba and approached its king and challenged him to a game. Among them was the young King of Shams, vassal of the King of Sheba, who wanted to win back the independence of the country forfeited by his father in battle.

He was a beautiful man, golden faced, golden haired, golden limbed. The King of Sheba found the sight of him pleasing and his manner even more pleasing because there was a diffidence about him, a sort of acknowledgement in the turn of his smile, the flow of his gestures, that he was up against a master – *the* Master – and could easily lose. Somehow, his humility enhanced his appeal as an opponent. Such a man is stronger, more daring, than the idiot who approaches undaunted, unmindful of reality. So the King of Sheba welcomed the young king and he spent many hours talking to him and entertaining him and discussing matters of both states until finally he began his formidable game.

Before he started, he asked: 'You are sure you want to play?'

The young king nodded vigorously. 'I do, my liege.'

Sheba gave him a second chance. 'The cost of losing is high,' he reminded him. 'Your kingdom to the winner.'

'You are a wonderful emperor, my lord,' said Shams. 'And my kingdom has improved vastly since you oversaw it. But I must at least try to redeem it for my heirs. With your friendship and guidance it will prosper even more when it is back in my hands. For a kingdom, in the tradition of my country and most others, does not belong to the king. It is a divine trust, to be nurtured and improved before being passed on to the next generation of carers.'

Sheba nodded. He liked this young man more and more. He would not mind losing to him. His kingdom was already large enough and rich enough and beautiful enough. He would even be glad for this young man to have his own country back. A thought crossed his heart but his mind steadied it immediately. No – a game was a game and must be played fair and square, so he would not, deliberately, lose. Indeed, how could he? For the simplest riddle can be an inordinate dilemma to one who cannot solve it. So, he closed his eyes, made himself comfortable in his seat and reached into his mind for the first enigma that popped in. And this was it.

> *More creative than the Creator, more destructive than the*
>   *Destroyer*
> *Higher than highest, lower than lowest*
> *Hotter than fire, colder than ice*
> *Brave men run from it, cowards face it*
> *The hungry refuse it, the dead eat it*
> *What is it?*

The young king latched on to the clues that offered an opening. 'The dead eat it and the hungry would have to refuse it. Is it dust?'

The King of Sheba shook his head in frustration and the curls in his beard wriggled and bounced. 'No. No. No. The dead do not eat dust. They do not eat at all, do they?'

The young king thought hard.

'What's higher than highest?' fired the Sheban king, exasperated. 'Who can be more creative than God the Creator – what is more destructive . . .? Is anything hotter than fire or colder than ice? Tell me, what is it? Go on, tell me?'

'Well, the sun might be hotter than fire – but colder than ice . . .?' The young king hung his head and did not notice the Sheban advisers shaking their heads at their king. He was bound to break the laws of the game. They knew he only wanted to help his young opponent, but his attempts could be misconstrued: his critics might say it was a trick to throw the King of Shams off scent.

The young king shook his head, resigned. 'I'm sorry,' he whispered. 'I acknowledge defeat. I cannot think of an answer. I can think of nothing that brave men would run from and cowards would face.'

The Sheban king's face scrunched up in frustration. He jiggled his fingers and wriggled in his throne and clenched his eyes so tight they began to water. He had it! The boy had the answer – he just needed to detach himself from the question, take courage and answer. 'Would you like to hazard a guess?' he demanded, almost choking on his words.

The young king shook his head. 'My mind is empty.'

'But you just said it!' cried the Sheban king. 'You used the word!'

The young king shook his head. 'Tell me the answer,' he said, quietly.

The Sheban king couldn't speak for a moment. 'Nothing. The answer is "nothing". If only you'd tried just a little harder. Still, that's the way with riddles, isn't it? There but not quite clear.'

The King of Shams rose with dignity from his seat, took off his belt of sovereignty and laid it at Sheba's feet. Beside it he placed his sceptre. Then he reached up to remove the crested torque of gold from around his neck. But the King of Sheba stopped him.

'Why are you in such a hurry to give up your kingship?' he demanded. 'You are entitled to another chance.'

The young king looked determined. 'I want no special dispensation.'

'Well you can be sure you'll get none. What are you to me more than just another one of my many vassals and thousand guests? True, I enjoyed your company but I have a favoured guest most nights. No, this is the normal pattern. All part of the game. I will set you a test. It is full of trials and tricks but if you achieve your quest and manage to come home sound in limb and whole in mind, I will give you back the kingdom of Shams. If not, it is mine. The trial will be hard, so you have a choice. You can surrender now and save your life or you can play the game and perhaps redeem yourself and your kingdom.

The young king bowed low. 'I will accept the test.'

'Good!' exclaimed Sheba, a look of relief flooding him and lighting up the eyes of his courtiers. Here was a diversion! Here was a chance for the young king to win at the game of fortune. There was not a man in the court who was not behind him, urging him to win.

'You should know,' continued the King of Sheba, 'that you risk life and limb.'

The young king bowed again, in acknowledgement. 'I have no wife or child to support. My kingdom is already beholden to you. I have nothing to lose, all to gain.'

'Then go on your way and may the sun guide your path. Remember, the journey to Mauza is well trodden. Our merchants come and go in three months. There are hills to climb and forests to negotiate but the route is well established and travel is easy. Still – a well-trodden path makes its own travails. Our merchants are the richest in the world, known for their fabulous goods. So the same path is beset by brigands and opportunists out to make a quick fortune. Your life is in danger: don't doubt that for a moment or you will lose your advantage. But that is not the hardest part of the journey – after all, many undertake it for their own advantage. No, the second chance comes with a higher stake. You must complete the return journey within thirty days. If you do not, you die.'

The young king stretched himself to his full height and in that moment Sheba's king, his courtiers and the rest of the kingdom felt a deep yearning for his success. On the back of that yearning, he set out on his journey.

Well, the young king rode out of Sheba and into the desert. The sun blazed ahead of him, blinding him so that he could not see very far ahead. But his horse continued, fleet of foot, eyes shaded, at a speedy pace until all at once it let out a terrified whinny and reared, clawing the air.

Shams clung to its neck, scanning the dunes for sign of the trouble. But all he could see was a cloud of dust a few yards ahead. What was it? he wondered. Had his mount sensed some treacherous quicksand and saved them from drowning in a sandy undertow? But no. As his eyes adjusted to the glare, he saw two twining shapes wriggling in the dust.

Two enormous serpents reared up, the sand sliding from their wide backs, fangs snarling, tongues curling, hisses mingling. The king stared. What was he to do? Well, first things first. He should calm his horse down, steady it. As he soothed

its mane, wiped its frothing muzzle, offered it water, he kept a
chary eye on the battling serpents. He studied their every
move but they remained oblivious to his presence.
Unobserved, and out of immediate danger, the king made his
decision. He would intervene, but in order to stop the fight, he
would have to kill one of the creatures.

He watched, alert for a sign that would tell him which of
the serpents deserved to die. He could not tell which of them
was a fair fighter, which not, which of them began the fight
and whether he was justified – so he decided to play a game of
chance: he would simply shoot the first of the two to raise his
head to the right of a certain sand dune directly behind. He
fitted a diamond-tipped arrow to his bow and waited until
the white serpent twisted its massive head to the right, towards
the dune. Then instinctively, the young king abandoned his
decision, took careful aim at the black serpent and let his arrow
fly. Its tip pierced the small space between the eyes of the
black serpent, and with a mighty spitting noise it leapt up in
the air then died back like a fire quenched with water.

The white serpent stopped a moment, observing the young
rider as if reflecting on his deed. Then, with a look which
may have been gratitude, it plunged into the sand and disappeared downwards towards the core of the earth.

The king continued his journey with lightning speed and
spent the rest of his twenty-nine days whipping aspiration
and exploiting opportunity until at last he arrived back at the
boundaries of the country neighbouring Sheba, with a desert
expanse and a city still to traverse before dusk. Stopping only
to water and feed his loyal horse, he clung to hope and the high
road even more than he had done during the preceding days.
Then suddenly, as he was halfway through the desert and at
the very same spot where he had intervened in the battle of the
serpents, his horse reared, whinnied and, as before, came to a
stop.

This time, when the young king looked over his shoulder, he
saw a princely rider accompanied by a curtained palanquin.

'You saved my life,' said the prince. 'I want to repay you.'

'Forgive me,' countered the king, 'but I don't recall seeing you before. I need no payment – but I am in a hurry and if I stop to talk, I won't reach my destination in time.'

'Sheba by dusk?' laughed the prince. 'I'm afraid that's out of the question. Without my help, that is.'

The king tightened his horse's bridle. 'Your help?'

'You do know me,' continued the prince. 'The white serpent? I am the Prince of Jinns and you helped me get rid of a very dangerous adversary. You saved my life and I want to repay you.'

'Thank you, but if you don't let me get on my way, there will be no one to repay,' replied the king. 'If I don't reach Sheba by sunset, I will forfeit my life.'

'Nonsense,' said the Prince of Jinns, briskly. 'You saved my life: I'll save yours. I want you to marry my sister. She is the Queen of the Jinns and will be a great asset to you.'

The Prince of Jinns dismounted, walked over to the palanquin and drew up the curtain. There behind it sat a young woman. Her beauty was of the other world and she was so luminous, Shams thought the evening sun must have given her his lustre as he faded. He felt quite faint with desire.

'I presume you approve,' beamed the prince, reassured by the king's obvious emotions. 'She is wise and well versed in the ways of humans. She will ensure your future.'

The king stared at the Jinn woman, speechless.

The prince's smile turned into a chuckle. 'Well. I can see you're not fit for much now. But if I don't do something about it, I'll have caused your death – and where would that leave me?'

The young king still stood tongue-tied. The Jinn reached out his arm and it grew and grew and grew until it reached the belly of the horse. Then he raised up both horse and rider and delivered them to the centre of Sheba's capital. Back to earth, the young king recovered his senses and urged his horse more and more swiftly until he reached the palace gates. Suddenly he had so much to live for. Not just his kingdom but his beautiful new bride-to-be to rule beside him, children, a future!

A huge cheer went up as the gates were heaved back and he was helped off and escorted to the king.

'Well done,' the King of Sheba applauded him. 'You're back and you can live as a free man again. If I had a daughter, I would give her to you. But I do not. So go home and live in peace, and any time I can help, I shall be glad to do so. Our future games will carry harder penalties but I have to confess that this was the most enjoyable match I've ever had and you the most worth opponent.'

So the young king married the Queen of Jinns and the Jinn explained that he had deliberately set up the fight in order to test the young king's superiority among men before selecting him as a worthy husband for his sister. In time they had a beautiful daughter named Bilqis. And all that Bilqis did not inherit of her mother's wisdom and magic, she learned by the time she was ten. Then, having passed on all her knowledge to the girl, her mother also handed over rulership of the Land of Jinns, and died.

So it was that Bilqis became mistress of immense wisdom. She could intuit the past, predict the future, coin maxims and unravel riddles. Besides, she could read omens and explain phenomena and discern the meaning of events, past, present and future.

Soon afterwards, the King of Sheba sent the King of Shams a proposal of marriage for Bilqis. 'I am far too old to be a physical husband to your daughter,' he said, 'but this is the only way in which I can make her the Queen of Sheba. She has no equal in the world and Sheba deserves a queen like her.'

The King of Shams knew his friend must have thought long and wisely before making his suggestion. He agreed to the match and Bilqis became the queen consort. As soon as the girl began menstruating, the King of Sheba summoned his priest and the priestess of the temple of the Mother Moon and Bilqis was consecrated High Priestess and Sovereign Supreme of all Sheba. The king tutored her in the ways of sovereignty and watched with pleasure as she proved to be the perfect choice. Under her rule, the kingdom flourished and grew and the people loved Bilqis. But all that changed the day that the old king died. For his son, who had bowed before Bilqis for two years, was not content to remain a prince for the rest of his life.

Cunningly, he persuaded a powerful group of Shebans to oppose Bilqis. But Bilqis, born as the result of a series of games, was a canny player herself. She knew what her stepson was capable of. She had played with him as they grew and she had seen the darknesses in him. He had flouted rules and violated nature when his father taught them to listen to the rhythm and flow of the earth and its creatures, to hone instinct and vibrate to the time and motion of its currents. That was the way to draw in the wisdom of its mighty and enduring force. That was the truest source of wisdom. But all this was lost on Bilqis' stepson. The only instinct he knew was the one that swelled and seared his loins. Bilqis was forced to bring all her wiles and guiles to bear to protect her royally decreed virginity from him.

Bilqis listened to her finely tuned instincts and knew exactly what she was doing when she went into court and made her announcement.

'It is understandable for a male child to covet the throne. He considers it his birthright. If his mother clings to it, then he feels obliged to become violent. Sheba has a past tradition of noble queens, I know, but I am happy to hand over the kingdom to my son.'

True, she told them, he had not been schooled in the ways of sovereignty as she had – but he was the son of a wise and wonderful man and he would no doubt learn swiftly. As his mother, she would be glad to advise him if he required her guidance.

The Shebans were disarmed. Those who had spoken against her, regretted their words. Those who wanted her as queen fretted and reproached themselves for allowing her to abdicate. But Bilqis soothed them all, devoting herself to the service of the temple. And all the time she nurtured her powers of thought and insight and magic and learned the lessons left behind by those who had possessed the wisdom and knowledge of infinity.

The king, her stepson, meanwhile, grew more and more debauched. Mainly, he liked to hunt. But he did not target the animals of the jungles – wild, ferocious creatures or fleet edible ones. No, his pleasure was to pursue and rape the wives of other men. There was little any of them could do to stop their king. Often, they would think of taking a delegation to Bilqis but then they would hold back. They had not helped when she needed their support; with what face could they ask her to rescue them now?

Then the king's attention turned to the most beautiful, the most desirable woman in the land. Bilqis herself. It was unnatural, whispered the people. She would punish him terribly, muttered his enemies. Incest was reserved for the gods – how could the king even dream of it? But the king denied incest. The young woman had never slept with his father. The whole land knew she was a virgin. She was not his real mother. She was a good few years younger than himself. This was not incest, whichever way you looked at it. And so it was that he arrived at Bilqis' temple and demanded marriage. Now, the people thought, holding their breath. Now, Bilqis' stepson had gone too far. Now she would turn the power of her wrath against him. Bilqis was known to be just and virtuous. Now, at last, Sheba would be safe from its evil ruler.

Bilqis, mistress of the game, walked out to the front of her temple. 'I'll marry you,' she smiled and went back in.

The populace was in a state of shock, followed by bitterness and anger. Immediately the tongues began wagging again. The longing for power had made her insane. Her ambition to rule made her diabolical. But then what could they expect – was she not the daughter of a demoness? Stories proliferated of her hairy legs and her supernatural knowledge of magic and the black arts. And as Bilqis put on her wedding robes and underwent the marriage rituals, many thought they saw a demonic aura surrounding her – a horned, creature with slit pupils and yellow irises glowered through her eyes. Others claimed that at some angles they saw her true image, a wrinkled, decaying hag beneath the marble-smooth fourteen-year-old skin. How else could the wisdom of aeons reside in a slip of a girl? She had held them all enthralled. Now the scales were dropping, jolted by her naked ambition to be queen again. Now they could see her for what she was.

She had tricked her father, then the Sheban king and now the young king too. They held their heads in their hands and waited for disaster. This woman whom they had hoped would be their salvation was to join hands with their oppressor in unholy matrimony and complete their destruction.

Bilqis knew what they were thinking. But she did not let it disturb her. It was just one of the burdens of monarchy and she had to bear it patiently. She had chosen a game of skill and part of it was to give away nothing. She remained impassive, stayed aloof from the accusations and machinations and played the part of a royal bride on display. It was the hardest day of her life; being strong, she realised, did not mean that she did not feel pain – only that she did not let it show. By the end of the day she would have made her toughest move and won – and so she maintained her equilibrium.

As she lay alone, in the heart of the night, her new husband came to her, lascivious with wine, penis erect. He grabbed her by her hair and threw her on the bed, then hurled himself at her. Bilqis thrust out her hands and struck his chest. The next moment, she felt his warm blood on her hands, then on her face and chest. She struck again.

'Die,' she said. 'In the name of all the women and men you have killed for your pleasure.'

When she was sure he was dead, she let go of her heavy, gold dagger. It fell on her left foot and severed her toes but Bilqis did not even notice as she dragged herself to the doors. She walked out on to the terrace of the palace and clung to the rope so that the gong heaved over and over again with the weight of her.

'Rejoice!' she shouted. 'I have killed him. Your persecutor is dead.'

Then she swore a mighty oath: 'Never again will there be bloodshed in Sheba. There is a peaceful option for everything – together we'll find it.'

From that moment on, Bilqis put her mind and soul into the reformation of Sheba. Now, four years later, it was prosperous and peaceful and its people more content than ever before. And though, outside the kingdom, the odd rumour ranged about Bilqis' demonic nature, her goat-legs, her hoofed feet, her own subjects knew the truth about her and loved her like a mother and a daughter rolled into one.

If Solomon wanted to play games, Bilqis would be happy to oblige. She would offer him such a match that it would be remembered for aeons to come. She clapped her hands and laughed and her laughter tinkled like a waterfall through the grounds. Then she said a prayer, sobered herself suitably and summoned her advisers.

'I have received this letter from Solomon of Israel. How shall I deal with it?' she asked, handing it to them.

After usual formal salutations from one sovereign to another, Solomon aggressively asserted his credentials as the King of Kings chosen by the One and Only Almighty God that he worshipped, and commanded her to attend his court to pay him homage. If she did not, he threatened, he would send his kings and their legions against her – and these comprised the beasts of the fields, the birds of the air and the demons, ghosts and other creatures of the night. The monsters, he claimed, would strangle her in bed, the animals kill her and the birds dispose of her flesh.

What a bizarre invitation: the man who sent it was clearly frightened of what he did not know. One thing she could understand much better now: if Solomon sent the same 'invitation' to the other monarchs, those living near him in particular, it was no wonder they responded with war – and even those who did not, would, by their lack of response, invoke attack from Solomon. You could see why the man spent half his life in battle. No one had taught him that even slavery can be sought sweetly.

Bilqis knew then that there were deep conflicts within Solomon. The man who interacted with the wisdom and sweetness that Tamrin described could hardly be the same one who had written this note exposing terrible vulnerability and fear and – yes – indiscretion and blatant aggression towards her when she had done him no harm, nor offered any threat.

Tamrin now told her that Solomon was behaving in this uncharacteristic way because Bilqis was a woman. If there was anything to fault in Solomon, in his experience, it would be the man's attitude to women. Tamrin had noted that, occasionally, he would toss a deprecating joke about women into his heady, absorbing conversation; casually, lightly, even jokingly. After all, his courtiers laughed – if indeed they noticed it at all. But to a man of Sheba they were offensive and Tamrin wondered if he detected some pungency, a certain bitterness behind the lightness. But for all his fabled wisdom Solomon was apparently oblivious to this. Bilqis could see he had a blind spot.

'What kind of remarks?' she demanded. 'I need to understand this man before I'll have anything to do with him.'

'Well,' began Tamrin, 'he suggested that women were unreliable, immoral and inferior.'

Bilqis was amazed. 'And the women of Israel don't protest?'

Tamrin looked uncomfortable. 'You have to meet Solomon to understand. They believe every word he says.'

Bilqis' eyes were full of questions.

'He has written a book filled with statements condemning women.'

Bilqis decided she would act unexpectedly. Playing games was her forte. The alternatives Solomon offered her were obeisance or contempt. Both diminished her. She would choose a third. One which showed respect and friendship but preserved her sovereignty. For why – why in the name of all living things under the sun, would she give up her dominion because some king demanded it? Only a lunatic would ask it. And Solomon was not a lunatic.

But first she would consult her council. 'As you know, Your

Majesty,' they advised, 'we have not fought a war for some years now. But we still have our military skills and possessions and if you want us to prepare for battle against Solomon, we are ready to fight. We wish to fight. But the final decision is yours.'

Bilqis, Queen of Sheba, reflected a moment.

'You know how I despise killing,' she said, at last. 'When kings attack countries, they leave behind a trail of destruction and death. War releases the lowest instincts in the noblest men. Worse of all, no one wins a war – the cost of both winning and losing is far too high. So instead of fighting, I'll send envoys with gifts of peace and friendship. My next decision will depend on Solomon's response.'

Bilqis filled a ship with the wood of ancient cypress trees and the fabulous incenses of Sheba. She included a large, lustrous pearl – the most magnificent to be found in the ocean – and this pearl was unpierced. Let Solomon make of that what he would. At least it would please him; at most he would read in it the symbolism of Bilqis, Queen of Sheba, unmatched in beauty, unique, virgin, unconquered.

But Solomon reacted strangely. He took Sheba's gift as bribery, or a show of wealth, or an insult to humiliate him. He thundered and roared and bellowed and blustered, threatening to march on Sheba with his minions and legions and kings and countries and to drag her from her throne by the hair of her head and dash her to the ground at his feet. Inside, Solomon was slightly scared and absolutely intrigued by the Queen of Sheba. When he had calmed down a little, he realised that much of his anger came from disappointment. He desperately wanted to meet Bilqis – and since she had turned down his invitation and, instead, sent him a pearl to taunt him with her unconquerable nature, he would have to find another way of meeting her.

So Solomon sent another message. This time it was softer and sweeter and Bilqis prepared to make the journey.

'Tell Solomon,' she commanded the hoopoe, 'that I shall soon leave Maarib to make the journey to Israel. And because

I am Queen of Jinns as well as Sheba, my journey will be much shorter than the usual seven years from Sheba to Israel.'

As soon as Solomon heard the news, he summoned the jinns. 'Who can go to Maarib and bring back the throne of Sheba before she reaches Israel?'

Many jinns offered and Solomon dispatched a powerful creature who promised to return in the time it would take for a flower to open its petals at dawn – an invisible instant, a mysterious moment that happens in secret. Solomon was satisfied. He would use the throne when the time was right.

As she travelled, Bilqis made sure she learned more and more about Solomon and his family and his background. She knew for sure that he was determined to be adversarial. She was in no doubt that this would be the ultimate battle. Solomon would make an impressive opponent and Bilqis must not be overwhelmed. So she thought carefully of the things she had discovered about Solomon. It would show her the way into the man's mind and heart.

When Solomon was born, the womb of his mother Bathsheba was still warm from her first child, snatched from her because of her sins. Poor babe – why was he made to give up his little life because of her adultery with David? And did his death pay for her husband, slain by David? When Solomon came, Bathsheba could not allow herself to love the new infant. What if he was taken from her too? A dead child for each parent, each deed. Then, suddenly, it was too late and she could not feel the love any more. It was frozen like a stream in winter, turned to ice. When she looked at Solomon she saw a jibe, a jeer, a taunt from the Almighty, a shade, left here to remind her of what she had lost, what might have been. All Israel praised the prodigious child, saw that he was wisdom incarnate, that he would bring glory to the name of Yahweh, swore that he would not simply continue the hallowed traditions of his tribe but refine them and raise them to new heights. That Yahweh Almighty would speak through him. But all Bathsheba could see was a travesty of justice. That a child was dead . . .

So, while the world sang Solomon's praises, his mother used every excuse to swoop on him like a crazed falcon. When she hurt him, he wanted to strike back, wound her, punish her for making him suffer for a tragedy that was not of his making. He was barely a toddler when he interrupted her at prayer to announce that her soul, or that of any woman, was no more important than a wood-shaving. Bathsheba had abandoned her prayers and grabbed him by both shoulders, shaking him furiously, threatening to have him stoned to death.

The young Solomon hardened himself. He no longer admitted to the pain of his mother's hatred. And he closed himself off to the hideous goings-on in his family. When his half-brother Amnon raped their half-sister Tamar and the family wept and wailed and tore their clothes and rent their hair and ground their teeth, Solomon remained indifferent. Women, he thought, women – where there is a woman, there is trouble. When Absalom, Tamar's twin brother, ran away in fear of his life after he had killed Amnon for violating his sister, David was inconsolable but Solomon was detached.

Oh, it hurt him to see his father's grief at the loss of his beloved heir, but then Amnon had been tempted by a woman and who should understand that better than David who, in a different way, was also incited to violence when he lusted after Bathsheba? Perhaps David loved his other sons better because they were more like him. Solomon was different; Solomon, cut off from the love of both parents.

But when Absalom was found hanging from a tree by his own, wild tresses, Bathsheba changed, as if suddenly she realised she had a living son and not just a dead one. She demanded that David appoint Solomon heir to his kingdom. Perhaps, too late, she felt some twinge of love for her son. Perhaps she needed to assuage her own guilt. Solomon had conjectured long and hard, agonising over why David, weak and broken, had agreed. Was it because he felt Solomon had some merit or simply that there was no one else?

Was it any wonder, then, that Solomon's Book of Proverbs

was filled with cruel words about women. He was writing with the blood of his broken heart. If he could only rid himself of the distrust and bitterness engendered by his mother, he would see that women were as mutli-faceted as the best-carved diamonds – alluring, pleasing, infinitely precious if sometimes dangerous and cutting.

Sad, though, how he sought to find his mother through his many wives, to conquer her through marriage and intercourse, to wound her through desertion by marrying more and more and more. No doubt, each woman was a disappointment. Who can meet the expectations of a husband hoping to find both wife and mother in one woman? And what woman would dare to stand up to Solomon the Great, Solomon the Wise? To be as powerful and commanding as his mother? To let him see his mother's fire flashing through her eyes, her fury consuming him and turning him for a moment into a terrified child, so that he could seize the moment, withstand her attack, curb and subdue the harridan? Only then would he disengage from his devastating mother-memory and start to feel a grown man inside himself.

'Perhaps that's why I excite him so much. Maybe that explains his aggressive messages,' mused Bilqis.

She was exhilarated by the thought: it meant Solomon recognised she was his equal. Somewhere in his depths he might even have conceded her superiority. The whole act of demanding a visit from her was a way of affirming his power to himself: 'I subdued the Queen of Sheba' . . . If he was studying her as carefully a she studied him, he would know by now that she was highly regarded in the many kingdoms with which she had negotiated trade and safe conduct.

Flipping through the book, she sometimes shrieked with fury, sometimes giggled with incredulity as she travelled to Israel.

'A beautiful woman without a loose tongue, is like a gold ring in a pig's snout,' he said in one place. Somewhere else he described an immodest woman as a cancer. He denied there was such a thing as a perfect wife.

'Don't any of his wives take exception to this?' Bilqis wondered, trying to work out why he kept marrying if he truly believed his own words. He compared the female temperament to harsh death, and described women as a trap, an encumbrance and a shackle. But their wiles only worked on those who sinned against God.

'Then you must be a dreadful sinner, Solomon,' she mused, 'because you have more wives and concubines than any man I ever heard about. You poor, poor man. What did you mother do to you? Because surely none of your wives is strong enough or clever enough to make you so bitter. Have you ever tried giving your soul to one of your wives to see how she can make it shine? How joy and ecstasy is so much more enduring than the thrill of the orgasm? I could show you, Solomon, but only if you give me the soul you're so determined to shield from women.'

At every step of the journey, Bilqis received information about Solomon, and evaluated it. When at last she arrived at the borders of his country, she felt prepared and ready to do sport with Solomon, the wisest of men.

When Solomon saw Bilqis, he lost his breath. He forgot that her throne, brought all the way from Sheba to his palace, sat prominently placed by his own. He forgot the massive sheet of glass that covered the orchard floor where he had arranged to welcome Bilqis. He even forgot they were in an orchard. As she lifted the veil over her palanquin she was more alive, more vibrant, more exquisite than any woman he had seen before. And with more than two hundred wives and a thousand concubines at his disposal, he knew how exceptional she was. He was overcome. But only for a moment.

As she stepped out of the palanquin, Bilqis felt a thrill. So this was Solomon. Well, physically, at least, he was no disappointment. She was dazed as she surveyed the ground she had to cover to get to Solomon. And she saw that it was wet.

Strange, she thought, steadying her mind, that Solomon should choose to see me in a drenched field instead of his palace. I wonder what his game is?

Spontaneously, she clutched at her skirt to raise it so that she would not get her hem wet as she walked across to him. Tentatively, she placed one foot on the drenched ground. It was not wet at all. Why had Solomon covered the ground with glass? But of course! He wanted to verify the rumours he had no doubt heard about her demon-nature. Did she really have the feet of a goat? Well, let him conjecture. She smiled inwardly at his trickery. If things go to plan, he's going to see it anyway. Better now than later.

Nonchalantly, she yanked the hem of her skirt higher, revealing her ankles. Then, from beneath lashes trained into curls with generous coatings of antimony, she darted him a sly glance.

Solomon looked horrified at what he saw. He tensed, then furrowed his brow, relaxing. Bilqis' eye followed his as he gazed at her foot. She saw the reason for his wonder. The mutilated toes were reforming and her foot was suddenly whole again. Bilqis moved it. The sensation was back! She leaned forward and once again felt the support that had been lacking for so long. Then she rocked back and forth and deliciously, sensuously, wriggled her toes. What a miracle! Her foot was suddenly healed – after four years of mutilation!

But what was it that had shocked Solomon? Surely not the magical healing? No! It was the fine down on her legs. So it was true that the women of Israel duped their men by removing the hair of their bodies by artificial means. Their priests had decreed that hair growing on the places covered by clothes was a sign of evil. But did they realise that the secret held them hostage to their men? Solomon might be repulsed by the down on Bilqis' legs but would that be reason enough to ignore her other charms? She thought not. But she would solve that problem when he put it to her. And she knew that he would find an opportunity.

The Queen of Sheba walked slowly towards Solomon across the floor of glass. The two monarchs greeted each other with all the formal ceremony of state but the pleasure shone on their faces, glistened in their eyes, flushed their cheeks. Then Solomon ushered Bilqis to her throne.

'Do you recognise this?' he asked, watching her expression closely.

So, thought Bilqis, exhilarated, the battle of wills and wits continues.

She cast a glance at the throne. It was hers. But she did not let her surprise show.

'It is so much like mine,' she murmured, 'that I cannot easily see how it could be another.'

Solomon smiled. So far, so good.

'Now,' he said, 'I have another question to ask. Why was it that you sent me a thousand children of each sex and every one of them dressed alike and, I'm told, born at the same time?'

'Why, my lord,' replied Bilqis. 'I want you to distinguish the girls from the boys.'

'Hmm,' Solomon stroked his beard. Then he ordered his eunuchs to offer the children some nuts. Huge trays full of nuts were carried in and placed, row upon row, before the seated children. As the eunuchs stood back, there was a scuffle. The children moved as one to the trays and grabbed the nuts. Bilqis shook with laughter and Solomon laughed too. The boys pushed and shoved, elbowing their way forward but the girls, sure that there would be plenty for everyone, stood aside until the boys had finished. Then as the children retreated to their seats like an ebbing tide, he motioned Bilqis to watch carefully. The boys spread their legs, poured handfuls of nuts into the hammock that formed between their thighs and shovelled them into their mouths by the fist. But the girls kept their thighs pressed together and picked the nuts up between their fingers and thumbs and placed them politely in their mouths.

'The girls are modest,' Solomon said to Bilqis, 'the boys are not.'

Sheba nodded, smiled. Solomon's pleasure pleased her. But even more, she was delighted that he was meeting her expectations. The feat with the throne had been spectacular.

'Now another riddle,' she said. 'Here it is. Seven come forth but nine go in, two offer the drink but only one accepts.'

Solomon was taken aback. 'That is the idle prattle of women on a moonlit night!' he flared.

Bilqis rocked gently in her seat. Was Solomon fishing? Was he unsure of his answer?

'Have you been present at women's moonlight talks, Solomon?' she demanded. 'Perhaps you join your women – your wives and your concubines – on moonlit nights.'

'Do you want to insult me?' Solomon asked. '. . . or are you unaware of our laws?'

'No offence meant,' wheedled Bilqis, her tones silky. Perhaps Solomon did know something about the female mysteries, after all. 'But if you have not been with women on moonlit nights, then you cannot judge the quality of their conversation.'

Solomon cocked his head slightly. 'I know enough to tell you this. The seven that issue forth are the seven days of female bleeding which can be drawn out by the full moon – when, according to my faith, a woman is forbidden to a man. Should she conceive, her pregnancy lasts nine months. Both her breasts offer nourishment but, usually, there is only one infant to receive it.'

Bilqis beamed. 'You are as wise as they say, Solomon. You know how scientific women's talk can be. Here's another one.'

Bilqis raised her arm and immediately several young men entered in somersaulting, juggling and dancing.

'Tell me, Solomon,' Bilqis asked, leaning back in her throne. 'Can you tell me which of these boys are circumcised?'

Solomon made a gesture to the priest and Bilqis watched as he disappeared. Some moments later, he reappeared with the Ark of the Covenant. At once, some of the young men abandoned their performance and bowed low before it while the rest looked on in surprise.

'The ones who bow are circumcised,' Solomon said, smugly. Bilqis inclined her head in acknowledgement.

'Have you any more enigmas?'

'A wooden bowl, an iron spade. When the spade scatters rocks, rivulets flow.'

Solomon smiled slowly. 'A cosmetic box, no doubt made from the fine wood of your cypress trees, Sheba. It contains crushed antimony stones. And when their paste is drawn through your lids, your tears flow.'

Now Bilqis knew for certain that Solomon had taken the trouble to learn something about feminine ways, despite his disdain for women. She decided to test Solomon's knowledge of the earth's mysteries.

Bilqis gestured to her servants and they carried in a tree trunk with neither roots nor branches.

'Which end of this trunk sprang from the roots, Solomon, and which held the branches?'

'Lay the tree trunk in the water,' Solomon commanded. Two large men carried it over to the pond and laid it on the surface. Everyone watched as the trunk dipped in the water to half its depth, then resurfaced, see-sawing. First one half, then the other, rocked up and down in the water. Then slowly, like the scales of a dishonest merchant, one end of the trunk sank below water level and the other bobbed above.

'The roots have sunk,' announced Solomon. 'The branches are buoyant.'

Without preamble, Bilqis continued.

'It comes from the earth, like the dust which feeds and enriches it. But it flows like water and lights up the home.'

'It is the oil from Naphthonia, known as naptha. It contains a luminous mineral.' Solomon smiled and looked at Bilqis. She sparkled with energy and there was an excitement about her, as if she was enjoying his success as much as he himself. Solomon was dazzled.

Bilqis lifted one shapely leg and folded it beneath her on the throne. Again, he glimpsed the down on the legs. But he forgot again as she shifted her top half closer to him, leaning her chin on her palm.

'A storm wind fills its top, it groans in protest. It graces the rich and disgraces the poor. It venerates the dead and demeans the criminal. It is gratifying for fowl but affliction for fish. That's my riddle. Can you answer it, Solomon?'

'The answer is flax. It makes sails for ships, which groan
when they fill with the wind that bears them out to sea. It is
woven into linen which is the pride of the rich but when it gets
old, it is passed on to the poor and its tatters disgrace them. To
fowl, its seed is food, but fish are trapped and killed in the nets
woven from it.'

Bilqis clapped enthusiastically – elated – like a teacher
cheering her prize pupil. The courtiers held their breath. Had
she stopped quizzing their monarch, this bold, child-queen, or
was there more to come?

Bilqis looked Solomon straight in the eye and told him how
much she admired him and how delighted she was that he
had solved every one of her riddles. That he knew about
nature and artifice and could distinguish between them but,
even more important, he understood the process of their
transformation from one thing into another.

'You are cleverer than I believed,' she admitted. 'Your
wisdom is superhuman. And the praise I've heard about you
doesn't do you justice.'

Solomon looked humble. 'I'm human like any other man –
conceived through the pleasurable coupling of my parents,
formed in my mother's womb for a period of forty weeks.
When I was born, I fell on the same earth as the rest of
humankind, wailed the same wail, breathed the same air. I
was fed, dressed and raised as every child is. From the beginning of time all humans have been the same, even kings. We,
all of us, enter and leave life in the same way – through birth
and death. But I'm grateful for your compliments and accept
them as a token of your generosity.'

'All the same,' Bilqis repeated, 'I set out to see if you were
all that people said. My own merchant, Tamrin, praised you
highly: your wisdom, your kindness, your knowledge. But I
had to see for myself. And, as I said before, the reality far
outweighs the reputation.'

'But your wisdom, Bilqis, bubbles out of your own being,
like a brook that will no longer be stifled below earth. Mine is
begged from my God, the One and Only, it is his gift and

bounty. Yours is in your veins, your breath. Your heart is bountiful, your mind open – that is why you had the largesse to visit me, although my invitation was far from diplomatic.'

A thrill of pleasure surged through Bilqis. This was the side of Solomon she had intuitively known, which she had longed to meet and unite with. And she could see that Solomon felt the same.

'You are more beautiful than I imagined,' Solomon confided. 'I was quite overwhelmed when I saw you. But I was puzzled by your legs. Do you think, Sheba, that the growth of hair on them is a sign that the burden of the crown and country is unnatural for a woman . . . that your body is adapting to the maleness of the task . . .?'

'I don't think so,' smiled Bilqis mysteriously. 'Women have often ruled Sheba. You need not doubt my femininity. Did you know that most women never let their men see that they have hair on their bodies? Perhaps this little feminine wile is still a mystery to you?'

'Then why don't you remove it, Sheba?'

Bilqis twinkled. 'Why should I?'

'To restore the manhood to your men.'

'My men have all the manhood they need. They are not made more manly by changing the bodies of women.' She brought her face close to his, baiting him.

'But say, for the sake of discussion, that I did agree to remove it, how would you propose I do it?'

'With a blade.'

'No male weapon has ever touched my body,' replied Bilqis, fixing her eyes firmly on the dagger at Solomon's hip, then letting them wander, suggestively, to his crotch. 'Nor will it except as a gesture of alliance. You know how I disapprove of war.'

Solomon did not miss the point but he chose to evade her implication and replied literally. 'It may cut your ankle. And we would not want to spill your precious blood.'

'Nor yours, Solomon – because once drawn a sword can harm either party.'

Bilqis had shot a dart at Solomon's manhood but she did not allow him to retaliate.

'Tell me about your god, Solomon. Why do you choose him to worship? In Sheba, the sun is our God. We can see his bounty. He preserves life, makes plants grow, provides warmth, fire for cooking. And he's more bright and enduring than anything else in the universe.'

'My God created the sun and everything in the world,' Solomon replied passionately.

His emotion wrenched at Bilqis' heart. She remembered his past. This God was good to Solomon and in return Solomon loved him in the place of both his parents.

'Tell me more,' she said, gently.

'The sun, the moon, the stars and earth – he made them all. He honours me by sending me injunctions. He has instructed me to build his tabernacle. He is the ultimate power and authority.'

'Then,' said Bilqis, disarming Solomon, 'I'll worship him with you.'

In spite of this, over the next days, Solomon made no approaches to Bilqis and it was not for her to initiate sexual relations with her host. Bilqis waited. What did Solomon want from her? she wondered, as he showed her through his palace and his possessions. She could tell from the gentle brush of his body against hers, from the way he took every opportunity to touch her – around her waist to manoeuvre her through an archway, under her elbow to support her, on her hand to help her to her feet. Often, too, she caught him staring at her, eyes smouldering like glowing embers. She could feel the heat emanating from him and creating a blaze in her own body, the flutter of breath catching in his throat at the nearness of her. She could see his gaze fix on her and his mind with it – and she knew, unerringly, that he saw, thought and heard nothing except of her.

Bilqis waited because there was an intense, luxurious pleasure in waiting. Then she decided she had waited enough and it was time for a tactical move.

'Tell Solomon,' she instructed the hoopoe, 'that I have been here a long time and learned a great deal from him. I shall never meet anyone like him again and I will never forget him. But I have a kingdom of my own and the time has come for me to return to it.'

'Your Majesty,' the hoopoe told Bilqis with hoops of delight. 'Solomon is devastated by your message. He is quite crazed by the thought of losing you. He has begged you to stay long enough to have a last meal with him.'

'Tell Solomon I accept his invitation,' Bilqis told the hoopoe. Then she wrinkled up her nose. 'No, make that "his gracious invitation". And ask him to prepare for my visit.'

Bilqis' appearance belied her inner state as she faced Solomon. A thousand butterflies fluttered their colourful wings inside her, there was a pleasurable humming in her veins and her groin was infused with a warm, sensual feeling. The king reached out and took her hand and Bilqis was astounded by the life and feeling in this single, small piece of her. She could hardly meet Solomon's eyes. But, she reminded herself, I'm a queen – the Queen of Sheba – I meet any other monarch on equal terms. And when she forced herself to look into Solomon's eyes, she knew she was no queen looking into the eyes of a king but every woman looking for the first time into the soul of the man she loves and with whom she longs to be physically united.

Solomon led her into a chamber; purple and gold with the colours of royal passion, aglow with precious gems, the air scented with incense, moist with fragrant essences. Bilqis felt intoxicated. For the first time ever, she was completely alone with Solomon. As he plied her with food and poured exotic drinks down her throat, course upon course was presented to her, salted meats, followed by peppery fish; fruit nectar followed by dry wine. The strong seasonings mingled and burst in Bilqis' mouth. Solomon had planned the meal well. Anything less flavourful would have lost its taste. For everything was a whirl inside.

But Bilqis gave nothing away. She could not. Her virginity –

the virginity of the Queen of Sheba – the virgin, twice widow, was far more precious than sexual yearnings. No, she would only gift her virginity to Solomon when she was sure he knew its value. So far, the signs were good – he treated her with respect while conveying the excitement and pleasure her closeness brought. He had enhanced both their passions with finely judged discretion. And through his behaviour he had allowed her to hold herself aloof and free to make such indications as she chose about her own feelings.

The food was cleared away and Bilqis rose to leave. Sudden panic seized her. What if Solomon let her go without inviting her to his bed, without ever making love to her? Was this holding back just another game? Was it part of his seduction contest? If so, he was making a terrible mistake – because without the proper approach, Bilqis would have to return a virgin. All that passion wasted!

Should I, she wondered, give him an indication of what I expect?

But what did she expect? If only she knew. Marriage, perhaps – a political alliance sealed by marital union. But would this marriage mean any more to Solomon than his two-hundred-odd others?

Bilqis held her breath as Solomon approached her. 'Stay with me tonight.' His eyes were wild. 'For the sake of love, sleep in my palace tonight. A bed has been prepared for you.'

Bilqis' heart jumped, then fell like lead to the bottom of the sea. Another bed! But she reminded herself of Sheba and that she was its queen.

'I will stay,' she said, refusing to allow her slender neck to be weighed down by its own need. 'But only on one condition.'

'Anything,' promised Solomon, grasping her hands, fixing his eyes on her lips.

'You must promise not to take my virginity unless I give it freely.'

Solomon's face became emotionless. 'Of course,' he replied. 'If you swear you will not take anything from me without permission.'

Bilqis' laughter tinkled like a hundred fountains, her nose wrinkled in amusement. 'I? Take anything of yours without permission? Tell me, what would I steal, Solomon? Your jewels? Your draperies? Your seal, perhaps?'

Solomon's expression did not change. Bilqis was so delighted at his ready promise, his implied willingness to woo and seduce her rather than make demands, that she put aside the game-playing, the contesting, the riddling.

'Yes!' she cried, elated. 'Yes, Solomon, I promise not to steal anything from your palace.'

Then Solomon came to Bilqis and held her close a moment before wishing her good-night. Bilqis was a whirl of emotions: wishing one moment that Solomon would take her, the next, flattered by his restraint. One instant disappointed that he could resist her, the next thrilled by the meaning of his temperance.

She tossed and turned in her bed, tormented by a terrible thirst, watching Solomon behind his curtain of fine muslin. What was this terrible thirst? she wondered reaching out for a pitcher and finding none. Was her body telling her about the searing need she felt for Solomon? Look at him, still and silent. Asleep, thought Bilqis. She stroked her legs. Smooth legs, prepared as a gift for Solomon. How could he sleep, knowing she was so near him? Well, he was used to women, hundreds of them sleeping beside him, around him, near him. But, she thought, pride surging through her, this is the only time he will meet an equal.

She also thought of all that equality implied – Bathsheba, Tamar, Solomon's past – the pain of his childhood and the way he had been forced to close off his emotions, contain his expectation. Now, here was a new experience for him – a queen in her own right and one who neither displayed nor felt an atom of fear. Who treated him as her equal. How would he cope with a woman like her? What would he be letting himself in for, if he trusted himself with her? He had told her already that he could not give her any less than his soul, if anything. But she remembered the words he had written in his book. *Do not give your soul to a woman and let her trample on your strength*. And this time, instead of anger, Bilqis felt pity.

The same pity had prompted her to depilate her legs with the miraculous substance brought to her by the jinns: sugar crystals, soaked in the juice of limes and cooked over a slow fire. The sticky mixture laid over the skin pulled away the hairs without resistance. Her legs felt encased in their alien smoothness. But Bilqis was not like all those other women, who traded their hair for bondage just to pander to the fantasies of their menfolk. No, she had taken care that Solomon knew the whole truth about her. She had refused his offer to be dominated by a sword. So the pearl remained unpierced by metal and in return Bilqis did not impugn his masculinity. Piercing Sheba would be a daunting task, even for Solomon. So, she suspected, would be the job of emasculating Solomon. If only he knew it. But Bilqis had no desire to ridicule his manhood. If the act of depilation would convince him of this, it was a small sacrifice for her; to him it would be a panacea.

Her heart softened as she thought of his trials and she stood up so that she could see him better. Ignoring the searing thirst, she walked gently over to Solomon's bed and stood gazing down at him. She could hear him breathing now, deeply, evenly. There was no doubt he was asleep. But he slept like a king, awake to danger. As she approached, he stirred slightly, his lids flickering, his mouth twitching very slightly at the corners. But he continued to sleep. Clearly, he trusted her. Bilqis' heart felt full and she wanted to be close to him. She lifted the fine muslin curtains that enclosed his bed. She felt a tug. Her gown had caught on something. Bilqis turned to disentangle it and there, beside Solomon's bed, she saw a silver salver bearing a thin-necked pitcher.

Water! thought Bilqis and, without reflecting, she bent down and poured some into a cup, savouring the sight of the clean liquid as she raised it to her mouth. But before she could drink, a hand clutched her arm.

Bilqis' heart leapt. Solomon! He was awake. Lovingly, she looked at him. But his look was of triumph, not love.

'Sheba,' he reproached her, 'you've broken your promise.'

Bilqis stared at him, surprised. 'My promise?'

'My water. You took it without asking.'

'You were sleeping so peacefully. I couldn't have woken you just to—'

'You broke your word.'

'Surely, Solomon, even a slave can't be reprimanded for taking a glass of water.'

'Therefore you, Queen of Sheba, should be exonerated? I don't agree. You promised not to take anything without my permission. You broke your promise.'

Bilqis found words difficult. Her mouth was dry and swollen. Her wit drained away. All she could feel was a burning, desperate thirst. She shook her head in disbelief.

'Have it your way,' she managed to whisper. 'Just let me drink the water.'

But Solomon held on to her hand. 'I will release you from your promise if you release me from mine.'

Bilqis was no longer thinking. All she wanted was the water. 'I agree,' she cried out. 'Just let me drink.'

So Solomon released her hand, took the goblet from her, raised it gently, lovingly, to her lips. And as she drank, her head thrown back, her lips sucking eagerly at the goblet's rim, he created sweet poetry and stroked her back with firm, sensual strokes.

When Bilqis had finished drinking, he caressed her, soothed her hair, kissed away her resistance. And Bilqis, finally in Solomon's arms, knew that he had tricked her. But she was content for one night to overlook his trickery, because her need for him was as great as his for her. Bilqis acknowledged that the mistake was her own. She had forgotten, for one vital evening, that Solomon was a game-player first, a lover only second.

'Wine, hot peppers, salt – in abundance,' she murmured, as the first rays of light began to break through the skies.

Solomon looked shamefaced as she watched, eagle-eyed. 'I had to be sure.'

'You had to win.'

'I could not bear you to go. You were so aloof, so haughty.'

'You had only to ask. I wanted your respect. No false promises, no unnecessary gestures, no vulgar seduction. Just for you to express your desire.'

'This was my way of doing it.'

Gently, Bilqis disentangled herself from Solomon. 'You've had your way. Now, I must return to Sheba.'

Solomon fell to his knees. Solomon of two hundred wives and a thousand concubines, clutched at her garments.

'You can't leave me now, Bilqis. Wasn't our love as sweet as honey and as rich as the scent of flowers? You're the woman I've searched for all my life – you can't leave me, not now. I want you to have my children. I want you to be my queen. My only queen, crowned like me.'

Bilqis cast him a sidelong glance. 'A better woman than most, would you say Solomon?'

'Without a doubt,' Solomon affirmed.

Bilqis raised an eyebrow. 'I'm trying to recall,' she mused, 'where I heard that though some men are definitely better than others all women are as bad as each other.'

Solomon covered his face in shame. 'It was before I met you.'

Bilqis turned away from him. 'We each have our weaknesses, Solomon. I made love with you even though I knew you had tricked me.'

Solomon looked hopeful. 'So why . . .?'

'You should know the answer to that. You've made love to hundred of women – good enough to lie with but not to take as equal partners.'

'You've used me,' Solomon accused her. 'You've exploited my love and now you're casting me aside like a useless shell.'

Bilqis looked into his face, concealing her pain behind a glass sheet of coldness. 'All's fair in love and war, Solomon. Your wisdom impassioned me. And I needed a wise man to father my child. Now, it is done, I must go.'

She touched Solomon's face, superior. 'If we stay together,

there can only be war. Your way, not mine. Appeal to your wisdom, Solomon, not your virility or your pride, and you will know I'm right. Your wisdom can withstand the toughest test but you still have a lot to learn about love and trust. We were never meant to remain together, only to transform each other by exchanging wisdom.'

Solomon laid his cheek on Bilqis' head, clutched her like a frightened child. Tenderly, Bilqis moved away and walked back to her camp, her head held high.

The journey home would be a long one and she had to prepare.

Medea

Medea watches Jason as he crosses the courtyard to her house. The women of the city stand at the gate in clusters. Watching, waiting. How is Medea? Poor Media! They want to see her. They want to commiserate.

Jason holds his head high, carries his shoulders proudly, walks arrogantly, looks resolute.

As if he's a hero, Medea thinks, grimly.

More than anyone in the world, she knows the man behind the heroic successes, the fame and the fortune. She can remember Jason as a stripling, fresh off the *Argo*. How full of hope he was then, purity and determination shining from his eyes as he set out to right a wrong, to reclaim Iolcus from the usurper Pelias. Another life, another time. The past: a fresh and beautiful youth landing on Colchis with his heroes, on a quest for the Golden Fleece. How he strutted and postured even then – she could remember, so very well. He was like a satellite of the sun: golden, fiery, vibrant. And sun-worshipper that she was, she fell in love with him. Her own little Helios, she called him. With him she could reach great heights.

But Medea could see through Jason's bravado to the fright-ened, vulnerable youth beneath. How terrified he was of the trials that Aeëtes was going to set him. And well might he be, because the Fleece was a divine gift from Aeëtes' grandfather, Helios, the sun himself. Aeëtes, considering it an appropriate offering, had consecrated it to Aries, God of War and appointed Medea its High Priestess and guardian. But it had become the main source of Medea's quarrels with her father: defiantly she flouted Aeëtes' order to kill all foreigners who landed on Colchis. Besides, who could kill these heroes? These beautiful, skilled young men, the *crème de la crème* of human society, the gems that glittered in the Hellenic sun? She certainly could not.

As protector of the Golden Fleece, Medea feared no hero. She was well able to guard it and keep it safe. But would Aeëtes trust his own daughter? No, though she tried continually to reassure him that if all else failed, her powerful magic would still keep the Fleece safe. She had, after all, learned from her aunt, Circe, the greatest of all sorceresses and the great Hecate, creator of all magic and, some said, Medea's mother. See how she had proven her devotion a hundred times since she and Jason had escaped from Colchis with the Fleece.

But how can you convince a coward that courage is a virtue, persuade a wounded man that loss of blood is beneficial? Besides, everyone knew kingly stubbornness was impossible to overcome. Aeëtes was convinced that the simplest way was to kill all foreigners before they began their quest for the Golden Fleece. And he always took the simplest route. Medea knew that men, and most especially kings, needed shows of strength to prove their effectiveness. Aeëtes was no different. But still, she stood fast against the killing of foreigners and the schism between them deepened, grew embittered and festered like a putrid wound.

And this newest wound now, that Jason had inflicted on her. You could not see from looking at him that he had done wrong. There he was striding into her home for all the world as he had stalked into Pelias' palace all those many years ago, demanding his throne.

'What do you want?' she enquired sharply, as he entered her chamber.

The anger leapt and darted inside her chest, ripping through her throat and into her brain. Flames of fire flashed into her vision as she bit on her tongue to hold back her recriminations. Let Jason speak. Let him put his case.

Jason held up his hand in a gesture of peace. Look at him – already assuming the displays of royalty. Jason learned fast, she knew that. But she would have liked to see his head bowed a little, his gaze averted, his shoulders stooped – some semblance of penitence, some acknowledgement of wrongdoing. But no, that would not become the future king of Corinth.

She swallowed hard to get rid of the taste of blood in her throat. 'Didn't you have the pluck to tell me yourself, Jason? Couldn't you have had the decency? Couldn't you find a moment to slide out from between the thighs of that royal whore? How old is she? Older than your sons, I hope?'

At least now, she had forced his gaze down. 'I've come to tell you that I have every intention of looking after you and the boys. Just because I'm marrying again doesn't mean I'm going to abandon you.'

'That's rich, Jason. That's bloody rich. Zeus! If I'd known what a mealy-mouthed little wimp you can be . . .'

'Abuse doesn't make anything better, Medea . . .'

'Oh yes it does. It makes me feel better. How can you stand there, so sanctimonious, so pious, telling me you're going to look after me and your sons? You know as well as I do, Creon has just been here telling me to get out of Corinth. I'd have had to leave now, this minute, if I hadn't begged him on bended knees to give me a day! If that's how you'll look after us, I prefer the wolves. At least I know to hide from them. Their own father! If you had stood firm, Creon couldn't have come here to banish your sons. You should have stood up to him, Jason, for your sons if not for me.'

Jason looked weary. 'It's your own fault. You've done nothing but rant and rave since you heard about it. Your anger is so poisonous . . .'

Suddenly, Medea slumped. 'You have poisoned me, Jason. I'm poisoned. You brought us here to Corinth where we don't know anyone. You agred to marry the king's daughter. Couldn't you have been honest enough to tell me yourself? Why did I have to find out from the petty street-gossips? How do you expect me to react?'

Jason shrugged. 'Not by cursing Creon and his line, certainly. But that's your way, isn't it, Medea? If people act against your expectations, you can't hold back the curses and tirades. I've told you repeatedy, it'll end in grief. But would you listen?'

'Don't talk down to me, Jason. You've grown tired of me and you've found another, younger lover. Shouldn't you have told me yourself? Is it the action of a hero, to let his wife and children hear such news from slaves and servants?'

'I did it for you, Medea. I thought you'd understand that. I thought you'd be pleased. We're strangers in this country. I've made an alliance with the king. Your sons will be brothers to the future king. You could have lived in a palace in great honour. How can you say I've wronged you?'

'Oh, so kind of you, my lord,' crooned Medea, sinking into a deep curtsy. 'Such a hardship for you, marrying a young princess. I'm so grateful you've rejected your wife and your children for her. So grateful. Wonderful for your sons to know while they wander about without a proper roof over their heads that their father has provided them with kingly relations.'

'That's right, Medea, mock me. You've always mocked me. Are you surprised I have to look elsewhere for support?'

'Oh so it was support you were looking for, was it? And which part of you, exactly, does Glauce support? The small of your back – or, no, your loins, perhaps?' She turned wearily away. 'Just leave it, Jason, tell me where you want me to go with the boys. Somewhere we won't be pursued by Creon's hounds.'

'Tell me where you want to go. If there are friends who you think will receive you willingly, I'll send them word.'

She laughed, bitterly, jerkily, silently, not with her heart but her body. 'You tell me. Where can you think of? Somewhere free of political problems, somewhere the king doesn't need the friendship of Creon or Corinithian allies – can you think of a place like that?'

Jason was stung, and stung back. 'Colchis. Aeëtes doesn't have to fear Corinth. He's across the Bosporus in a foreign land. Hellas has no truck with Colchis. And Creon is a fair man – he can't judge Aeëtes for offering refuge to his own daughter.'

Medea whirled and spat in a single movement, like a recoiling spring. 'How low can you fall?'

'This is nothing but sexual jealousy, Medea. You can't bear the thought of me with another woman. You've never loved me.'

Never loved him! After she had given up her country for him; after she had abandoned her father and killed her brother to help Jason's ship escape from Aeëtes' pursuing fleets. How could he throw her favours and sacrifices in her face as if they were faults? True, she had never let on to Jason how much she missed home, how she longed to make amends to her father for her betrayal – but she had done what she had to do. She had done it for Jason – and, most important of all, she had done it for love. Behind love marched the minor army of reasons: the greater good, the pre-determined future, the punishment of past ills, the reward for services rendered.

And she had loved Jason – still loved him – with a passion and ardour that had never reduced by an atom. Yet here she was, looking at him diminished almost beyond recognition. Inflated by the size of his alliance. How easily men forgot the sacrifices of women. How quickly they changed their loyalties to their children, mistaking sexual mirages for happiness. Jason, who had longed for sons and celebrated for weeks at the birth of each one, was abandoning them now for children not yet born. What of the oaths he'd sworn to them in his own mind? He would never abandon them. They would be the kings of his heart and mind for ever. He would not let history repeat itself. They would never feel abandoned by their father as he had been by his.

Medea looked blankly at Jason. He was talking. He was

saying something, offering some explanation. But she couldn't hear him, only the rise and fall of his voice and the movements of his mouth as he spoke on. Her mind worked rapidly, analysing, assessing her next move. One thing was for sure: she would never get him back. And even if she did, she would never forgive him for the many, many betrayals.

How much Medea had lost for the love of Jason and how easily he had forgotten. The sea and sun of her native island raged and flared alternately in her mind. She had missed Colchis these past days, quite naturally, since she was once again in exile. But now the magnificent Black Sea taunted her: you were the one who chose to go, Medea. You gave up your native seas for the love of a man. And the sun, her great-grandfather burnt into her, branding her being with the words: you abandoned your forefathers, Medea, you chose to befriend the enemies of your land.

Medea responded with all her being. 'Don't you see I was part of Hera's plan. It was she who wanted Pelias killed – I was her instrument.'

But a woman like Medea is an instrument only when she chooses to be. It was not for Hera that she killed Pelias; it was for Jason. Everything was for Jason from the moment she saw him, Medea was for Jason. She had not just betrayed her father, she had betrayed her allegiance to Aries when she poisoned the dragon to let Jason take the Golden Fleece. And she, its High Priestess and protectress, had killed for Jason. She had thrown her twelve-year-old brother to the sea monsters like a sacrificial pig. And she had watched, triumphant, as her father's fleets scattered and stopped, abandoning chase of the *Argo*, while they retrieved the dead boy's limbs to give him a decent burial. True, Medea, initiate supreme of the greater mysteries, knew that death was simply a stage in the continuum of life. But it took heart to plunge a knife into your own brother, to decapitate and dismember him.

Astonishingly, Jason did not seem to think so. He assumed she had done it easily. And she, puffed like the *Argo*'s sails, inflated by the love of this godlike mortal had danced to his tune, pandered to his fantasy. His admiration had made her greater, more powerful, more unassailable than ever before. When they had arrived in Iolcus, she could see that his list-lessness came from being dispossessed. The throne that Pelias occupied was moulded to Jason's shape. He belonged on that throne as petals belonged on flowers; his separation from it was like morning failing to follow night. Pelias, evil Pelias who had sent him on the death-defying quest to fetch the Golden Fleece, was like a mutilating fungus on the mother plant, like a cataclysm that kept dawn from breaking. She had to remove him. She would be doing nothing wrong. It was for the good of the land, the good of the cosmos. Hera approved: she had known all along that Pelias was evil. Was it not Hera who had set Jason on his quest, brought him to confront Pelias in the first place?

Medea met Pelias' daughters. She delighted their hearts with quinces, grapes and exotic cuisine from her native land beyond the Bosporus. And she entertained them with tales of her home. In particular she told them about Hecate – dark Hecate who prowled the nights of the absent moon, looking everywhere at once with her all-seeing eyes, sniffing out men's deeds and transgressions with her sharp sense of smell and her canine instincts. How Medea conjured up images of the Sacred Bitch, roaming the pathways and stopping at every crossroads to bless her devotees. Mistress of Magic, Power of Sorcery, she nurtured the young and rejuvenated the old.

Once, Medea told them, she had heard about a sick, old man boiled in a miraculous elixir brewed by Hecate – and he came out of it young and healthy as a hero.

'Is it true?' asked one daughter.

Medea shrugged, laughing gaily, dangling grapes above her guest's open lips.

'Who knows? I learned the recipe but it would take a daring person to try it out. I do know that executed with an open mind and a pure heart, Hecates' magic never fails. And then this magic is dear to her, the magic of revival, the recycling of life, rebirth.'

She saw Pelias' daughters thrill with fear and anticipation. She saw their eyes wide with expectation. She could hear their unasked questions. Is it true you're a witch? Would you perform the spell on our father?

But Medea would have no obvious part in it. Tales of treachery towards her family were current and frequent and she had no intention of feeding the fires that could become her own tomb if she now got involved in regicide. So she made safe her fireside.

'The spell is only effective when it's performed by a near and dear one.'

'So,' they said, 'we'd have to do it ourselves, if we wanted our dear father to be young and healthy again?'

Medea nodded, let herself shudder delicately. She put down her grapes, pursed her lips. 'It will be hard and I don't envy you.'

Their eyes shone with eagerness. Their lips parted with ardent expectation. 'But it would work? Pelias would be rejuvenated?'

A nod from Medea made up their minds. And on a night darkened by the absence of the moon, Medea demonstrated the magic to them by boiling the head of an old ram in a huge cauldron. Pelias' daughters took the elixir and the cauldron and repeated the spell.

Jason should have been crowned king. The throne was his by rights. Only Pelias, left to guard it till his nephew's return, had allowed his old limbs to become melded to it, welded to the power and glory of kingship. He deserved his horrible death. More so, because he had greedily concurred with it.

'Don't you think,' protested Medea, as the crowds of Iolcus hounded them out of the kingdom, 'that Jason has a right to this throne? He is Aeson's son. Have you forgotten how Pelias stole his throne?'

But Jason's rights were shadows in the murk of yesteryear. What loomed large was a murderous plot and Medea at the centre of it. Hera, where were you then? Or was I just your pawn?

Women like Medea are never pawns. She had wanted Pelias dead as surely as his subjects now wanted her gone. She had acted out of love, not logic. She had made mistakes. She should have used her magic. She had unlimited stores of it. Pelias could have died in one of a hundred other ways. And so it was that they were in Corinth and she twice exiled.

Well, she would not make the same mistake again, that was for sure. She had been punished for ignoring the divine gifts of her native soil and resorting to tricks, like mortals. Now she would look upwards to the heavens, throw open her arms and welcome in the great powers. She would delve deep into her own womanly magic, access her most profound sense of justice. She would avenge the wrongs she had suffered.

It was as if she was immersed in the depths of her beloved Black Sea, drawing strength from it. Jason filled all her six senses, blotting out everything. In that moment, she experienced love reach boiling point and becoming hate. Alchemy worked, opposites balanced, ardent love sustained passionate loathing. Without it the plan would not have formed in her mind. Medea faltered, she fell to her knees, she let herself feel the great love that had brought her there, that underpinned her tortured rages, her unbearable grief. She looked up at Jason, her tears flowing freely.

'Jason, I'm truly sorry for my behaviour. I simply could not bear to lose you to another woman. After all, I gave you everything you wanted – from the moment of the first contest to the moment we left Iolcus. And I would give you more.' She paused, let the tears come. 'But no, you've decided to take Glauce for your wife. I accept that, though I don't pretend to understand. I accept that there are things between man and woman that always remain secret, no matter how close they are to each other. And I also accept that it is impossible for me to stay on in Corinth after my behaviour. Medea the witch, the foreigner, is too threatening . . . But Jason, what about our sons? They haven't harmed anyone. They're not asking for revenge or even a stake in your new kingdom. But they love their father. Let them stay. Don't force them to live fatherless and unprotected for their mother's misdemeanours.'

Jason hesitated. Medea struck.

'Remember how it was for you, Jason? Not knowing Aeson? Remember the questions you asked Alchimeda, how you yearned for a home, for the love and guidance of a father? How can I replace that, Jason? I beg you, let your boys stay.'

'But are you willing to give them up?' Jason was uncertain.

'I am. What you predicted has come to pass. My rages have ruined me. I'll leave; let them stay.'

'Where will you go?'

'To Athens. Aegeus will protect me.'

Jason became restless. He paced to the door, paced back. Medea could feel her natural magic beginning to take effect. Jason was like a caged beast. Medea had jailed him in the bars of his own past. She could see how their young faces altered in Jason's mind until they became his own.

'It's useless,' he spluttered. 'Creon won't agree.'

'But Glauce will. She loves you to distraction. She'll do as you say. I know she will.' Medea knew her plan had worked. Now she had to help Jason realise it.

'How can you be so sure of Glauce's reaction?' he demanded.

Heroes weren't renowned for their intellect, Medea knew. Jason would respond to flattery.

'We both love you, Jason. I know the power of your love. It made me want to give up everything for you – without your asking.'

Jason's brow creased a little. He nodded. 'I'll speak to Glauce. But you must promise to abide by her decision.'

Abide by her decision! It was a wonder Jason did not hear the fierce sizzle as fury flooded out to quench Medea's elation. But she bowed her head, to conceal the intensity in her eyes, measured the tips of her fingers, one hand against the other.

'You are too modest, Jason. I agree to your request because I know you'll succeed.'

Visions flashed through her mind. Jason going out to face the thousand warriors. Jason dodging past the unconscious dragon. She had said the same words then. But how different she had felt! Now she was sending him on a quest. One that would sweeten her bitterness.

Go Jason, go! Fly with the wings of Eros on your heels. Go to fulfil my plan.

Aloud, she murmured, 'Let me make the first gesture of peace. I'll send Glauce a gift to delight her heart. I'll send her my wedding gown. The softest weave, stranded through with the gentlest morning rays. And my bridal coronet. You remember it, Jason. It was a gift from Helios. Its gold was brightened by his own light. How it glistened and flashed . . .'

Jason averted his eyes, uncomfortable.

Squirm, you monster, thought Medea. Squirm, but I'm not letting you off my hook. The more you squirm, the more you tear. I'll get inside you and possess you so that I'm never out of your mind. You'll never be free of me. Never. No matter who you marry, no matter where you rule.

'Why do you want to give away your treasures, Medea? Keep them for yourself. You may need them.'

'Need them? You don't think I'll be a bride again, do you, Jason?' She stopped, suddenly assailed by a vision she had seen this morning.

Another time, another place. The future: Aegeus of Athens by her side; a bridal procession; Medea hailed Queen of Athens. Oh, she'd marry again, she knew that for sure. But she would not need the magical robes or the coronet. She had plenty of treasures in her cauldron. For now, she was content with Jason's guilt. Her determination took wings.

'I would like Glauce to have them. If for nothing else, then as an inducement to accept my boys.'

Jason bowed his head in acquiescence, hesitated for a moment before pressing his lips to Medea's hand, then was gone.

Medea went hastily up to the roof of her house and bolted the heavy door behind her. Swiftly, surely, she constructed an altar from the consecrated stones which travelled with her everywhere, from Colchis to Iolcus, Iolcus to Corinth. She touched them reverently, laid her head on their coolness, absorbed their energies. Then she began her work. She brought together herbs and minerals, chopped, singed, brewed, poured the potion out of her cauldron into an exquisite goblet. Then she placed it on the altar, directly on top of an exquisitely woven dress and addressed the powers of darkness, the powers of light.

'Hecate, Great Goddess, Divine Bitch, heal this, my wounded womanhood. Come from Thrace, Divine Crone, come from Colchis, Mistress of Magic, Power of Sorcery, Mightiest of Goddesses, triumph of the strong, Judgement Incarnate. Punish those who steal the rights of others. Those who violate the precious bonds of successful marriage. I want to make an example of this arrogant young woman who has prized a man above her sisterhood. And through her I want to punish Jason. One woman sacrificed for the benefit of thousands is a sacrifice well made. Bring success to my endeavours. I lay this brew before you, concocted from the purest herbs, cleansed by my own hand, sanctified in your name. Bring them potency, Mother. Goddess of Death, gather my sons in your arms, safe. Mighty She-wolf, tear apart their enemies.'

A hiss like a puff of air. The contents of the cup bubbled over, drenched the garment, its smoke permeating every fibre. And when the smoke had sunk into it, the dress glowed as if a soft light was illuminating its folds.

Then Medea addressed the sun. 'Great Helios, father of my fathers, bless your daughter in her mission. Aid your High Priestess who has guarded and honoured the Golden Fleece without fail. I lay before you a coronet of gold. Send it your most potent flames. Make them unquenchable. Make them greedy for revenge. Bring me success in my intentions and take me safely from Corinth to Athens.'

A beam of lightning flashed down from the skies and consumed the coronet. Smiling with satisfaction, Medea bowed deeply to God and Goddess, waiting until the fire died down and the coronet smouldered into embers, regaining its original shape.

Then Medea placed each of her enchanted gifts in a separate box, made of carved cedar-wood, and summoned her sons.

'Go to your father,' she ordered, handing each one a box. 'He wants you to stay with him in Corinth. And when he visits Glauce, give her these gifts. They will soften her will.'

Medea's heart bled as they looked at her blankly, buffeted by the hot wind of ill-fortune that had invaded their heads and withered their minds and will. What will? They were like the walking dead; had been since they had heard their father had abandoned them for another woman, was already building estates on the shaky foundations of future sons. How could Jason speak of loving them, remarrying to ensure their future, then accept Glauce's decision to banish them?

They were better dead. Even better, dead at his feet, killed by his actions. Then he would swallow bitter gall for the rest of his days, wander homeless, friendless, selfless until he died, forgotten and unsung. After all, who was Jason any more, but the hero who achieved his quest through the will of a powerful woman? What had he ever done that deserved praise or glory except when Medea stood behind him? In spite of that, he had repudiated her, humiliated her. Now, she would cut him where he bled most.

Tenderly, she embraced her children, smoothed their cheeks with cupped palms, stroked their hair, wiped their tears.

'Whatever happens, don't forget that I am protecting you. Don't let yourself get angry. Don't be sucked into any quarrel that may flare up. Just hand Glauce these boxes and stand back until you receive your instructions. If you follow my orders, you'll be safe.'

She gave both boys a drink of the wine blessed at Hecate's altar and sent them on their way. It was a strong draught, the same she had given so long ago to the dragon who guarded the Golden Fleece. It would work slowly and fortify them in both body and mind for the dreadful ordeal ahead.

When her sons had left, Medea went into the courtyard and addressed the women who had been gathering there for days, some from curiosity about the famed sorceress, some from sympathy for a wronged woman.

What would Medea do? they wondered. True, she had a vile temper but hadn't she deserved some respect from Jason? Not one of them would deny wanting to rip her husband limb from limb in Medea's situation and not one of them would dare to fulfil her want. Medea was their will, Medea was their hope. And Medea knew it.

'Women of the city,' she beseeched them, standing proud and straight. Her quiet dignity made them weep more than her tears could have. 'Keep my secret. I know that as a stranger to your city, I have no rights. But I ask you as a woman, abandoned on a stranger's doorstep. You know how Jason has treated me. You saw Creon stalk into my home and order me out of Cornith. So tell me, is there a single one of you who feels, deep inside her, even if she won't speak out in her grief and humiliation, what I am feeling?'

Not one woman spoke, but the tears in their eyes told Medea a hundred tales. Relief suffused her body as she inhaled, confident in the knowledge that she had secured their loyalty.

'Since you understand me, I have a favour to ask. I have sent my sons to Glauce. They go in the spirit of conciliation, with gifts for her, poor puppets, hoping to help Jason persuade her to let them stay in Corinth.'

The women surged forward to help and Medea turned momentarily away speaking almost to herself. 'Foolish, foolish Jason! Does he really believe, after all these years, that I would leave my sons to the fickle mercies of a woman like Glauce? That I would allow him to separate me from them? No, Jason, no. The next few hours will tell you what I'm made of. What bitterness and what tenderness lie side by side within me. You're blind not to have seen it yet. So blind. You watched me sever myself from my father and kill my own brother. But you lost yourself in the sweetness and healing of me and forgot that nothing gets between me and my goal. You were too arrogant to stop and wonder if that wrath could ever turn against you. Well, you'll soon know that my aim is remorseless and true and I point it at the point in the heart where the hurt will be deepest.'

The women looked in wonder at Medea. What was she muttering? What would she ask them to do? Medea turned.

'Look after my children when they are with Glauce. Protect them from her and the courtiers of Corinth, even Jason. They don't know the consequence of the gifts they carry. Remember that, I beg you, and carry them back to their mother. Will you do that for me?'

The women did not question Medea. They did not stop to ask about her gifts or why her children would be in danger. They simply acquiesced. Medea was looking out for her children. Each one of them was willing to turn she-lion for her children.

'Your children are innocent, Medea. We'll bring them back to you.'

Medea thanked the women, then reached for her goblet and drank deeply from the magic draught. The next moment her limbs grew heavy and her mind went mercifully numb. For the next few hours she would elude the hideous anticipation of grief and tragedy.

The people of Corinth were wild wolves, their eyes aflame and red with the fire that Medea had sent, so the women told Medea.

The boys presented their gifts to Glauce and she accepted them greedily, curious to see what Medea could offer. She hated Medea with a loathing fuelled by jealousy but she was curious about the land of Colchis and its magical objects. She snatched the first box from the boy's hand and opened it. Oh, the flush on her cheeks when she anticipated wearing the wedding gown that brides of the sun had worn before her. Graspingly, she opened the second box. Oh, the radiance of the magnificent coronet as it lay there sparkling and inviting.

'The boys,' Jason whispered.

'The boys! Yes – the boys! Yes, let them stay!' What did she care? What did self-absorbed little Glauce care? Corinth was a big enough place and even if she let them stay in her palace, they'd be swallowed into its huge spaces; she would never have to tolerate them, set eyes on them even. They would be no threat to her or any future heirs to the Corinthian throne. By the time she'd finished with them they'd forget any link to the throne they'd ever been foolish enough to imagine. That poor, rejected old woman they called their mother didn't know what a mistake she was making, leaving them here. Well, now Glauce wasn't just getting shot of the old crone but the sad old witch had even parted with her most precious possessions. Obviously, she wasn't half as clever as she liked to make out.

The women of the city could hardly remain faithful to Glauce. She was the woman they all feared in their own lives. She was the bauble that could entice their husbands away from them. She was the quagmire that could lure them and suck them under. And in that moment Jason was all their husbands, innocent victim of her evil temptations.

'No!' Medea reminded them sharply. 'No. Don't forget that Jason is the one who wandered. Jason is the one with a wife and children. He could have refused Glauce. The fault is his.'

But, the women told Medea, Glauce nurtured a poisonous hatred towards her, a fiery hatred which grew even as they watched.

Medea laughed softly. Her magic drew its potency from malice. Or she would not have let her sons carry it. Even Jason, misguided as he was, would not be harmed by the magic. Weak he might be; malign he was not.

And so it was that as Glauce had pulled Medea's gown over her head and smoothed down its folds, her hatred permeated it. Its fibres began to light up – at first a filament here and there. Saffron orange, catching, spreading; spark turning to fiery tongue; tongue licking gluttonously, along the warp, across the woof, even further. By the time she had placed the coronet on her head, Glauce was a human flame. The coronet branded itself deep into her skull. Glauce screamed. Jason leapt forward, trying to help. With dazed faces, the boys stepped back.

Creon exploded into the room, flung Jason away and clutched at Glauce. She thrashed and flailed against her father's ageing bones.

'No, my love!' yelled Creon. 'Let me save you.'

He grabbed at the coronet but his fingers caught fire. He pulled at the gown but its fibres melted into his skin, corroding his flesh. Creon looked at his daughter, his little girl, and all he saw was a carcass rotting on its skeleton. But still she screamed, still Glauce retained the strength to hate. Her naked eyeballs swivelled towards Medea's boys. 'Kill them!' she screamed. 'Kill Medea's children.'

'No!' Jason bolted forward to protect his sons. 'This is Medea's doing. She's exploited them. Leave them alone.'

The courtiers lunged at the children, knocking Jason away, and as Creon lay down to die with his darling child, they tore like wild animals at Medea's children, wanting to avenge the Royal Household.

'Their eyes were red,' continued the women of the city, 'like Agave's women, wild as savage beasts when they were ripping apart Pentheus.'

But the women of the city had remembered their promise to Medea. They were suffused with the power of the Divine She-wolf as they snapped and growled, their fangs bared in defence of their young. Filled with Hecate, Mistress of the Seas, they surged forward as one, surrounding the boys like a vast, frothing ocean and blanketing their limp, bleeding bodies with their own.

'Have you brought me my sons?' wailed Medea. 'Where are my sons?'

The women of the city moved aside, like great breaking waves. There lay Medius and his brother. There they lay, lifeless, innocents. Why had she let this happen to them? The question was reflected in the eyes of every woman standing

there, magnified a hundred times. Why had she let the innocents become part of her revenge?

'I gave them my magic brew,' she told them. 'They knew
nothing of all this.'

'The gods have mercy on their young souls,' murmured the
women as they recalled the blank expressions on the faces of
the boys, their frozen movements, their dullness.

Medea thanked the women, and when they had left, she laid
the boys out on the roof beside her. She smoothed their bodies,
soothed their limbs, caressed their faces. Then she turned to
look at the blazing sun, her eyes open wide, unhampered by its
brilliance.

'Father, Helios, send me your chariot! Give it wings. I must
take my sons and leave for Athens.'

She could hear Jason battering down the door to her courtyard as she placed the lifeless bodies of her sons into the
chariot drawn by winged dragons. But she did her work tenderly, gently, as if nothing mattered now except her love for
the poor, dispossessed creatures. Below, she heard the crash of
wood splintering, the clang of a bolt giving way.

'Well, well. So Jason still has the strength of a hero. His
might is not all sapped away by his dependence on women.'

She mounted Helios' chariot, moved in a blaze of light to
the edge of the roof.

'Medea!' screamed Jason, gaping up at her, his eyes streaming, his hair wild. 'What have you done, Medea? You've killed
my sons.'

'Alive? Dead? What do you care?' Medea's voice was cold,
crackling like a whiplash. It fell viciously on Jason's wounds.
'You wouldn't have seen them if they lived.'

'You're wrong!' The cry was wrenched from Jason. 'Glauce
agreed to let them stay.'

'Better dead than at her mercy,' sneered Medea. 'Better
dead with me than alive with you.'

'How could you kill them, your own sons?'

'To wound you, Jason. To tell you how I felt. Look at your
children's bodies and feel what I felt when you abandoned me.'

Jason's heroic frame was racked with sobs. Medea watched, contemptuous of his grief until at last, he raised his head.

'Let me have the boys. I'll give them a worthy burial.'

Medea revelled in the entreaty, in the succour that came from beggaring him to her will. 'Let you have them? But you were sending them away to wander homeless. They were as much your sons then as they are now. Why should I give them to you, Jason? Why should I do that?'

'They are my sons.'

'But you didn't want them when they were alive. When they needed you. Then they were my sons and there was no room for them in your life. Your royal life. Get out of my sight, Jason. Don't delay me. I have to bury my sons.'

Jason fell to his knees. His voice was like a burst reed-pipe as he begged. 'Let me touch them, Medea. Let me embrace them, one last time.'

'They don't miss your embraces now, Jason. They don't need you any more.'

With a final look at the ruined hero, Medea jerks on the reins. She has no time left. In a shower of sparks, the chariot takes off. Medea sits back as it soars into the sky. If she had waited a moment longer, Jason would have seen the waning effect of the magic draught. The boys are beginning to stir and stretch.

Medea will see to it that they wanted for nothing.

Granya

You know who Granya is, for sure. She's the one who some describe as the 'nasty one'. And was she nasty? Decide for yourself.

Just look at her now as she twirls and whirls, dancing, kicking out her shapely legs. A flash of the ankle here, then a curve of her hip or calf, writhing, swaying. Not shirking her responsibility to her guests just because she's the princess, the belle of the banquet, the reason for the gathering. Oh, she's exquisite and doesn't she know it! The world is hers to command – at least all Ireland. For Granya is not merely beautiful, but also the betrothed of the greatest of all hunters, the uncrowned king of hills and wilds and protector of the land, the great Finn McCool himself.

And what, you might ask, is one so young doing engaged to one so much older? Well, the truth is, with men like Finn, age hardly matters. He is a hero – one of the greatest – and Granya fit to be his heroine.

She chose him herself. It wasn't that anyone forced her. Cormac, her father, High King of all Ireland, had started to wonder if she would ever accept any of the magnificent and splendid young men who beat a path to Tara. However handsome they were, however rich, however heroic, Granya would look disdainfully at them and insist she would only marry a man as great as the High King himself.

'No such man exists,' insisted Cormac. But Granya proved them all wrong. And Finn was her prize – as regal, as loved and even wiser and more powerful than Cormac himself. There was many a fay and fairy woman willing to marry Finn but he refused steadfastly to marry, saying he would never be harnessed to one female.

Now here was Granya, dancing with glee as she waited to meet her future husband for the first time. The woman who had changed his mind, and without even meeting him.

That was part of the reason for the liveliness, the confidence that shone out of her eyes. If she was good enough to make Finn turn his back on a lifetime's promise never to marry, she was good enough to achieve anything. She deserved it all. She thoroughly enjoyed the wide-eyed young men, heroes, some of them, as they struggled not to meet her eye, not to look at her too boldly. She kicked higher, higher, her hands on her waist, the challenge in the tilt of her chin, the blink of her lashes, her curving smile.

And they fell, one after another, in love with her. Gazing at her beauty, enraptured. Granya's lips softened into a smile. Her eyes rested, a moment's reward, on each of the young men surrounding her. The Fianna, those great and glorious fighters – how she had them in thrall.

Weep your hearts out, you fays and fairy women, she sang in her head. Just weep your hearts out. Or stay away from here – because you see, when Granya dances, young men have eyes for no one else.

And then she saw him as he entered with her father. Finn, the hunter, the wise man, the uncrowned king of the wilds. Finn McCool of Alvin whom no woman, it is said, had ever turned down. Granya craned her neck, strained her eyes. She saw her father and with him a tall, well-built man, dressed smartly and moving with pride. Beside him, two others. One was young enough to be his son, the other young enough to be his grandson.

Panic-stricken, Granya turned to the Druid standing by her.

'Which one is Finn?' She followed the Druid's gaze as it came to rest on the tallest, most powerfully built, the most handsomely dressed of them. Her heart sank. He was old. She had agreed to marry a man old enough to be her father. Not a single soul had told her Finn's age!

Her thoughts were like trapped animals. They ran this way and that but there was a pitfall on every route. If she refused him, the old hostility between Cormac and Finn would surely flare up again, worse than ever before. If she said nothing, she would be enmeshed in a loveless, luckless marriage like a fish on a hook, twisting, thrashing and ripped to shreds before she ever got away. Of course, she could kill herself – but that, too, would bring disgrace on her father and antagonise Finn.

Then her thoughts were stilled. Cormac was introducing Finn to her. Finn bowed his head. Just his head, note, not all of him as people generally did before the High King of Ireland and his family.

Granya marshalled her thoughts, played the princess that she was. And there was, no doubt, something about Finn. In spite of his age she could feel why he excited other women. It was as if his hair was woven from silver strands, his skin burnished with time, his eyes deep with wisdom and his heart . . . She stopped short. She knew nothing about his heart except that his revenge was relentless, his punishment merciless and nothing stood in the way of his intention.

Finn apprehended her gaze as it travelled up and down and around him. 'You are as beautiful as they say, Granya. White as snow, fragrant as a flower and bright as the sun. As far as your appearance is concerned, you exceed the reports. But what of your mind? Is that also as marvellous as they say?'

A challenge, thought Granya, captivated for the moment. I'm beginning to like this man. He's offering me a challenge.

Finn held out his arm and she took it and let him lead her
out into the green parks of Tara.

'You won't mind if I put a riddle or two to you?' asked
Finn.

Granya laughed. 'I love riddles. But you must not mind if I
give you the correct answers.'

Finn smiled and Granya thought she noticed the mildest
amusement in his smile – indulgence, even. She felt a rush of
irritation but restrained herself. The perplexed face of
defeated foes was thrilling and made her laugh from the centre
of her being. She prepared herself for the cut and thrust that
would follow.

'Indeed, Granya,' said Finn gently, 'it doesn't matter if you
don't win, as long as you know you have tried.'

Granya bristled as Finn stopped by a flowering bush and
looked at the flowers, studded like shining white snow crystals
set alight by the kiss of the sun.

'What is it, Granya, that is whiter than snow?'

Granya's answer was a master-archer's arrow. 'Truth.'

Finn looked reflectively at his wife-to-be, then walked on.
He looked around him, enjoying the splurge of spring colour
that brightened every bush, every mound.

'And which of all these colours is the best?'

'The colour of childhood is the best of all.'

Finn's expression did not change. He continued to enjoy the
colours. Granya looked into his eyes but found them shuttered, though their lids were open. She tried to engage his
glance but it was blank.

I cannot marry this man, she thought, panicking for a
second time since seeing him. He is not even here beside me.
It's as if I don't exist for him. He's drawn a screen between us
and I'm trapped behind it. It dawned on her that Finn was the
hunter through and through, and here and now she was the
quarry that challenged his prowess, threatened his reputation.
He could not allow himself to feel, for the feelings that came
could be of pity or justice and they would interfere with his
determination.

For the first time in her life, Granya felt fearful. A picture flashed in front of her eyes of herself, running, running pursued by Finn, his hounds, his all-seeing eye. Then his voice, posing one riddle after another like a hunter's whip, lashing relentlessly.

'What is hotter than fire?'

'The face of a hospitable man with no food or drink to offer.'

'What tastes more bitter than poison?'

'The reproach of an enemy.'

'What is best for a champion?'

'His deeds to be high, his pride to be low.'

'What is the best of jewels?'

'A knife.'

'What is sharper than a sword?'

'The wit of a woman with two lovers.'

There was not a flicker on Finn's face – no pleasure, no disapproval. Granya took a deep breath. The devil was in her again and she made up her mind she would not be intimidated by this man. She had a sense that he was establishing rules, assigning standards. The pattern she set now was the one she would have to live by for the rest of her life with Finn. And it was better she showed him her strongest side while he was still able to withdraw from their agreement. Then, if he objected later to her behaviour, she could remind him he had not protested when he still had the choice.

'Were my answers the right ones, Finn McCool.' It was a statement, not a question.

Finn turned away. 'They were good answers, daughter of Cormac.'

'But were they right?'

'To be right is not as important as it might sometimes appear. To be good is always honourable. And I'm telling you, your answers were good ones.'

'But, Finn, were they right?'

'You must understand, I studied for years with the great bard Fintan. He taught me about poetry. It was while I was with him that I tasted the three drops from the salmon of knowledge. That was a very great blessing indeed and one that few men are honoured with. That knowledge included the ability to see what no man can see – into the future, into the distance. It also included the ability to pose and interpret riddles.' He turned and faced her and now his eyes were no longer shuttered. Granya thought she saw a threat gleaming in them. 'It is no disgrace to you if your answers are not right.'

'So I'm wrong.'

'There's no shame in being wrong, especially if you are a woman.'

'Why is it that you can't give me a direct answer, Finn McCool? If I'm wrong, tell me.'

'You are very young.'

'True. And I have never studied with a legendary bard like Fintan. So if I'm wrong, I can accept it.'

Then Finn made his greatest mistake.

'You are a woman, Granya. A very beautiful woman. And a clever one. Has no one told you that the best thing for a woman is to find a man to guide and protect her? Once she finds such a man, she need never trouble her wits again.'

Granya hardened. 'I am strong enough to accept that I'm wrong, Finn,' she said coldly. 'But are you strong enough to accept that I'm right?'

Finn turned and walked towards the palace. Granya followed.

'So, am I to believe I am stronger than you, Finn? Because your reaction tells me I'm right.'

'You are young and wild, Granya,' responded Finn, tight-lipped. 'And you have a lot to learn. But you'll find me a good teacher.'

Granya tossed her hair back, raised her face proudly, 'Some time soon, Finn, you must let me ask you a riddle or two.'

She ducked past and entered the halls of Tara before him. All eyes turned on her and she took the same delight in the frank, open staring of some of the Fianna as she did in the pointedly averted gaze of others.

That was when she noticed Dermot.

He was looking away from her into a dream; a strange and beautiful dream. Granya realised, incredulous, that his lack of interest was genuine. She paused beside him, smiled, greeted him. He looked, not at her but, jolted by her closeness, through her. She addressed him. He answered gallantly but remained distracted.

Granya turned away, her fists clenched into balls, her eyes stinging with the affront. Her blood gushed angrily through her veins, buzzing and humming in her ears as she walked over to Finn's Druid.

'Who is that man?' she asked, breezily.

'It is Dermot, grandson of Duibhne,' replied the Druid. 'His other grandfather is Angus Og.'

'Angus?' Her eyes widened. 'You mean Angus Og of Brugh na Boine? Angus the Love God?'

The Druid nodded, amused by her strong reaction. 'The same. Angus brought up Dermot as his own after his father Donne had disgraced himself.'

'Is it true what they say about him? He has a love spot on his forehead and that any woman who looks at it will fall in love with him? Is that why he keeps his forehead covered with his hair?'

The Druid nodded. 'But there are other things that Dermot would prefer to broadcast. For instance the number of times he has saved the lives of his fellow members of the Fianna, even Finn.'

But Granya was dug into her investigation like the root of a mighty oak into the ground, intent on growing. 'And is it true that he can love a woman better than any other man from Ireland to India?'

The Druid's unease told Granya she was right. 'That's what they say.'

'And you know it's true?'

'I know I've heard it.' The Druid shifted uncomfortably, suspicious of Granya's questions. 'But I've never spoken to him about it and so I can't say for sure.'

Granya's eyes sparkled. 'You know well, Druid, because you've seen the women's faces after he has pleasured them. You know it's true. And I don't know why it is that Finn and his men find it so hard to answer a question directly.'

She was off across the other side of the room without waiting for the Druid's reply. Dermot was handsome, courageous and famous. She paused an instant on her way to him and looked at Finn. He was also handsome, courageous and famous. And he had the wisdom of the two worlds after having studied with Fintan the poet and imbibing the three drops from the salmon of knowledge. By sucking on the back of his thumb, he could acquire answers no one else knew, know things that had not yet happened. He could scry: by gazing into the still waters of a bowl he could see where people were hiding. And he had a wit to challenge hers. He was an appropriate match for her in every way. But there were questions about people and relationships that never entered the equation when marriage proposals were made and accepted. Important questions such as the nature of the partners-to-be, their attitudes, their ways, not just of behaving but of being. Matters that could affect the future of a marriage.

Tonight Granya had discovered something about herself – that she was no shrew to be tamed by Finn; and something about Finn – that he had a mean streak about him.

'Perfect in every way,' she murmured, 'except for his ungenerous soul.'

She continued her progress across the room until she stood squarely in front of Dermot. She placed her hand on his shoulder and he looked up at her, enquiring.

'Take me away from here, Dermot, take me away from my father's home and from Finn McCool who is old enough to be my father.'

Did Granya imagine it, or was there fear in Dermot's eyes? 'I want you to take me away from Finn and from this marriage,' she repeated.

Dermot leapt to his feet, backing away. The moment was

charged. The friends sitting near him stopped talking, transfixed. Had they heard right? They stared at Dermot, waiting for his reply. He said only one word.

'No.'

Granya was bewildered but she saw Dermot's friends watching and quickly gathered her wits. 'Then I put a *geis* upon you. You are bound to help me or you will be destroyed by magic.'

Dermot was adamant. 'No.'

'I am asking for you help.' Granya threw down her trump card. Dermot paled as she continued speaking. 'It's a woman's duty to herself to know where she can get help when she needs it. I know, Hawk of Ess Ruadh, that you are sworn not to refuse any woman who asks for your help.'

'I'm not sure this is a genuine request for help,' Dermot protested. 'It sounds to me like a deceit.'

'It's not your business to investigate the motives behind a request.' She turned to his friends. 'You have heard me ask for Dermot's help. Should he comply?'

The young men told Dermot that he was obliged to fulfil Granya's request.

'And what if I prefer to be cursed than to betray my leader?'

'But you are not betraying your leader,' demurred Caoilte. 'You are simply helping the princess.'

'By helping her, I betray him.'

'Finn will understand,' soothed Finn's grandson, Osgar, 'when we explain the circumstances.'

Dermot looked at Granya. 'This is an evil thing you're forcing me to do. I'm damned if I do it and I'm damned if I don't. I warn you here and now, I won't replace Finn in any way. I'm obliged to help you but I will never love you or touch you while we are together.'

Granya tossed her head. Her look crackled with challenge. We'll see about that when the time comes, she thought. But for now, if it makes you feel better to think you can resist me, that's fine with me.

Later that evening as everyone sat around the table feasting and drinking, exchanging stories, jokes and riddles, Granya wondered if it was slighted pride that was pushing her to conquer Dermot. Was she responding to the primordial challenge of male to female, some shadowy love dance that preceded the mating game? But no, she was sure it went deeper. True, it was Dermot's disregard that first captured her attention but when she had looked closer she had seen into his soul, caught sight of the dream his eyes had been fixed on. She wanted to be part of that dream. And if she had to bend the rules to achieve it, then she would. What better use was there for her wit and wiles?

Granya clapped her hands and ordered her serving-maid to bring in her enchanted jug, the one which never emptied. The jug was brought and Granya placed it in front of her announcing that she would honour all the guests by serving them from the magic pitcher. The round of glasses began, each one passed along to be filled, then passed round again to be drunk. And into each glass, except Dermot's, Granya added a sleeping potion. By the time she finished pouring, a deep sleep infused the dining halls of Tara and before long all the heroes and warriors closed their eyes and let their heads loll. Only Dermot remained awake and, across the table, Granya looking at him, her face solemn, her eyes determined.

She rose to her feet, walked over to Dermot, took his hand. 'It is time for us to leave.'

'Granya, do you realise what you're asking me to do? You're asking me to betray my dear friend and leader. You're asking me to give up all my companions, the chance to perform glorious and heroic deeds. Finn is not the greatest hunter of all times for nothing. Once he makes up his mind, his prey can't hide for long. We'll be fugitives until we die, running, hiding . . . It's not too late to change your mind.'

Granya was offended. Dermot was still unwilling to look into her dream and see himself there. She accepted that Finn was a worthy and powerful friend and provoking him by running away with his future bride on the day of their engagement was no casual thing to do. But she too was giving him up – she too would share in the dangers and the disrepute. Surely Dermot could see that Finn was unsuitable for her. He must have been out of his mind, asking for her hand!

But such things were often part of fate's strange route to meetings and partings. His proposal had brought Dermot to her and though he so resented being with her now, she knew that soon he would thank her for her boldness.

'Let's go, Dermot, my mind's made up.'

Dermot stood up, his movements leaden and resigned. Hurt pride pinched and tugged at Granya's heart. Here she was offering Dermot her hand and her companionship, prizes for which hundreds of men as good and better would have risked their lives, and all she got from him was the bowed head of resigned acquiescence. The pinching and tugging continued as they left the palace of the High King, Tara, the place of Granya's birth, her sunny bower, her green groves.

Would she ever see Tara or her father again? Given the circumstances of her departure, probably not. But this surging, crashing desire she felt for Dermot would give her no peace. So, when Dermot drew her into the shadow of Tara's walls and urged her to change her mind, she clung to her intention.

'Never,' she hissed. 'Never will I marry Finn, even if you leave me to my own resources.' Then she sighed. 'You really don't feel it, do you? This bond that ties us together? Do you feel it at all?'

Dermot shook his head. 'The only bond I feel is the one that you are using to imprison me. Before that I didn't even notice you. I'm not a man for banquets and royal courts; my mind was elsewhere.'

Granya remembered, insulted. 'Perhaps that was why I chose you rather than another man, Dermot. Because you ignored me.'

'Then you are just a wilful woman and I want no part of you.'

'You really do believe this is some whim, some skittish female caprice. Well, it's not. I know about you, Dermot. I've heard tales about you. Your deeds with the Fianna, your kindness to

the wild and ugly daughter of King Underwave . . . I can't say
I saw the love spot that Time herself gave you, but I know that
I saw you and wanted you. It was as simple as that.'

'Simple!' bellowed Dermot, red with anger. 'There's nothing simple about it! Do you know what our lives will be like?
We'll be chased relentlessly by Finn and the Fianna. We'll live
on the run, in perpetual fear of being caught and punished.
Tell me, what's simple about that?'

Granya turned away from Dermot, hiding her tears. This
was a wretched way to start their life together. Love demanded
is love degraded but how else could she have secured Dermot?

'We should leave now,' she ordered. 'In a few hours they'll
miss me and start a search. We must hurry or we're lost.'

'We are lost anyhow,' said Dermot, bitter.

'No!' Granya was petulant. 'This may be the start of something good in your life.'

'My life was good enough as it was,' Dermot barked. 'My
first allegiance is to Finn and I am doing this under duress.
Just remember that I have no intention of being your lover.'

Granya had tolerated enough. She might be in love with
Dermot, but she was not a mat for him to wipe his feet on. She
was doing him a favour in guiding him towards his true destiny, even though he didn't know it yet. She would not be
abused for it.

'You'd be wise to remember I get what I want, Hawk of Ess
Ruadh.' Her voice was cold and the chill sank into her bones,
making her shiver. She gathered her cloak closely around her
and drew herself up tall. 'Now, since you're here to help me,
do your job and take me away. You'll find horses in the field on
the west of Tara. Choose two to ride and take two along as
spares for when our mounts grow tired.'

'Don't you think the horses would alert Finn and the
others?' demanded Dermot, impatient. 'Besides when they
wake and find we've fled, like thieves in the night, the horses
will be easy to track.'

'Then we'll go on foot.'

'I hope you don't expect me to carry you on my back?'

'I said, didn't I, that I'd walk?'

'Is there no way I can make you change your mind?'

'None. So we might as well be on our way.'

Granya knew the countryside as well as she knew the parting of her hair and the curves of her limbs. She led Dermot through hedgerows and tracks that lay hidden between swamps and pot-holes, so narrow and treacherous that the tip of a shoe landing out of place could mean a murky end in a bog that had devoured many a human before them. But Granya was sure-footed and Granya was swift and they were miles from Tara before dawn broke. As the first bird sang and the first fingers of light streaked the sky, she looked around her and saw that they were now in a place she had never seen before.

'I have led you far away from Tara as best I could, Dermot. And now it is up to you to protect us both.'

'They'll soon be out searching for us,' replied Dermot. 'Is there a direction you prefer?'

'I trust you, Hawk of Ess Ruadh, I'm content to follow you.'

Dermot led and Granya followed until, as night was falling, they approached a forest. Granya suggested they sleep there so that they would be safe from Finn's men for the night. But Dermot shook his head in frustration.

'No forest in the world is dark and thick enough to hide us from Finn.'

'Tell me how he'll know where we are.'

'By filling his shallow golden bowl full of water and looking deep into it. The movement of the water will settle into shapes which Finn can distinguish. From these he deduces where to look.'

'So,' snorted Granya, disdainfully, 'Finn can't know for sure where we are. He can only deduce.'

Without another word, Dermot worked hard gathering branches, chopping wood, tying up brush until he had built a small dwelling for Granya. As night drew in she went into her side of the hut and lay thinking of Dermot and the events of the day. He said he did not love her; well, he was still mourning the loss of his former, glory-hunting days. He said he did not want her. But she could see from the concern on his face that he did care. It could be that he hunted, made a fire and roasted fowl to keep up his own strength. But why had he worked so hard on building her the hut? Poor Dermot, he was riddled with guilt and racked with confusion for hating and desiring her at the same time.

Granya lay awake, piqued by Dermot's resistance. He was stubborn and ungrateful. Here she was, offering herself to him and he was turning down the prize for which hundreds would gladly risk their lives. In the deep of the night, she called to him.

'Dermot come in and rest.'

Dermot came.

'Daughter of Cormac,' he growled. 'I will lie down beside you, but only because my body is tired and I need my strength for this journey to which you have condemned me.'

Dermot held up a bone which he had saved from the carcass of the fowl. 'This bone will lie between our bodies. It will keep the boundary between you and me.'

'How many times must you tell me that you don't want me?' Granya snapped.

'You are not a woman to give up easily.'

Her pride wounded, Granya shifted to the outer edge of her bedding. 'I'm also a woman who can bide her time.'

Soon Dermot's breathing grew heavy and deep and Granya knew he was asleep though he slept with the lightness of the breeze skimming tips of grass – a hunter's sleep, skittish and on the wing. But to her, sleep didn't come at all. She was not one to beg and Dermot would know her worth when he saw how Finn abandoned all other glory-seeking to win her back.

As the birds began to chatter and the skies grew a paler shade of black, a cry tore apart the peacefulness of the forest. Then another. Then a third.

Dermot sat up at the sound of the first. By the time the

third call fell on his ears he had distinguished the cries as the warnings of his friends. Finn was on their trail!

'Let's run,' cried Granya, triumphant. Finn was here!

'I'm a warrior. I don't run.'

Granya was provocative. Would Dermot run with her or would he fight Finn for her? Either way, he would irreversibly become her knight. 'You're bound to save me.'

'So I am and I'll find a way without running.'

Dermot thought rapidly, checking the strength of the tallest tree near them, getting ready to hide Granya in its branches when, suddenly, he was hurled back by a massive weight. A huge dog reared itself on its back legs and placed its paws on his shoulders as if embracing him, joyfully licking his face, making small, excited noises.

'This is Bran,' explained Dermot, 'Finn's hound – she's been sent to warn me that Finn is close by.'

'Then we must leave immediately,' urged Granya. But Dermot insisted he would stay and see them. If they could not understand his reason for doing what he did, well then he would have to accept that many years of camaraderie had taught them nothing about his character.

Dermot pointed to an enormous oak. 'I will help you into that tree. Hide in its branches until the trouble is over.'

Granya revelled in the attention. Still she tested her powers of persuasion, pressing and wheedling, coaxing and insisting that Dermot should come up the tree with her. But her appeals fell on unyielding soil.

Granya was piqued. 'You're the grandson of Angus, but how you take every opportunity to revile and reject love!'

'I don't revile or reject it,' Dermot responded. 'I've had love – in short sweet bursts and in exquisite continuity. But this – this awful situation you've got me into – this isn't love. This is wanton and wilful and evil. It will bring misery and destruction for everyone. Love can't be forced. You clearly know nothing about it.'

Dermot reached up to a high branch and levered himself into the oak. He consolidated his foothold then stretched down and drew Granya up after him. The hounds of the Fianna were barking louder. Swiftly Dermot settled Granya in a fork at the junction of two strong central branches which proliferated into a sturdy mesh like a massive hammock from which there would be no danger of falling.

'Don't be rash, Dermot. If you die, I'll stay here until I'm dead too.'

'What's wrong with you, woman?' growled Dermot. 'Can't I even die without your permission?'

'In the name of love, Dermot . . .'

The oak shook violently as if a strong wind was trapped within it.

'Angus!' Dermot gasped.

'I wondered when you'd think of me,' grumbled Angus. 'For all your talk of honour and chivalry, Dermot, you're disgracing the great traditions of love. How can you refuse this beautiful young woman who has put her trust in you?'

'She's forced me from my home and my friends and everything I love. How can you expect me to love her?'

'Stuff and nonsense! Don't be so arrogant. Love rates above all emotions and commitments. You wouldn't be the first, you know. Tristan fell in love with Mark's betrothed. Naoise eloped with Deirdre. And what about Lancelot and Guinevere? No, you're not the first and you won't be the last. This is a great and ancient pattern – the young, new lover displaces the old. You are lucky that Granya chose you.'

Angus Og, God of Love, raised his huge cloak and invited them in. Granya crept under it, nestling in his protective presence. Dermot hesitated a moment, then turned quickly away.

'I must stay and fight Finn. And if I succeed, Granya, I will come for you. If not, then Angus will be your protector.'

The last Granya saw of Dermot was a flash of silver in the sun as he leapt off the tree on to the ground, preparing to take on the Fianna. And from that day to his arrival in Brugh na Boine, she was like a phantom. She felt nothing, saw nothing, did nothing, only waited, willing Dermot to remain alive and come back to her whole and healthy. Then one day, not long afterwards, Dermot arrived to fetch her.

Granya hatched from her cocoon of grief and suspense, a butterfly, so ecstatic and full of the joy of life that she flitted and sparkled and spread happiness and colour with every moment and every gesture and all Brugh na Boine seemed to light up with her feelings.

But then they were on their way again and Dermot's bitter mood continued as days and nights passed into weeks, weeks into months, months into years and all the time they remained on the move and Finn and his men were never far off. A fine chicken bone told him that Dermot had kept his distance from Granya; a piece of unbroken bread told him her virginity was intact. It infuriated Granya that Dermot insisted on broadcasting to Finn and his men that he, the great lover, had resisted her so long. Still, what of it? Granya exulted in Finn's persistence, growing more confident with every encounter that Dermot was the cleverer fighter. If only he could acquire some of Finn's ardour, the passion that goaded him into pursuing her after all this time.

But did her thoughts have the slightest impact on Dermot? Not a bit! With the approach of every danger, he offered Granya the chance of recanting, returning to Finn. After every escape, he told her how useless their lives had become. But Granya's resolve grew with each admonition. She would bend Dermot's will. She would make him love her.

And so it was, still loveless and unreconciled, that they arrived at the forbidden forest of Duvross.

'By whose authority is it forbidden?' Granya challenged, curious.

'It's been forbidden since recorded time.'

Granya sensed that Dermot was hedging. 'If there's no reason, we should disregard the rule.'

'There's a tree here which bears lethal fruits.'

'A whole forest lost for one poisonous tree? That's absurd. And you don't even care to question the reasoning behind it?'

'For mercy's sake, woman, don't you ever accept that life is not a garden to burst into bloom every time you want to smell something sweet? The forest has always been forbidden. The tradition has been observed for generations. Let us look elsewhere.'

'There's no time to go elsewhere,' insisted Granya. 'Night is falling and where better for a few days' respite than a forest which no one dares enter?'

Granya ran into the forest of Duvross. Dermot ran after her, grabbing her arm to stop her. But he never uttered the words he was going to say. Granya saw his look change to one of resignation, as if he knew only too well that all his argument and persuasion would be lost on her. When Granya made up her mind, she stuck to it.

'You must promise me something,' he insisted, holding her close so that she could feel his breath on her hair, feel his chest, tense and hard. 'Never pick or eat any of the fruit of this forest unless I give it to you.'

Granya looked at Dermot. His face was intense with concern and anxiety.

'And if I do?'

Dermot's grip tightened. 'If you do, I'll leave now.'

'Still longing for Finn's forgiveness,' she said, bitterly. 'Do you still deny that he's the one in the wrong now? Is he too foolish to understand that fate meant us to be together?'

'It was Granya, not fate, who threw us together. You've wronged me, Granya and I'll never forget it.'

'Then you're as foolish as your friend and perhaps you should leave me to my devices.'

As she turned and walked away, Granya saw from the side of her eye that Dermot was stricken. Dermot was weakening. For a while now, he had not cursed her nor told her to return to Tara. Nor had he made any effort to abandon her though he knew she was safe and could perfectly well survive on her own. Unlike him, she did not long for her old life but thrilled in the game of hide-and-seek, of life and death. Yes, for all her discomfort, she gloried in Finn's determination to get her back. Each battle confirmed her female power, and her resolve to conquer Dermot grew deeper, stronger.

You may well ask where it will all end and if Finn will eventually give up his pursuit but for now, two young men arrived in Duvross, sent by Finn on a quest to bring back Dermot, dead or alive.

'We are the sons of Morna,' they began, not knowing their host was Dermot himself. 'Morna and McCool have been enemies for generations.'

The two kinsmen had gone to Finn to call a truce and cement a new bond. Finn agreed readily if, like all members of the Fianna, they passed a test set by him. They could capture Dermot and bring him back to the Fianna, or fetch him the berries of the fairy tree of Duvross.

'The magic fruit,' said Dermot. 'Do you know how dangerous it is? Did Finn tell you?'

'Finn told us everything. It cures illness and the signs of old age and, like the best wine, it gives the eater a constant sense of well-being.'

'Did Finn also tell you that, like wine, if taken in excess, it causes madness? Only, the madness of the berries never wears off.'

'Why do you undermine Finn?'

Why had he never told her about the miraculous properties of the fruit? Granya fumed. Why had he told her only about its dangers?

'The tree is guarded by Sharvan, the surly ogre of Lockham. His sole task is to protect the berries from humans. No man has a chance against him. He can only die if he is struck three times with his own club on the gold torque around his neck.'

The sons of Morna looked at each other and laughed. 'It seems to us that you're the one who wants to protect the tree from newcomers, not Sharvan nor the fairies.'

'Perhaps you should think about fulfilling the other condition,' goaded Dermot. 'I have been wondering why Finn set you such a difficult task.'

'We said before that our father killed his father and it would take a big deed to put old hostilities to rest.'

'It's a very sad thing I have to tell you but tell you I must. Finn himself killed your father. By the ancient laws that is revenge enough.'

'Why do you insist on maligning Finn?' roared one brother.

'Finn wants you dead,' declared Dermot. 'But you won't listen to the truth. So fight me and take my head back to Finn or battle the ogre for a fistful of berries.'

'We'll fight you,' thundered the two men, rushing at Dermot. But after little more than a skirmish, Dermot tied the two men up and Granya approached him haughtily.

'Why didn't you tell me about the magic berries?'

'I told you what you needed to know.'

'But you told the strangers the whole tale.'

'They had to know the danger of their mission.'

'You thought I'd make you bring me some.'

Dermot clenched his teeth. 'That would be no surprise.'

Granya could not have been more wounded if Dermot had struck her. 'You think I'd be frivolous enough to endanger your life on a whim?'

'You've done nothing else since you set eyes on me.'

Granya felt quite crazed by the unfairness of his remark. To him, she was still the wilful, stubborn king's daughter who wanted her way come what may. And what if she did want her way? She was Granya, was she not? Beautiful Granya who could choose any man she pleased and had turned them all down for Dermot. Suddenly she was fed up with his inflexibility, his inability to see what he was rejecting. Surely, anyone else in his position would have applauded her qualities, her constancy, her refusal to complain.

Night after night, she endured the humiliation of that wretched chicken bone, that unbroken bread – sterile symbols of a withered friendship with an obstinate man. She had seen him look longingly at her in the night, many times. She had felt him pull the covering over her shoulders – and she had longed for him to acknowledge his love. But he always disappointed her. Hot tears were the only human warmth she had.

Her brain throbbed, her skin stung, her whole being melted into an amorphous mass that threatened to bubble, froth over and spill away.

'You're right.' Her voice was thin and sharp as a sword when she spoke but inwardly she heard a crazed howl of passion, the earth lamenting its own destruction. 'I want some of those berries. And if you don't get me some, I'll fetch them myself.'

Dermot blanched. 'We've lived safely here for so long because I promised Sharvan that I would keep away from the tree. Are you asking me to break another promise?'

'I'm asking you to do nothing. I've put up with your carping for a thousand years because I fell in love with you. But I want those berries and I'm going to get them.'

'You will not.'

'I will so, grandson of Duibhne. And until I do, I won't sleep a wink, or even lie down until I die or have the fruit.'

'Untie us, Dermot,' begged the sons of Morna, 'and let us watch you fight Sharvan.'

So Dermot untied the men and set off for the rowan tree. Granya wanted to call him back but crazed as she was, tears flowing, hair streaming, she convinced herself that she hated Dermot. She would not relent and take back her threats. What would be the point, now? Dermot already despised her for a stubborn, wilful woman who thought of no one but herself.

As she waited for Dermot's safe return, Granya's mind was a battleground, her heart a storm-torn sea. Then she saw two specks in the distance and recognised them as the sons of Morna. Their eyes sparkled and their words shot out of their mouths like fireworks. First of all, they said, Dermot had approached the ogre respectfully, with a request. He did not wish to violate his pact and asked Sharvan for a handful of berries. Without warning, Sharvan swung his massive club at him and as Dermot staggered back, Sharvan grew careless, confident that no human could survive such a blow. But

Dermot seized the giant's club and struck him three times on the great torque.

'Dermot killed Sharvan,' marvelled the men, 'but he needs your help.'

Granya flew from her hut like a feather on the wind and didn't stop until she reached Dermot's side. In that moment she would gladly had forgone the magic berries. But Dermot looked at her with empty eyes and pointed to the rowan tree.

'Take as much fruit as you want.'

Granya caught her breath sharply, brought a cold, hard sheath down over her heart and looked at the tree as it glowed and shone like a thing made of precious metals and gems.

'The tree frightens me, Dermot,' she breathed. 'I'll only eat the berries if you pluck them for me.'

So Dermot plucked the berries and all four of them shared. Then the sons of Morna packed a few and took them back to Finn.

Well, Finn knew instantly that Dermot had helped the sons of Morna, and he arrived in the forest of Duvross with the bravest and best men in all Ireland. They stormed into the forest and there, in the distance, they saw the shimmer and shine of the rowan tree. Granya watched from the tree as Dermot lay asleep beside her.

Finn seized the trunk of the tree and began to shake it furiously, shouting: 'Come down, son of Donne. Come out of the tree. Face your retribution.'

Granya retreated deep into the shelter of the magic tree as Finn sent up nine warriors, one after another, to fight Dermot. As the first of them reached into the branches, the boughs of the tree were agitated by violent gusts of wind.

Angus Og! thought Granya. He's here to help Dermot.

The berries, or Angus' magic – one or the other must have put Dermot into a deeper than natural sleep. By the time he opened his eyes and took stock of the situation, he saw the nine men lying dead at Finn's feet. Finn had impaled each one on his spear, taking him for Dermot. Angus had worked his magic and deceived Finn. Now Finn saw that he had killed his own men and his already swollen blood-lust doubled.

'Come down and fight me, son of Donne!' he bellowed. 'Or will you hide in your tree like a little frightened sparrow for ever?'

'Why does he call you son of Donne?' Granya demanded.

'Donne my father, crushed a boy between his knees and killed him. He has been in disgrace since then.'

'Why did he do that?'

'He believed that Angus loved the other one better than me.'

'Come with me to Brugh na Boine,' pleaded Angus, interrupting.

'For once,' Granya begged, 'ignore your code of honour.'

For an instant, Dermot softened. 'The boy my father killed is now the Green Boar of Beinn Gulbain. Until he comes for me, I won't die.'

So it was that once again Dermot defeated Finn and once again he and Granya were on the run until they found a cave at the edge of the sea and made it their home. Still, Dermot would not relent and take Granya into his arms and still Granya was determined to have her way.

She lay awake at night asking herself why Dermot did not love her. Was she no longer beautiful, or desirable? Had she not proved her loyalty? One night, as the questions raged in her mind, Granya did not even notice the waves grow and grow until they rushed past the mouth of the cave hissing and spitting. When finally the spray drenched her body, she reached out to turn Dermot over so that he would remain dry. But Dermot pulled violently away from Granya's touch. Before she could protest, through the curtain of water and foaming spray appeared a tall, heavy man.

'I am Ciach. My boat was tossed ashore. I wonder if you'll let me share your cave until the wind subsides. Then I'll be on my way.'

'Welcome, stranger.' Dermot lit a fire and made the man comfortable. He appeared friendly enough and eventually Dermot grew drowsy from the warmth of the fire and his eyes closed.

Granya kept an eye on the stranger. Outside, there was a lull in the storm. Ciach stood up and collected his belongings. He smiled gratefully at Granya and she smiled back. Without a word, he lifted her in his vast arms and began to walk away. Dermot stirred. Granya said not a word, but watched intently. Dermot saw Granya in Ciach's arms and jumped to his feet, sword in hand. His eyes blazed and his manner was wild. Suddenly, a demon was in Granya. Now that she was in another man's arms, Dermot was jealous. Well, let him suffer a little of what he had made her endure. She snuggled up to Ciach, smiling.

Dermot rushed at Ciach, trying to wrench Granya from him. Granya's anger blazed. How dare Dermot act so possessive? How dare he? Dermot, who had reviled her and refused her at every turn. What right had he now to attack any man for holding her in his arms?

'He gave me more in a moment than you have in ten years, Dermot,' she raged.

'Shut up, woman,' barked Dermot. 'You're a death knell to any man you favour. You have the blood of hundreds on your hands and you don't show a shred of remorse.'

Granya's eye fell on the knife embedded in meat on the spit and, without thinking, she snatched it up and flung it at Dermot. But though it found its mark, he didn't flinch or show any sign of being hurt. Instead, he attacked Ciach with such violent, ferocious blows that he brought him to his knees in one moment and in the next to his death. Then he walked out into the storm and stood looking out at the sea.

Granya felt wretched. She was a creature of passions: when they overcame her she did not reason any more. But now, watching her beloved Dermot standing on the edge of the cliff with the sea roaring and bellowing at his feet, she was filled with remorse.

He's right, she thought, reflecting on their past. What have I brought him but misery? He might have been happy if he'd accepted my love. But he only ever reached for the heartache.

It's best that I let him go.

She went out to Dermot, who was still watching the sea, so bereft and vulnerable.

'Come into the cave,' she implored him. 'Warm yourself by the fire. I have something to say.'

Tenderly, she touched his shoulder. Dermot's hand covered hers. He whirled around, his eyes reflecting the convulsions of the sea. 'What do you want from me, Granya?' he said, desperately. 'Will you make me love you, then leave me, like you left Finn?'

'Oh Dermot,' Granya wept, 'I've stayed with you all these years because I love you. If you can't see that now, you never will.' She reached out with her other hand to wipe the drops glistening on his lashes.

The next moment he wrapped her in his arms, holding her close. Granya dared not believe the time had come. She could feel the warmth of his body as he murmured in her ear.

'You're the smoke from a burning fire, Granya, you'll drift away as soon as it's lit. You're the early morning dew, you'll disappear with the sun's first rays. You're the victory dream of a warrior travelling to battle, you'll fade as he wakes.'

'I'm none of those things, Dermot. I'm your true love. We're flower and fragrance, the stream and the river, the bird and the wind. We were meant to be together. That's why I've loved you since we met.'

But Dermot just clung to her, kissing her hair, her forehead, her eyes, muttering on about how she would leave him once he confessed his love.

'Hush, hush, Dermot.' Granya led him to the fire. 'Warm yourself and eat a little to restore your strength.'

But as soon as she moved away from him, Dermot became withdrawn. He looked dully at the spit.

'The meat isn't carved,' he said. 'I can't eat.'

'Then I'll carve you a piece,' replied Granya, reaching for the knife. But the knife wasn't there. She remembered with a shock that she had thrown it at Dermot.

'Where is it?' she asked, terrified at what she might hear.

'Where you put it,' replied Dermot.

Granya breathed in, stretched out her hands. 'Then give it to me.'

'Take it yourself.' Suddenly, Dermot seemed to come to life, watching her, testing her.

Granya walked determinedly over to him. She saw the knife embedded in his thigh, grasped it and pulled. Dermot stood up. This time, Granya saw the candid desire in his face, the love in his eyes. This time, she knew the moment had come. Easily, she glided into his arms. They sank to the ground. At last Granya had won Dermot.

'And I was coming to release you from my *geis*,' laughed Granya.

'Well if you had,' grinned Dermot, 'think what you would have lost.'

When Finn eventually tracked them down to the cave, he found no chicken bone and the piece of bread was broken.

He's taunting me, thought Finn grimly and he followed Dermot all the way to Brugh na Boine where he had taken Granya to ask for Angus Og's blessing.

Finn could not attack the house of a god, but it was not long before Dermot came out to meet him. And this time, though he did not know it, he was fighting Finn, the Fianna and the magic of the Druidess Bovmall who had once been Finn's nurse.

As he emerged from Brugh na Boine he found himself in a cobweb-like mist, its sticky strands obscuring his assailants and distracting him. But it was soon clear that this was not enough to assure victory for the Fianna. So Bovmall cast another spell. She found a leaf and tore a hole in it through which she flung spears at Dermot. From the roof of Brugh na Boine Granya saw each spear find its mark on Dermot's body.

'Where are they coming from?' she wondered in panic, as Dermot turned this way and that to escape the volley. But soon Dermot saw that all the missiles were coming from the same direction. Some powerful magic was working against him. He stood up straight, looked sharply in the direction of the attack – and saw a floating hole in the mist, edged with the green of a torn leaf. He threw himself on the ground, flat on his back, out of range of the hole. Then he lifted his spear, aimed carefully, and let it fly.

The Druidess fell back with a loud howl. The magic broke, the volley of darts ceased and Dermot's wounds healed. Finn ordered the Fianna to withdraw and regroup. But Angus Og declared that it was time for a truce. Though Finn was unwilling, he knew he could not oppose a god. Grudgingly he acquiesced and entered Brugh na Boine for a feast which lasted a year and a day.

And in that time, Granya married Dermot and they gave birth to their first child.

Dermot built Granya a house that sat in a glen surrounded by lush greenery, a gushing river, benign, rolling hills. It was a spot that the gods would envy. Granya was the happiest woman in the world, bringing up her children, loving Dermot and enjoying his attention. The years of running had been a terrible trial and she loved the comfort and tranquillity of her new life.

Then, one day, Finn returned. Dermot and Granya gave him a warm welcome. But though Granya prepared a welcoming feast and her hospitality was faultless, she was not altogether comfortable with Finn.

'Nonsense,' teased Dermot, confident in their love. 'You just don't like to think he's forgotten you.'

So Granya said no more about her worries. Then, one night, she was awakened by a noise out in the mountains. It was the sound of a chase.

'It can't be,' said Dermot, incredulous. 'Who hunts in the deep of night when the quarry can hide in the dark?'

But the noise persisted and Dermot decided to investigate.

Granya ran to the highest window of her home and gazed out. There was Dermot in the distance, walking through the glen, up the mountain path to where Finn sat. And, a short while later, here was Finn striding towards the house. Granya did not know when Finn arrived and when he mounted his chariot and left. All she could see was a large animal approaching Dermot. It looked like a boar, only it was green. And its head was round and smooth as a mole's where a boar's ears would have stood out on top. It was the Green Boar of Beinn Gulbain and it was Dermot's death.

With a scream, Granya ran out into the night. Through the trees she ran, her face scratched, her hair torn by branches, her feet in shreds. She ran through the thickets and thorny briars to the mountain path until she reached Dermot. But she never saw him alive again.

Nor did she see his broken, mangled body. For Angus Og was waiting with his grandson in his arms. Around them shone the mystic light of the Tuatha Dé Danann, the ancient gods of Ireland. Dermot looked peaceful.

'I can't return him to you, Granya,' Angus told her, tenderly, 'but he will go with me to the world of the gods and there he'll live for ever, untouched by sickness, untroubled by human suffering.'

Then Angus Og told Granya that Finn had visited them with only one purpose in mind: to kill Dermot. He had used his powers of divination to find out that Dermot would die at the hands of the Green Boar, then he had located the beast and lured Dermot out in the dead of night to confront his death. How he had taunted him! How he had mocked! But Dermot had stood firm and met his end like a true hero.

If Granya's grief was limitless, her fury was also infinite. She gathered her sons around her and explained the circumstances of Dermot's death.

'You are all grown men now and brave warriors. Go out and avenge your father. Finding Finn won't be easy. One day you hear he's in the west, the next he's in the east. He is capricious, he follows his whims. But however long it takes you, find him. And when you do, kill him.'

By now Granya's daughters were married and the loss of

Dermot and the departure of her children made her lonely and restless. She waited desperately for word from her sons. Were they safe? Had they found Finn? Or had he found them first and killed them with the aid of wiles and magic as he had killed Dermot?

When Granya saw a lone rider approach one day, she ran down to greet him. Would he have news of her boys? But when the dust settled around the stranger and his mount, she saw Finn. He leapt from his horse, bold as brass, and strode up to her.

'I hope you will make me welcome, Granya,' he challenged.

Without a word Granya walked into the house and ordered a welcome feast. Why was Finn here? Had he come to tell her he had killed her sons?

For Granya, the meal was like a trial by fire. Finn stared at her, full of desire, and grasped her hand frequently. And how the compliments flowed from him – like coins from the purse of a money-lender. Vulgar and ominous. But for the sake of her sons, Granya forced herself to endure Finn.

When at last dinner was over and Finn bade her good-night to go to his room Granya decided she would not let him sleep under her roof then find the next day that he had murdered her sons.

'Have you seen my sons, Finn?' she demanded. 'Have you killed them? Because if you have you are not welcome in my home.'

'I have not seen them, fierce Granya,' he replied, calmly. 'But if I had, they would not be alive today. Because I know they're out to kill me.'

Granya sank back in her chair, relieved. 'Then I bid you good-night, Finn.'

Granya fully expected Finn to leave the next day, but he stayed. And the next day, and soon she felt a fire rekindle inside. It's the loneliness, she told herself, and as long as I can keep him with me, Finn will be away from my sons. But it was more than that. Granya was alive again! She could feel her old power return. Once more her sense of mischief surged through her blood. And when Finn entered her room one night she let him come to her bed. Not because of her sons, but because by now she wanted him.

Finn was rough and demanding, not like Dermot, gentle and tender. But he brought her pleasure too. Soon she began to look forward to his caresses, his demands, the wildness of their nights together. Granya felt young again, revived with the vigour of love and love-making. So when Finn asked her to marry him, she accepted his offer, locked up her house safe for her sons and went with him to Alvin.

'This is where you should have come years ago, Granya,' Finn said gruffly. 'And how many lives you would have spared.'

'Ah,' said Granya, triumphant. 'But you know, Finn, none of those lives was as important to me as the lives of Dermot's sons.'

Lamia

Do you know Lamia? Who is she? She is a snake-woman, all slither and venom, who comes in the night, steals children and devours them, crunching their tiny bones in her gargantuan coils. Is that who Lamia is? Or is she a shadowy creature, woven from the darkness of night, lurking in its most dreadful depths? She uses the moonlight to delude men, bathing in its pools and streams so that she appears, incandescent, to unsuspecting men. She takes them to her palaces of dreams, enfolds them in her irresistible arms, entwines them in her pleasure-giving limbs. She shows them ecstasies beyond imagination, beyond illusion and promises them they will be with her for ever. But in the light of day, she vanishes. *La Belle Dame Sans Merci*, leaving behind robbed manhood scrabbling in the shattered ruins of the dreams she made.

So, who is Lamia? Is she the distant dream of glory – the certain knowledge that every fantasy can become real? Or is she the fantasy that destroys?

Her story begins long ago. Long, long ago. Before anyone ever sought to record her tale, perhaps even long before the science of writing was invented. So we can start where we like, to pick up the threads of her life.

Lamia was no older than thirteen or fourteen. Dana, her beloved maid, was with her but she felt alone. Absolutely alone, as night, infinite and frightening, enfolded her in its mystery.

She stood by the fire, so close to it that it singed her lashes and the wisps of hair that sprang from the drying skin of her forehead. She stepped nearer the fire, her hand on her pregnant belly, urging his image to appear in the flames. Dana moved forward, anxiously.

'My lady, step back, you'll harm yourself.'

Lamia did not hear her. 'Come,' she breathed into the fire, 'come to me. Your child is due any day and I want you to be near me when he's born.'

Dana put a cool hand on Lamia's shoulder. 'He will come, my lady. But you must be careful of yourself – of the infant.'

The infant jumped in her womb as if it had heard Dana. Immediately Lamia stepped away from the fire, the spell broken, her heart leaping in terror.

'Dana! What was I doing? Why did you let me . . .?'

'You wouldn't be told, my lady. I did what I could. But never mind. You are safe and no harm has been done. Come, let me take you to your chamber. Let me bathe you and tend you and then you can rest.'

Lamia relaxed in the bath. She could see the baby's powerful movements on her belly, like some sea creature, causing waves and undulations on the surface but never allowing itself to be seen.

'He'll love it, I'm sure he will.'

'And it's on its way into the world, that's for sure.'

'Do you think he'll get here in time for the birth, Dana?'

Dana turned away, reaching for the thick, soft towel. She wrapped it around Lamia's cloudy black hair and rubbed gently.

'Why won't you answer? Did you hear me, Dana?'

'I did, my child.'

'And do you think he'll come?'

'He's . . . Who can say, my child? He is supreme king.'

'That means he can come if he wants to.'

'Of course, my lady.'

'I hate it when you do that, Dana. Do you think he won't come?'

'I think that with the world's affairs to tend to, he might well forget the birth of a single child.'

Lamia lashed out like a wild animal. Red weals appeared on Dana's plump cheek, the trails of Lamia's nails.

'He loves me.' The words came out in a small, piteous sound, more like the mewling of a kitten than the roar of the wild beast that had lashed Dana's cheek.

'Well, then he loves you.' Dana stood up angrily, holding up a large sheet to swirl round Lamia's wet body. She didn't touch the cheek which swelled and smarted and seemed to grow hotter by the minute.

Lamia loved Dana more than anyone else in the world – even her own parents. True, Belus and Libya had given her life and all the accoutrements of glamour and luxury that anyone could offer. But Dana gave her love. Pure, unstinting, unconditional. She had given up everything to stay with her and nurture her – even the chance of marriage and children of her own. And what was her age? Eight, maybe ten years older than Lamia.

But in that moment she didn't see Dana's blazing cheek, her wounded heart, her crushed pride, her intensifying concern. Because she had an idea.

'I will send a message to remind him that I'm to have a baby and that it is due any day now. And that it would be wonderful to have him here.'

'*You can't send him a message.*' Everything of fear and impending doom was in those words, and Lamia heard it.

'Oh you're a prophetess of gloom today, Dana. What harm can it do?'

'What harm can it do, my lady? Think for yourself what harm it can do.'

'Well, tell me.'

'You are talking about the supreme ruler of—'

'But doesn't that make it so much easier?'

'Easier? The news would spread like wildfire. The queen will probably know before he does. Haven't you heard how she deals with her rivals?'

Lamia tossed her hair. 'Zeus won't let her hurt me.'

Dana was grim. 'But if Hera gets hold of it first, will Zeus ever get your message?'

'I'll make sure it's done very secretly.'

'Hera discovered Zeus' infidelities with Leda and Danae without a single message. Her eyes and ears are everywhere. There's no such thing as a secret message. Messages proclaim themselves to everyone. The simple act of sending one broadcasts the liaison. Would Zeus thank you for an indiscretion like that?'

Lamia stamped her foot and the towel fell from her body. Dana smoothed soft, soothing oils on it and rubbed it to a velvet shine.

'I hate being in this situation, Dana. I hate every moment away from him.'

Dana squeezed her hand. She knew how much Lamia had changed since Zeus had come crashing into her life through the casement of her chamber, the curls of his beard glistening, his gold hair ablaze in the setting sun. The child hadn't a hope in the world of resisting him. Who could – the Supreme God in all his glory, visiting her, a virgin, barely past puberty?

Afterwards he lay with her, promising he would always love her, that he would never desert her. And she believed every word then as she did thereafter. He came, she sobbed and told him how much she missed him, he explained he was beset with the business of running the world and she accepted his excuses. Then he went and she was thrown back on her wretched state.

She swore every time a gap of more than two weeks elapsed that she would break away from Zeus, that she would find another, more suitable partner, someone her own age and befitting her status. Someone who would be by her side more often than Zeus and, when he was not, for he would surely be a brave and courageous soldier or at least an important ambassador, he would tell her where he was and send her romantic messages about his safety and about his love for her. If he did not, then she at least could send a message with impunity.

Over the past months she had taken to eating in her room, refusing invitations, and keeping her ears peeled for any news, any gossip, any shred of information about Zeus. The mention of his name conjured up fantasies of his infidelities with other women. There were many of them in the Greek empire who hinted or insolently claimed that they were mothering Zeus' progeny. At one moment she believed all of them were telling the truth while at others she swore they were brazen-faced upstarts trying to justify lurid encounters with their slaves. For the thought that Zeus had other women like her scattered through the length and breadth of the Greek empire was more than Lamia could bear.

'I'm more to Zeus than a female to beget a royal line upon,' she sobbed to Dana. 'Don't you think so? Or surely, he would have abandoned me once I had conceived. We know he only visited Leda once and as far as we know Danae never saw him a second time either. Besides, he visited them in disguise but he comes to me undisguised.'

Dana busied herself with whatever she was doing. It was better to play deaf or foolish at times like this. But she longed to take Lamia in her arms and tell her as gently as she could that Zeus was playing with her. That he had no intention of remaining faithful or of extending his protection. He moved in strange ways, did Zeus, and his ways were hidden from people like her and even educated ones like Lamia and her parents. But she remembered to pray hard every night that the secret would be kept and that Hera would never come to know of Lamia's relationship with Zeus. For the sake of her mistress and for the sake of the unborn child for whom the Goddess would doubtless set a terrifying trail of obstacles.

'Are you playing deaf and mute, Dana?' demanded Lamia, shrilly. 'Why won't you answer me? You think I'm wrong, don't you? You think I'm just another of his whores . . .'

Dana put her hand to Lamia's mouth. 'Ladies don't speak like that,' she admonished. 'Never say such things about yourself. There are plenty of others standing by to say them. Come now, to your bed and rest. Think good thoughts. Clear your mind and invite in Artemis so that you can bear your child easily.'

The first pangs came as night fell. Lamia tossed and turned and as the contractions grew stronger, ravaging her small body, she exulted. Her screams would grow so loud and so piercing that Zeus would hear them in Olympus or wherever else he happened to be and he would fly to her side. But as Nix dragged her velvety coat through all the darkest shades of blue to black and back to blue, Lamia's cries weakened.

Her pillow was drenched in sweat and tears, her mattress in blood, but still she whispered between every toss, 'He will come', and after every turn, 'Let him come to see his child born.'

The infant was a boy and he was beautiful. But dawn drew in and he went with Nix into her dark, mysterious world: where, no one knows to this day. Lamia was spent with the night's labour and she clung to his small corpse as she slept. Occasionally, when she opened her eyes, they looked blindly at Dana's anxious face, screaming the question 'Why?'

'Because,' said Dana at last, her whisper so soft that it was barely above the rustling of a leaf upon which a baby has breathed, '*she* has found out. There can be no other reason. He was healthy and bonny, and oh so beautiful. He could have fathered a race all his own.'

Lamia sobbed then. She put her face in her hands and she sobbed and she swore she would never see Zeus again. Belus and Libya held her in their arms and succoured her and slowly she began to go down and eat with them and join their companions. Young men began to pay court to her. Silently and secretly, both Dana and Libya said prayers to appease

Hera and when Lamia began to accept the overtures of a handsome young soldier from Corinth, they believed that Hera was listening.

That night Lamia returned to her bedchamber after midnight. She looked out of the window: the moon was full. She smiled a greeting to Phoebe, sent her a blessing and sang as Dana helped her out of her jewels and finery.

'I think, Dana, that he may be the one,' she said, honestly. 'I think this is how love should feel. He makes me laugh and when we touch he behaves as if I've done him a great favour. As if all the pleasure is his and he is highly honoured by my attention.'

'And is he right, my lady?'

Lamia pouted and shook her head vigorously. 'Oh no, Dana. Oh no. My whole being tingles when he touches me. And when my hand lies beside his, it seems to gain a life of its own, twitching and buzzing and urging me on to lift it and touch him.'

Dana smiled inwardly but made her face serious, her voice earnest. 'I think then, my lady, that he probably is the one.'

'Have you ever felt that way, Dana?'

'No, my lady. There's no time in my life for all that.'

'But that's terrible, Dana. You must make time for it immediately. And I will help you.'

Dana lifted the lace around Lamia's bed and parted it. Lamia sank into her mattress in the silvery light of the moon. She stretched out her limbs, hugging herself with girlish excitement. Would she see her young warrior tomorrow? Would he still feel the same about her? Would they get a better chance to be alone together? She pulled the blanket closer over her and turned on her side.

Something hard struck her in the ribs. She sat up, feeling around.

'Dana,' she called, 'Dana. There is something in my bed. Didn't you prepare it tonight?'

Dana came immediately. 'I prepared it myself, as usual, my lady.'

'Then your mind must have been elsewhere. There's something hard in my bed.' She pulled up her clothes. 'Look – that's where it hurt me.'

Dana scrambled around, her face close to the bedclothes, protesting against Lamia's accusations. Then, suddenly, she saw it. The gold of it glowed, and as she gasped and Lamia moved, the moonlight caught it and set the huge stone flashing.

'A ring!' exclaimed Lamia. 'A beautiful ring.'

'Of course,' gabbled Dana. 'Belus left the ring for you . . .'

'Liar! Belus doesn't have a ring like this. His entire treasury wouldn't pay for this ring.'

Suddenly all the life went out of her. 'It's *his* ring. He left it here.'

Dana snatched the ring from Lamia's hand. 'Then we must lay it on the windowsill so that he can take it back.'

'Take it back?' Lamia's mouth fell open.

'You must give it back, Lamia. Then he'll know you have an admirer who will soon be your lover and that you want no more of him because you've promised Hera . . .'

'I haven't promised Hera anything,' snapped Lamia. 'And she'll never frighten me—'

Lamia's eyes glittered with the tears – her baby's memory was with her still, not relegated to a dusty shelf of forgetfulness. The anguish came gushing back. Hera had killed her child.

'Please, my lady, please. Don't offend the Mother. She is the patron of marriage and fidelity. She is implacable if you violate her laws.'

'Shut up, servant. Remember your place and don't tell me what to do.'

'My lady you must listen.' Fear made Dana intrepid. Lamia showered her with blows that night but she didn't stop begging, cajoling, threatening. In the morning she lay a cringing heap on the ground and Lamia a sobbing, shaking form on the bed.

'If only, if only, I had stayed in my room I would have seen him again,' she lamented.

'But if you had been in your room, would he have come?' asked Dana, barely able to open her swollen eyes. 'Or did he choose this night to come because you were at last falling in love with someone else?'

'You're right, Dana.' Lamia threw herself from the bed, raised Dana to her knees, hugged her, asked her forgiveness. 'Of course you're right. But doesn't that mean he can't bear to let me go?'

Dana looked away. She was exhausted. 'You know best, my lady.'

From now on, she swore, she would simply do her best to support Lamia as she had always done. She would never again try to talk sense into her. It would serve nothing. But the very next night, she recanted.

'Aetolus is waiting for you in Belus' entertainment chamber, my lady, and his eyes are glued to the doors. Every time there's a movement, he starts up anxiously, then sinks back disappointed when he sees it isn't you.'

Lamia looked thoughtfully at Dana. 'I'm not so sure I should encourage him, Dana,' she murmured, grasping for excuses. 'He's so young and . . .'

Dana sputtered her scorn. 'Young? Young? He can easily give you five or six years, my lady. How old do you like them?'

Lamia pouted. 'I only meant it wouldn't be fair to encourage him if . . .'

Lamia did not go down that evening, or the next, or the next. But Zeus did not come all week and, once more, Lamia resumed the torment of waiting by the window, afraid to leave in case she missed his visit, terrified to divert her attention to a more suitable partner in case, this time, she lost Zeus for ever.

'He didn't come when you needed him most,' Dana reminded her, recklessly. The poor wretch never learned her lesson. How many times had she sworn never to give Lamia advice that she didn't want to hear? But could she ever hold to her word? Never! Her tongue always got the better of her.

And how she suffered as she saw Lamia flinch, now, at her words.

'I hate you when you say things like that, Dana,' she said, sadly. 'But I have to admit you're right. I don't think I'll ever forget how I felt when . . .'

It was the memory of her lost baby boy that made Lamia decide. Too many of nature's forces were acting against her. If she was ever to conceive again, she could only bear it if the father of her child was beside her and she was surrounded by respectability and calm. Not like the last time; she remembered the terror in the eyes of Belus and Libya. And sometimes the disbelief – could Zeus really be little Lamia's lover? Aetolus was a handsome man, with a sweet singing voice and a happy, loving nature. He would go to war, certainly when he had to. But he would be beside her as often as he could. She would be the most important person in his life, not merely another of his concubines – someone with whom to satisfy his lust before moving on to other, more demanding duties and relationships.

There was a glinting kernel of defiance in her heart: the thought that Zeus, too, could get his comeuppance, if she were to marry Aetolus and settle down happily with him to a life of pleasure and children and duty. If Zeus did not love her, then he would not even notice. But if he did – and his last visit suggested he might well – then he would regret the loss of her, bitterly.

'And what good would that do you?' Dana quaked. 'You are talking about the Supreme God— the ruler of Olympus. How can you speak like that?'

'You forget, Dana, that he is also my lover.'

'Was, child, was,' insisted Dana. 'Divine lovers can't be treated in the same way as mortals. It's a good thing for you to forget him and marry a human. Don't let blasphemous thoughts like these enter your mind.'

Lamia tossed her head. Dana's fears fuelled her resentment. Not even Zeus had the right to make her suffer so much.

That night, Lamia spent more attention on her toilette than ever before and glided down to her father's entertainment halls like a golden dream, preceded by soft puffs of essence of rose brought by traders from faraway places. Aetolus was hypnotised. Watching her that evening and the next few, Belus and Libya were convinced they would soon hear a wedding announcement. But Lamia began to grow tired of Aetolus' eagerness, his courtesy irritated her, his attentions palled. He was so young and worthy and *nice*.

'You cite those qualities as if they were bad ones to have,' Libya said, noticing Lamia's boredom.

'It's just, he's so unexciting.'

Libya's heart quaked. She knew that every night when Lamia returned to her room, she searched thoroughly for a sign from Zeus. Libya had been forced to appoint spies to get the information since that wretched girl Dana would tell her nothing about Lamia. It was a good quality in a servant, Libya knew, but if she had told them early enough, perhaps some of this catastrophe might have been averted. Or perhaps not. But she was no different from other parents in thinking she could throw an invincible net of protection around her young one if only she knew the dangers ahead. True, they might have tried to lure Zeus away with prayers and offerings but if he had chosen to ignore them, would they have dared to stand in his way?

Even if they had, how could they succeed against him? Bar of course invoking Hera's help.

Libya's heart quaked at the whisper of Hera finding out.

'And it is out of pity for the quaking of your mother's heart that I have held back,' snarled Hera in her chamber.

News had reached her that her husband was sniffing that other woman's scent again. When she had confronted him before, he insisted he had simply had intercourse with the girl to create a new line of men. Lamia was descended from an old race, one that predated the rule of the Olympians and Hera knew very well that it was part of Zeus' function, though she heartily disapproved, to impregnate the women of such races in order to achieve fresh, new ruling lines in his name.

'But her child is dead,' thundered Hera now. 'I saw to it myself.'

Zeus turned the colour of thunder and his silence resonated like a thousand twanging stringed instruments. All the gods and goddesses halted their activities for a moment expecting an explosion, wondering how best to avert Zeus' fury. But Hera was untouched by his show of wrath.

'And I'll do it again,' she spat, whirling around, making Zeus step back. 'And again and again.'

'As long as you continue to kill her children, I will continue to impregnate her.'

'And if she conceives and delivers a healthy baby boy, you'll leave her alone?' enquired Hera, her voice all mock sweetness and dark, venomous anger.

'I will. That's my method. It has always been.'

'Liar!' shrieked Hera. 'You returned to Lamia again and again after she conceived your child. Deny it!'

'If you already claim to know, why should I deny it?'

'You are denying it! The King of the Gods and no better than a cheating mortal. And weak and cowardly with it!'

'Hold your tongue, Hera,' commanded the King of the Gods, knowing, even as he was saying the words, that they were pointless. Hera would only stop when she had vented her rage to the full and finished saying what she wanted. He felt a small flicker of apprehension at the effect all this might have on Lamia.

Zeus knew that Hera would pursue him relentlessly, confront him with every visit he paid the girl, throw every possible trial in her way. She had already killed Lamia's first-born. But surely, the threat against further children was just that – a dire warning to head him off. Because Hera knew that, as the Divine Father, he had a job to do. As long as she let him get on with it there would be no further killing of children. It would be best to do the job quickly and let the girl alone. She would have the rest of her life to settle and raise the child in the manner suitable for a demigod. This Aetolus appeared to be just the right kind of mortal father for the boy.

Zeus would see to it that he would have a kingdom to rule soon after his marriage to Lamia.

But inwardly, he felt testy. There was something about Lamia – something that titillated him and called to him in a way that none of those others could.

That night, as Lamia slept, Zeus entered her room in a pool of light. She sat up in her bed, bathed in it, and slowly, as her eyes became accustomed to the glow, she discerned Zeus' face and form. Without a word, she leaned her head on his chest, the hot tears flowing from her eyes and sinking into his skin and through it into his heart.

If only, if only, Lamia could have know his thoughts and his intentions and his plans. Great plans, important matters which would have their effects on subsequent generations; which would put her, Lamia, on the pages of history and literature for posterity. But to Lamia they would have spelled bleak emptiness, a fame or notoriety that would have sounded the knell of panic. And would she have gone into his arms as readily as she did now? Would she have yielded to his caresses and his demands as eagerly and with as much passion?

She would never know.

Another pregnancy, another dead child, another visit from Zeus. Lamia could not remember how long this had been the pattern of her life. Ravaged in her mid-twenties, she sat glued to her window. She no longer knew which part of the vicious circle needed to be broken first, she rode such a treadmill of grief in her search for comfort. The death of the child meant another visit from Zeus, the visit meant another dead child. Succour and loss were stranded together in the same necklace of pearls: one caused the other.

So, Lamia suffered until she could suffer no more. There was nothing left of her but a shell filled with the remnants of anger, torment and grief. Sometimes she looked at herself in the mirror where Dana seated her as she tended to her, brushing her hair, cleaning her face, dressing her. And everything in the mirror was grey. Her skin, her hair, the great gaunt hollows which lurked beneath her eyes, under her cheekbones, on either side of her neck.

'You are the mother of death and destruction. Cursed, barren – you deserve nothing.'

Aetolus had given up on her long ago and found himself another wife. And still she waited for Zeus. Now, she decided, she would no longer wait for him to impregnate her womb, raging for new life. Or was it death?

One morning, she was woken by birds singing at dawn. It usually troubled her, that cheerful music, disturbing her sleep, mocking her as if to say: your life may be nothing but bleak desolation but the world goes on and what a happy place it is for those who deserve it. Then she would throw her blanket over her ears, smother herself in cushions and long for death to come and claim her. But she had heard that some people were so despicable even death shunned them.

That morning, Lamia crept out of bed and looked at the shiny lines dawn had drawn across the horizon. Protected by the darkness still lingering over the skies, she slipped out of her house and made her way to a nearby lake. There, she sat weeping and praying to Artemis, patroness of child-bearing, to Ananke of the Moirae, to Hecate, Great Mother of Darkness. Where were you when my babes were choking to death? Where were you when they needed you, I needed you? She begged them to send her some relief. She could no longer bear to see the constant procession of night and day march relentlessly through her life. She needed some respite, a moment's relief. 'Let me have a babe, just one, to love and fill up this gaping hole.'

Lamia's tears mingled with the sweet lake water: her eyes swollen, her emptiness opened up inside her like some dark, bitter chasm. She could no longer distinguish day from twilight or dawn, perhaps because her sight was weak from crying, perhaps because she no longer had the sense to recognise the changes.

But she was vaguely aware of the town coming to life. Of people and activity and movement. How she hated the ordinary activities of men and women and children. How she loathed the reminder that she was the odd one out. Sometimes, when she slipped away from the house and wandered through the streets, children threw stones at her and called her mad. At other times, people would move out of her way as if they were frightened. Once or twice she saw old women throw their mantles over the eyes of their young and pregnant relatives, saying that Lamia's accursed shadow might make them miscarry their own infants. Then Lamia would scream inside and sometimes aloud, lashing her breast and tearing her hair, running wildly in the streets, howling 'Hera! Hera! Give me back my innocent babes. Give them back to me!'

Physicians visited Lamia and sages and seers – and all predicted the same fate. Melancholy, insanity, endless suffering.

Lamia made her way home through a poor part of town where she would not be recognised. Her head bowed, her black veil pulled over her face, she glided swiftly along until she heard the cry of a baby. She averted her eyes. She couldn't bear to see, yet again, the humiliating sight of a mother protectively throwing a shawl over her infant to save it from Lamia's murderous glance. But she heard no movement. She walked on a few steps. Then returned to the spot where she had first heard the cry. There it was again, a delicate, tremulous wail, softer than the sound of a gull in the air. And again. More desperate this time.

She raised her eyes and saw it. A tiny baby in its basket, placed in the open courtyard to receive the morning sun. She waited, concealed by the mud wall of the hut. No one appeared. The infant's cries were beginning to come closer together. Its breath was getting shorter and shorter until the last wail disappeared in a mighty spasm of silence. The baby's face was distorted into a grimace. Lamia looked around, terrified. Where was his mother? His grandmother? Someone.

She drew closer. The baby's face was red, his lips turning blue. His little fists clenched as the flailing movements of his limbs weakened to twitches. Lamia could bear the tension no longer. She threw back her veil and lifted the baby from his bed, placed him over her shoulder, soothed him, rubbed his back, then laid him on one arm and slowly, following some deep instinct, applied subtle pressure to his stomach. Immediately, he wailed again. His breathing resumed, he kicked and howled.

Never, never, had the sound of a baby's howl been so precious to Lamia. It was proof of life, proof of her own ability to nurture an infant. She had lived so long with the knowledge of death, with the rumours of her own accursed womb, of claims that it was she who was somehow to blame for the deaths of her babies. Now, the baby's cries reassured her that her presence, her touch even, spelled reprieve and not death. She looked around, entered the courtyard, looked inside the window. She saw no one.

Lamia took the baby home and sat rocking him on her knees. All night, all day, she rocked him, caressed him, cuddled him, swearing Dana to secrecy. As always, Dana protected her mistress, though she pleaded with Lamia to return the baby to his parents.

'But I am his mother,' insisted Lamia. 'Don't you see? He's the answer to my prayers. I was given all the signs. He cried, he called me back to him. I was meant to take charge of his destiny and bring him back to life. He had no one else. I looked in the house. I could find no one. He was abandoned.'

'Not abandoned, my lady. It's harvest time – his parents were probably in the fields working or in the temples, praying.'

'And leaving their baby behind to die?'

'He's a bonny young lad.' Dana tried to appeal to a side Lamia had lost long ago. 'Working folk are forced to leave their babies behind some of the time. There was probably a grandmother somewhere who'd dozed off or gone to answer nature's call. He would not have been left for long.'

But Lamia was adamant. 'If I had not heard him and saved his life, he would be dead. A life saved is a life owed. So, by rights, this child is mine.'

'If that is so, at least send word to his parents. You of all people know how a mother feels when she loses her child. Put these people out of their misery. Tell them how you had to rescue the child. Make an arrangement with them.'

Eventually, Lamia agreed. Dana fetched Libya, and Lamia explained the situation. The peasant couple were sent for and at first seemed agreeable to letting the child grow up in the splendour and luxury of Libya and Belus' palatial home. Libya rewarded them handsomely and sent them on their way. The Fates had at last relented and there was a chance that hope would return to Lamia's life.

She concentrated all her energies on the infant, whom she named Bios, after Life himself, and she found his presence beguiled the hours more easily. Once, Dana thought she heard her chuckling softly to the child as she put him to her breast, imagining that the milk flowed out to feed him. But Dana kept the baby well fed with other milk so that Lamia's dry nipples were no more than a toy or a rattle around which to wrap his mouth.

Then one day, the baby's parents returned. They had heard about Lamia – how her babies died mysteriously. How she roamed the streets, insane, weeping, grey as a spectre and not yet twenty-two. They wanted their baby back. They could not sacrifice his life for riches, or the gods would punish them.

'Look at him,' Dana begged, cradling the child. 'Does he look ill to you? Or unhappy? Or wanting in any way?'

'We may never have another child,' the woman wept. 'Then where will we be?'

'But he's safe and happy,' Dana insisted. 'Why should anyone punish you?'

Libya and her advisers spoke to the couple for many hours, trying to convince them that the child should be allowed to stay with Lamia. She had saved his life, after all, and she cared for him devotedly. Her children had all died as soon as they left the womb but Bios was already several months old – his destiny would be different.

Still, they insisted, they wanted their son back. Libya prepared to request outside arbitration. She would bring to bear her wealth and power to secure the child for Lamia before her daughter even heard that his parents were back. But news travels fast, and unhappy news with merciless speed, and it was not long before Lamia knew that Bios might be taken away from her. Without waiting to verify the story or hear what Libya was planning, Lamia snatched up the baby from his crib and ran with him to her window.

She clambered on to the window ledge and stood staring down. 'If anyone tries to take my son, I'll jump to my death. And he will go with me because we can't be separated.'

A crowd gathered: among them Libya, trying to reason with her daughter, and the child's parents, begging for their baby's life.

Then came a strident voice cursing Lamia and her death womb. Cursing the day she was born, cursing the air she breathed. She would be better dead than alive. Even the teeming depths of the Great Megara would be polluted by her. The moment she touched that child, she had sealed its death in infancy.

All eyes turned to the voice. The hush was so great that the tiniest crackling of a twig could be heard. But who had spoken? No one knew, not even those who stood at the spot from where the voice seemed to come. Then a blood-curdling shriek from the window.

'Then that's how it will be,' howled Lamia. 'If he is to die, I will die with him. And if I'm responsible for his death, I don't care to live either. You have your way Hera! Rejoice.'

The next moment, she leapt from the window, Bios clutched close to her breast as they hurtled down.

Who knows – if she had not mentioned Hera's name, perhaps death would have reprieved her. As it was, she had publicly reviled her divine rival, who reached out and plucked her neatly out of death's way. The baby went alone and Lamia survived to suffer on.

Belus and Libya could do nothing to hold her back. Insane and uncontrollable, Lamia roamed the streets for days, stoned, pelted with rotting food, accursed and wretched. Months later, they heard that she had found a cave in the mountains where she lived alone. But even then, the story goes, when the urge to hold a baby in her arms became too great, Lamia crept from her cave, skulking around sleeping infants. When she found them alone, she carried them to her murky cave and held them to her nipples, until their sobs of hunger quietened and they fell peacefully asleep at her breast.

Death comes to all mortals and so it must, eventually, have come to Lamia. Or did it? For tales are told of a creature called the Lamia who appears in the night, bathed in a pool of light, beautiful as the moon, and tempts men to her bed. Far from the reach of the avenging Hera, she wreaks her revenge on the men she snares. For they wake up in the morning in her dark, murky cave, and the creature, half snake, half woman, who sneers at them, haunts their nightmares for evermore. Why did they lie with a strange woman? Why did they betray their own beloved?

But Lamia? Her womb is filled, live babies are born to her. Or so she thinks.

Morgan Le Fay

One moment I was running free in the hills and moors of Tintagel, the next I was sequestered in a convent in Broceliande, far, so far from home that there was no road to travel back even if I had the will to run, no messenger to signal Igraine's love to me from across the heaving sea. And soon no message left for me to send even if I'd had the means. The time between freedom and confinement was compressed like a hundred songs in a minstrel's throat.

Sometimes I was frightened that Igraine would disappear from the earth altogether like the song which ends when the minstrel stops singing and vanishes for ever when he moves on. Had my mother moved me on like a wandering troubadour? Did she want to forget the song I sang because it had turned bitter with the death of my father? Was I wrong to speak the truth to her? The truth of my feelings, the truth about what she had done? Ballads can sometimes be cruel but Igraine never wanted to hear the words of mine. Not once Uther Pendragon came on the scene. From that moment on it was Uther, your father this and Uther my lord, that – and where was Morgan? On the guilt-draped edges of her consciousness, reminding her, reminding her of dead Gorlois – her old lord, killed by the new one.

'Why can't you be like your sisters?' she demanded, her chin thrust out like a truculent child. 'They were happy for me to marry Uther.'

Why? I asked myself a hundred times. Was it because they didn't know about Uther's deceit? But even then, they knew Gorlois had been killed in a war of Uther's making. I always came up with the same answer.

'Uther got them kings for husbands. Margawse and Elaine can leave Tintagel to be queens in their own castles, else-where.'

'Oh, shame on you. What a jealous child you are, Morgan. How can you grudge your sisters a good marriage?'

'I don't, Mother. I want to stay here, in Tintagel.'

'Then why can't you make peace with Uther? He is your father.'

'He can't be my father. He can never be my father. My father was Gorlois, Lord of Tintagel.'

It's strange how the number three dances and revolves around my life. Even to this day. Of that time, three powerful images were retained in my mind, so vivid and so lurid that they caused a twisting sensation in the pit of my stomach and made me retch.

My father had left for Castle Terrabil to prepare for Uther Pendragon's attack, leaving my mother safe in Tintagel with my sisters and me. Late at night, I heard horses approaching the castle. The guards raised the portcullis when they recog-nised my father. He had returned with two of his most trusted knights, Sir Jordans and Sir Brastias. Father was ill. He spoke neither to his guards nor his aides and thrust his way through to my mother's chamber. I ran out of the room to meet him. He approached the foot of the stairs as I reached the top. Then I saw it – the first image in the light of the torches.

I can only describe it like this: my father's body was a case – an empty box – and inside was a stranger, completely formed, clothed in steel, fully armed. And beside him, bidding him good-night, were other strangers boxed into the bodies of Sir Jordans and Sir Brastias. It was a frightening sight and I knew it was a delusion. The box dissolved now, reformed now and at other times the strangers inside melted and reintegrated.

That was the first time I saw, actually saw, what is hidden from others. My eyes saw the truth. But at the time I was a girl of eleven, still wild and unschooled – and my father's 'little man' because he said I was so clever and adventurous and intrepid.

I followed the strange figure and as he entered my mother's room I snatched up a torch and stood by. Any moment now, Igraine would scream for help. Then I would burst in to rescue her. I'd burn the invader from my father and I'd save him and Igraine and we would all be a happy family again. But all I heard was my mother's squeal of delight when she saw the creature.

I waited, holding my breath. Mother usually slept deep and was drowsy for a long time after she awoke. But surely, she would see at once that this man was not her husband Gorlois, Duke of Cornwall? When she still hadn't cried for help after several moments, I wondered what to do next. Should I peep through the door? Had the man seized my mother and done something terrible while she was still drugged with sleep? Killed her, perhaps? Without waiting to think any further, I burst into the room, flailing my torch. That was when the second image was branded on my brain. My first sight of a couple *in flagrante delicto*. Mother was not asleep. There she was in bed with the double monster, arms and legs tangled, heaving and rolling, now he on top, now she.

I ran but the vision in my brain came with me. I shook my head to dispel it but it was branded there for ever.

The morning brought a messenger with the news of my father. Gorlois of Cornwall was dead. Wounded at Terrabil.

'Then who was with me last night?' wailed Igraine before fainting spectacularly.

Everything Igraine did was dramatic, alluring, sensational. Luckily for her, I was the only one who knew that she was speaking the truth. A stranger really had been with her that night when her husband was dying. Someone deceitful and dishonourable with whom she had made wild, passionate love and disgraced my father's memory.

Their wedding day was the third image. Igraine, my mother, standing beside her new husband, clinging on to his arm, catching every word from his mouth like pearls and rubies so that they might not roll away into obscurity. There was a blush on her face and a flush on her chest and she danced, eyes sparkling, full of such vitality and merriment that she looked like a girl and you could hardly tell which was the mother which the daughters. My sisters were thrilled and excited too but I had more attention from them than I had from Igraine. They tried to draw me out a little, that was when they noticed me at all. But most of the time, they forgot me too. And every time Uther was alone, I fixed him with a beady stare which made him drop his gaze and squirm. Once or twice I even managed to clamber on to his lap. I knew this made him uncomfortable and, in a strange way, frightened. But he could do nothing to get rid of me.

'How sweet,' exclaimed Morgawse and Elaine.

'How gorgeous!' echoed my mother. 'Little Morgan is making an effort. She was such a father's darling, you should be flattered.'

Flattered? It was the last thing Uther felt as I wriggled against his chest and raised my mouth to his ear. 'I know you. You're a fraud. You'll be punished.'

Uther recoiled as if I was a serpent stinging him. I was worse. A serpent, he could have slung off. But I clung to him like a leech and drank some of his life blood that day, I'm sure of it. And I kissed his nose and pinched his cheeks hard and told him he would die for injuring my father in so many ways.

'Sweet Morgan,' cried my sisters, not noticing Uther's uneasiness. 'She's such a strange one.'

Little Morgan, wild child of Tintagel. Strange little Morgan and her fascination with herbs and plants and stones.

Yes stones – and the stones were my salvation in those heady days when everyone was drunk with a wine that had no effect on me except to make me sad and bewildered. I would run down to the stone circles and hug them close and watch them drink my tears. And they let their songs echo in my mind and comfort me. Did no one care about Gorlois any more? How was it that suddenly all Tintagel, and all Cornwall, had become Uther's land?

'It's my father's,' I called loudly. '*My father's.*' But even the echoes of my father's hills and dales mocked me. 'Ather, ather, ther,' they called back as if calling the usurper's name. The maidens of the stone circle began to move and turn with the weight of my grief. They danced a dance for me of such beauty and such sweetness that I knew I was gifted and blessed and no worldly loss would ever destroy me. But when you're young, such knowledge comes at peak moments then washes away like the water of a gushing spring, through idling fingers.

No one asked me, not a single soul, how I felt. Gorlois was gone. There was a new duke at Tintagel, a new husband in my mother's bed, a new master in my home. But people don't just accept fathers as if they are pigs to be bought at market. My father's blood ran in my veins, not Uther Pendragon's. And I told him so at every opportunity. I sang the harsh ballad that my mother so hated – not just to hurt Uther but to remind Igraine that someone mourned Gorlois. That Tintagel resounded and thrived with *his* spirit, not this impostor's.

Of course, Igraine didn't know, until she was heavily pregnant with Arthur, that Uther Pendragon was the man who had deceived her the night of her husband's death. Then she was so relieved that it was her husband and not a stranger she had slept with that she no longer cared that he was not her husband at that time but a deceiver, her husband's enemy and the cause of his death. Igraine was malleable in those days and Uther did not miss the opportunity to strike against me.

'Morgan needs to be harnessed,' he told her. 'Send her to a nunnery. She's too clever for her own good and she has a vicious side to her. She needs it expunged through mortification and discipline. It is not a job for you or me. She must go elsewhere for her own sake.'

Of course, Igraine agreed. More surprisingly, she agreed to

give away her new son when he was born, so that Uther could keep a promise he had made to some sage. Arthur went within the hour of his birth, before being nurtured, without being named. A bearded man with long hair trailing to his waist came and took him away. I thought I had seen him before but I was too wrapped up with the anxiety of being torn out of my beloved Tintagel and thrown into the convent at Broceliande to give much thought to hirsute strangers. This one had mystical eyes. They lingered in my memory for a long while afterwards. The next time I saw them it was four years later, at the convent, and I was a young woman so distant, so different from that wild child of Tintagel.

The penances and drills of the nunnery had taught me to restrain myself, to contain my anger. I could pass for a refined young woman. I could read like no other woman I knew. I had perfected the arts of healing so well that I was better than most of the women who taught me. And I had discovered in myself a kind of wild magic. I could make things happen by looking, wanting, imagining or just simply by feeling. I had no doubt that was why Uther was dead and buried and rotting in some mound. But those were my secrets.

The nuns were congenial enough within the limits of their experience and their constraints. But their lives were governed by rules, hemmed in by restrictions – don't talk, eat, think, except what is necessary. Don't fall in love, don't desire, don't even imagine. They would surely have labelled my magic malevolent. They would have tried to crush the sensations that swelled and spread in me and told me the world was mine and there was nothing that was beyond my reach, nothing I could not have if I truly wanted it.

I proved it again when I sat by the lake and asked for a friend, a sister in spirit who would understand about my magic, share my ability to see. I looked into the lake, smooth and still as a mirror. My black hair caught the dancing light-reflections and shone back like a raven's wing. My skin was like the dusk. I couldn't discern the details of my face but I saw it grow larger as I stared into it and repeated:

'I want a friend.'

A ripple formed about my reflection, making it rock and swing until a round object bobbed up. A mass of tangled hair, a head, a face. So startlingly like my own. A sister in spirit, a sister in flesh.

'I'm Viviane,' she told me. 'They call me the Lady of the Lake.'

'I'm Morgan.'

Viviane smiled. 'Le Fay,' she mused. 'Of course. I've been waiting for you.'

'Waiting?' I was curious. 'Have you been looking for a friend?'

Now Viviane laughed. She threw back her head, floating backwards, shoulders glistening silvery white against the shimmering surface of the waters.

'I knew you'd come. We're destined to meet. You are the one on earth.'

'The one on earth?'

'Our job is a hard one,' Viviane continued mysteriously.

'Why did you call me the Fay?' I asked, suddenly remembering.

'Because, Morgan, you are a woman of magic. Surely, you know that?'

I felt that I had come home, not so much to a place as to a response, and the world inside me stopped teetering and found perfect balance.

It was here, on the shores of Viviane's lake that I saw the eyes again, reflected on the waters – disembodied. I shuddered. This was the man who had taken away Arthur when he was a baby.

'Why does he make you shudder?' Viviane asked, bobbing around in the water.

I shrugged. 'I'm not sure.' I had never loved Arthur. I had resented him throughout Igraine's pregnancy and this man had taken him so soon after his birth that I had never learned to love or even know him. But this man troubled me – his trailing hair, his waving beard, long robes, great tall height – they were saying something to me. I strained harder to hear.

'Morgan!' he said loudly. 'What are you doing here so far from the nunnery?'

'You mind your own business,' I retorted. 'Stay away from me.'

The man caught my piercing glare and shaded his eyes. He was picking up my magic. He knew I saw something that other people did not. But I willed myself to see beyond his hand. I watched as it turned paler than white, wispier than smoke and colourless as glass. My eyes bored through it, to his.

'Uther's friend!' I hissed. 'You were inside Uther's friend Jordans.'

I would have attacked him, pulled out his hair, torn him to shreds if Mother Annunciata had not arrived at that moment and hurried me away.

'He's a Druid,' she warned in hushed tones. 'You mustn't talk to men like him. They're the Devil's spawn. Evil to the core.'

'Evil, yes,' I agreed. But I said nothing more. The man knew that I had recognised him but his strange eyes stared past me to the head bobbing in the lake. The last I saw as I looked back was the sight of Viviane's shimmering shoulders as she kicked her feet above the waterline before disappearing. Then Mother put her hands over my eyes, blinding me so that I could no longer see the Druid.

'He's Merlin, the sorcerer,' Viviane told me the next day. 'He's been obsessed with me for years.'

'I hate him' I sulked, remembering how I could have damaged him if the nun had not come and taken me away. 'I want him dead.'

'Well there's a nice thought,' responded Viviane. 'And why do you want him dead?'

All I had to do was describe the vivid picture that was replaying in my mind of Uther and his friends disguised as Gorlois and his knights. It was like experiencing it all over again.

'I will punish him,' Viviane promised when I had finished my account. 'He destroyed a knight that day. For that I will destroy him when the time is right.'

'*You* will destroy him?' I was surprised by the passion in her voice.

'It is my job to protect the honour of knights,' replied Viviane. 'I am the keeper of their chivalry, their swords and their morals.'

I learned many lessons from the episode. For one, I began to get a profound sense of truth as intimated by the earth and by nature. Viviane had refused to kill Merlin because killing was not part of that truth. Animals must kill to eat, even human animals, but they rarely ate their own kind. It was only honourable to kill the hideous and obnoxious who polluted the world. Healing on the other hand was a skill to be valued above most others. If humankind could not give life at least they could preserve it. The nuns taught me to recognise herbs and understand their values. I learned swiftly and passionately and never passed up the opportunity to practise my art. Again, I noticed that I possessed a greater power than the herbs and poultices gave me. Once I brought back an ailing nun from the brink of death by putting a hand lightly over her heart, closing my eyes and conjuring up a vision of her sitting in bed, healthy.

Then one day as I was gathering herbs in the woods, I heard a voice that made me freeze.

'Girl!'

I crouched motionless in the tall grasses and shrubs. If I didn't move, maybe the owner of the voice would go away. But the man tramped through the undergrowth and found me. An unyielding hand gripped my shoulder.

'Don't touch me!' I swung round, my eyes following the bare foot, the white robes all the way up to the face. It was a kind face, beautiful with the ravages of time.

'I'm Taliesin,' the man told me, and his voice touched my ears like a lyric. 'I've come to teach you.'

'The nuns teach me.'

'Yes, but I will teach you what they cannot. I will teach you why the birds make and break their formations in the air. I will tell you the secrets of nature, why the rose is fragrant and the purple-veined mallow is not. I will take you into history and travel with you until you find your place in it.'

'And I will follow where your words lead until I can sing them more beautifully than you.'

His laughter was a jingling, joyous sound that filled the woods and vaulted to the skies. 'Perhaps you will, Morgan, perhaps you will.'

Fortunately, the nuns did not stop me seeing Taliesin. They said he was a good man, a holy man; not quite of their persuasion perhaps, but spiritual nevertheless. Merlin was a different kind altogether. If Taliesin could effect miracles it was through goodness and restraint that he had acquired the gift. Not, like Merlin, through the Black Arts.

I discovered that Taliesin had lived hundreds of years and travelled far and wide. He knew everything. The whispering of the grass told him the site and activities of wild creatures, the location and types of water within a given area and the distance of any structures, stone, straw, wood or wattle.

And I learned from him. I was the thirsty desert sand, drinking knowledge, turning fertile and sprouting my own oasis of erudition. I learned to predict and I learned to fly. I could turn myself invisible, disguise myself as an animal, a tree, a floating cloud. Most importantly I mastered the ability to tune into my own inner rhythms and discover what would make me happy, what would elevate me. But as I learned more, I realised that the distant shores of knowledge receded from me.

'It is best to stop,' I cried one day. 'There's too much to learn and not enough years in my life.'

Taliesin's smile dripped with insight and sympathy. I was distraught. I had begun to pride myself on my ever increasing springs of knowledge. Now, suddenly, I saw that knowledge was an ocean and I a trickle – I had not even arrived on its shores.

Taliesin's smile spoke to me now, as it often did. 'You have flown up with the wings of the raven, seen with the kestrel's eye – and you have observed that knowledge is boundless. Now that you know how much you do not know, your learning has truly begun.'

There followed an even more intense period of learning for me. Strange, when I look back it seems so short, but when I was in it, I lived a lifetime. Yet when Taliesin said he had given me all he had to give, I felt he was leaving me too soon.

'You are no longer a child, Morgan. You have become the Dark Woman of Knowledge. And now, you are ready to assume your responsibility. You know that Viviane, the Lady of the Lake, enables young men to aspire to knighthood. You will try the worth of kings. You will test their courage, their kindness, their honour and their skills. If they fall short, you will spur them to greatness. Remember that the person of the king affects the well-being of the land. A whole and healthy king means a prosperous and thriving kingdom. Your second duty is to use your special gifts of healing. You are the finest and most powerful healer ever born.'

I felt humbled by Taliesin's pronouncement. But the thought of testing the worth of kings delighted me.

I left the nunnery soon afterwards to journey back to Cornwall. Uther had died within two years of my departure; Igraine followed soon after. But the soil of Cornwall was both father and mother to me and I needed to return and feel it in my hands. After crossing the sea I procured a horse from a village at the port. He was a rough-looking beast but gentle and eager to please and I mounted him and began my journey. Travelling was easy for me. I didn't have to carry food because I knew every edible species of plant – which were most flavourful and which could give me the nutrients and energy to continue my journey at speed. Nor did I need to carry water. My ears were trained to hear the lapping of a stream or a pond even if it was several feet underground, or out of sight in the lee of a moor, a bush or a shed. Taliesin had taught me well. So it was with an open mind and a salutation in my heart that I looked forward to meeting the king.

As I took the road to Tintagel, I saw a procession ahead of me – happy people, carrying banners and flowers, cheered and sang as they went. At the very front was a knight on a white charger and beside him, on a beast quite as big and twice as lively, was a woman. She was the personification of spring. Her face, her palms, her fingers – each could be described with the name of a flower. When she moved, she scattered fragrance, when she smiled she made flowers blossom.

'Greetings,' I offered, driving my way past the marchers to the couple ahead. 'I am Morgan of Tintagel, on my way home after many years in the forest of Broceliande.'

'I am Guinevere,' smiled the young woman who was forward and brazen as a scarlet bloom. Her hand was like an exquisite Eastern flower called the lotus, as she gestured nonchalantly at the knight beside her, head tossed back like a sea anemone floating in the deep. A light flashed from her eyes and lit a spark in the man's. When she spoke his name, she rolled it on her tongue like dripping honey.

'This is Sir Lancelot, come to escort me to my marriage. He is the king's champion. I am the future bride of the king.'

The king, of course, was Arthur, the brother taken from Tintagel before I'd even had the chance to see his face. He had his father's features, but there was more of Tintagel than Uther about him. His breezy generosity, his welcoming manner, reminded me of Igraine and, yes, of Gorlois my father. But his humility was all his own. Neither his father nor my mother had given that to him: Tintagel's every stone, every plant, every stream shouted pride and self-possession. No, Arthur had bought his humility elsewhere.

Arthur welcomed me and invited me to sit beside him on the bridal dais. I was warmed by his delight. It pleased me to be his guardian and guide. He would make an able pupil. I observed Guinevere carefully. Was she flirtatious with all men, or did she save her coquettish looks and gestures for Lancelot?

In a way, I hoped the first was true, then I would be under no obligation to apprise the king of my misgivings.

The wedding ceremony was about to begin and though my instinct told me that the chemistry between Lancelot and Guinevere would result in a disastrous potion, I saw nothing to confirm this. Besides, I was distracted by Merlin, who walked into the hall just as the marriage was about to be solemnised. His eyes were still the same: frozen, devouring. And oh, what power they wielded over Arthur. The king became an infant in their presence. Merlin hypnotised Arthur. He held him a prisoner to his power. And humble Arthur – not yet aware of his own worth, no higher in his own esteem than a lowly groom – was grateful for it. He must be free of it, I resolved.

When Merlin had taken Arthur away from Igraine's anguished sobs and Uther's cruelty, he had not kept the infant for himself. Instead he took him to a distant cousin of Uther, a certain Sir Hector de Maris, and left him there. Hector was a good enough man and gave Arthur a respect for hard work and the job of squiring his own son Kay. That was where he learned the humility that was lacking in both Uther and Gorlois. His capacity for joy and life's simple gifts, he inherited from Igraine. She lived on in his sudden laughter, the light in his eyes, his tenderness for all around him. But like Igraine, he could see no fault in anything he did nor in any creature he loved.

As Kay's squire, Arthur accompanied him on all their expeditions. That was why he happened to be present at the contest for Excalibur, the sword which had stood bonded to a rock since the death of Uther. The best knights came from far and near, full of determination and hope, fuelled by greed and lust for power. They all failed to release it. Viviane had told me about the power of the sword: how only the purest and most noble-hearted knight could budge Excalibur and how it would slide sweetly and smoothly out for the chosen man. They all tried, huffing and puffing and pulling and struggling but no one succeeded. In the end it slid out on a coincidence.

Arthur had misplaced Kay's sword and in his panic he sought to replace it with the strange sword embedded in the rock. What a simple, distracted soul, not to have noticed the furore the contest had caused as the bravest and the best failed to release Excalibur! Arthur just stopped as he saw it, clasped his hands around its hilt and the next moment he had it before him.

Then Merlin came. And from that day he attached himself to the king like a sinister phantom. It was his job to guide and protect the Pendragon, he claimed. But wasn't this a sham, an ancient trick of king-makers to grasp the power behind the throne? Still, Merlin had waited long and he had waited patiently and it was unlikely now that he would relinquish his power without a struggle.

To me, he was the dark shadow that hung between my brother and me. I tried, gently, to alert Arthur to Merlin's schemes. But would he listen? No, like Igraine, he insisted those he loved and relied on were all good, all noble; those who spoke out against them were wrong. The word got out that I counselled Arthur against Merlin and Arthur's knights began to malign me. I was a troublemaker. I wanted the king's ear. And of course they were right. But is there ever an accusation so hard to fight as the one which is true in fact but hideously wrong in essence? It was true – I did speak ill of Merlin. He had caused my father's death. He had engineered my mother's rape and later her death too, from the twofold loss of her second husband and her infant son. I hated him. I feel not the slightest shame in admitting I hated him and wanted him dead. He had killed my parents, severed me from my source in the soil and streams of Tintagel and all Cornwall. Yes, I wanted him dead. I wanted Arthur free from his interference. Arthur's upbringing had not equipped him with the confidence to rule and judge for himself. But who had made a squire of the future Pendragon? Merlin himself. And as long as Merlin remained around him, Arthur would never acquire the assurance to trust in his own judgement. No, Arthur needed to be aware that he could make his own decisions. He had the purity and goodness to be king, but before the land would thrive and proclaim its well-being to the skies, the seas and all the lands around, he had to become secure and independent within himself. When that inner doubt and conflict disappeared and he spoke surely and strongly, the land would reply in the rhythms and cycles of nature's certainty. There was a link, the primordial link, between the function and person of a king and the activity of the soil and the subjects.

Merlin had to go. I could have killed him, easily, but Taliesin had taught me that I did not have the right. So I went to a nearby stream, stood on its banks and called to Viviane.

'You promised me,' I declared. 'You said you would punish Merlin for me. The time has come.'

True to her promise, Viviane appeared beneath the undulating swathes of water. For the first time since we had met, she stepped out from the deep.

'I'll keep my promise,' she said, her countenance grave. 'I do this for the honour of knighthood.'

Merlin had survived his celibacy by lusting after Viviane. He had fantasised and obsessed about her for decades but there was no female, human or immortal, as elusive as Viviane. He had attempted many times to seduce her but she had always evaded him. Now the prey turned predator. It took her no time to entice Merlin.

'Teach me,' she said huskily, 'about the secrets of the earth. The knowledge might be useful one day.'

And Merlin, inflated with pride and swollen with lust, did not stop to ask why Viviane, a goddess, a consummate magician herself, would need his guidance.

It gave me a measure of satisfaction to watch Viviane work her tricks on Merlin, the great sorcerer, the mighty sage. The illusionist who had facilitated the rape of my mother. And how he lapped up Viviane's words and her compliments and her smiles and her wiles! How he leapt and pranced trying to fulfil her every whim. He was as absurd as a shepherd boy trying to woo a queen, all fumble-fingered and tongue-tied and treacle-eyed.

And when Merlin was gone, we'd plan his punishment.

'Shall I turn him into an animal?' Viviane mused, gaily. 'A wild pig perhaps, to grunt and groan and snuffle and scratch in the woods.'

'No,' I was adamant. 'Kill him. I hold him responsible for everything that's gone wrong in my life.'

'Come now, Morgan,' Viviane replied. 'It was not all Merlin's doing. Uther must also be held responsible. Even Igraine, a little.'

The world would grow dark for me in those moments because I suspected that Viviane was falling in love with Merlin and would let him off lightly. But in the end it was she who came up with the idea. She would trap him beneath a large rock by the edge of the water. I relished the idea of Merlin in a dark hole, bereft of magic, impotent. Dead to all intents and purposes except that he retained consciousness – and that was the beauty of it. He would provide his own torture, his own suffering, and they would swell and explode to overwhelm his limits.

Now Arthur was free of Merlin, I saw him grow in every way. Guinevere was an able queen and though I still detected a definite *frisson* between her and Lancelot, I felt sure that they had the strength, at least for now, to consider Arthur before themselves because they loved him. I decided it was time to look for Avalon, the Island of Apples. The Fortunate Isle, Taliesin had called it.

'Nature moves in it,' Taliesin said. 'No one ploughs the land or plants the seed. It is self-seeding, self-harvesting. Grain, crops, fruit grow in plenty – the land is lush with grass and shrubs. And the same vitality that flows through the soil and the vegetation courses through the veins of its inhabitants and makes them live more than a century. The island is ruled by nine sisters who are kind and just and they are skilled healers and astrologers. One or more of them is abroad most of the time. You, Morgan, must one day find your place among them.'

But Taliesin never told me the way to Avalon.

'When the time is right,' he murmured, 'it will beckon. Follow the call and you will arrive there safely.'

Well, perhaps the time was not yet ripe when I went looking. At last, after many days I arrived at a ford. The stream slid over water-smoothed rocks and shingle-stones, so clear and so clean that the fish and the foliage could have been growing on the bank. Where the odd rock cluster grew dense and reared its head to the surface, the water foamed and frothed like fresh milk. But what was this? A dark stain spread to the centre of the stream, blotting out the bedstones, soiling the water, reddening the milk. Blood.

I looked round quickly, almost panic-stricken. The water approximately three yards upstream sometimes lapped over the bank, manipulated by a gust of wind or a large shoal of fish, and washed the blood in. I rushed over to look for its source. Was there some creature, human or animal, whom I could help?

I found only corpses. They were the slain bodies of warriors I recognised as Arthur's men. Their faces shone with honour and they had died with their swords drawn, standing. I was used to following my intuition in most matters so I laid down my stick and girded up my skirt. I would cleanse these men in the transparently running waters of the stream. I would wash their blood-sodden garments and make shrouds for them. And I would bury them like the heroes that they were.

I don't know how long I continued my task. I didn't notice when light passed into darkness or how many times night and day played their habitual game of hide-and-seek. I was aware of the occasional rider or walker passing me by and retracing his footsteps, perhaps for fear that he too might meet a gory death. At my hands, perhaps? I didn't blame them. How could they know my arms were tired, my knees bled and my back was bent over with the weight of my lolling head. Still, I washed and I washed and the smear that had alerted me to the mound of bodies was not submerged, for the whole stream was doused red with the blood of martyrs. The blood ran for miles with the swift current. The stones here would be streaked red for evermore. Blood, Taliesin had taught me, like the earth, contained a compound called iron oxide. It would create a natural memorial to the dead heroes.

When at last I stood up and staggered upstream to where the water was still clean, I saw Viviane's image.

'Rest, Morgan,' she whispered, tenderly. 'Your job is well done.'

In the mirror that Viviane held up to me, I saw a ragged, wretched woman, skin darkened with blood, grey hollows under her eyes, raven locks wild around her face and shoulders. Blood on her arms , her clothes, her face. I was the image of darkness, the spectre of death.

'Come in,' Viviane invited. 'Let me ease away your fatigue.'

But just then I heard a sound, looked around, caught a glint of metal.

'Another hero,' I cried wildly, withdrawing my foot before it touched the water. I ran, maddened to the place, threw myself over the armoured body, tugged at his helmet. Suddenly, the body sat up.

'I've been watching you.'

'Watching me?' I was bewildered. Then anger clenched my stomach in an iron grip. 'Who are you?'

'Don't be angry. I'm Urien, a knight of Arthur.'

'And you watched me prepare your fellow knights for their burial and didn't offer me a hand?'

Urien said he was ashamed. He didn't know what I was doing or what kind of creature I was.

'People have been talking these past days about a woman who washes corpses and sings and washes some more. They call her the Washer at the Ford. They say she is a mother, preparing her children for burial. Some said she had slaughtered them herself. I didn't dare interfere.'

I understood now how the haunting and terrible picture I made would caution a sensible man to keep his distance, even if he was a gallant knight. But now, the man lost all caution. He cupped his rough hands around my ravaged face and raised it to his own. His eyes were intense as he stared into mine, silver into jet, grey eyes into black.

'You are beautiful,' he said, looking into my red-rimmed lids, swollen from weeping, the smears of mud on my face. He could embrace the ugly as well as the beautiful. He was my knight.

No man had ever held me like this or spoken to me so intimately. I struggled to remember Viviane's quick evasions and skirtings back and forth from Merlin's fumblings. Nothing came. I was lost. Urien enfolded me in his arms, he soothed back my hair, daubed my face with the water from the stream.

'I love you, woman of magic,' he murmured. 'I want you with me always.'

Was this my destiny? Was I to marry one of Arthur's knights and remain earth-bound for years to come? Was I still so far away from Avalon?

His kisses told me I was.

Urien took me back to his castle. We married and I became Queen of Rheged. But I took a memento of the ford with me. As we walked away after burying the bodies of Urien's fellows, I saw a small raven, little more than a fledgling. He was hurt, and I picked him up and healed him. He flew with me as we rode back to Urien's castle, and with me he stayed.

Owein was born nine months after I met his father. He, too, grew to be a knight. And on his banner was a raven to indicate his descent from my blood. Owein, my son, could well be king one day. Even if Guinevere had given Arthur children, the right of his sisters' children came first. Guinevere did not, after all, have the king's blood running through her veins.

Arthur had developed into a splendid Pendragon. He had succeeded in uniting all the warring factions in England. Peace and prosperity reigned, proving that the king was robust and noble in his own person. But Igraine's legacy was profound in Arthur. He could not see evil unless it was at the other end of a sword. Nor would he be told. Rumours were rife in Arthur's court about the growing passion between Lancelot and Guinevere and though neither had physically betrayed the king, their hearts were treacherous. But Arthur either remained oblivious or turned a blind eye. Whichever the reason, it highlighted his weakness to me. It was time, I knew, to throw a few trials in his path, test his mettle but, most important of all, remind him that in a monarch, alertness meant the difference between life and death. If Arthur did not protect and respect his own honour, he laid the land open to shame. And what disgraced land can preserve its sovereignty? In a few short years of peace, Arthur had forgotten that predators were everywhere, watching, waiting.

My opportunity came soon. Urien was joining Arthur on a hunt about two days' hard riding from his castle, Camelot. Sir Accolon of Gaul, a knight who made no secret of his admiration for me, was to accompany them. As they hunted, I created a hart for them to chase. It dodged and dived, now within their reach, now, like an arrow, flying so far from them they only saw a speck. When at last the hart had led them to the waterside as I planned, Arthur met his mark and killed the animal. All three knights rode up to the creature but before they could pick it up they saw a wonderful ship anchored on the water. Four beautiful women came out of the ship and escorted them in.

I was struck in turns by dismay and triumph. Oh Arthur, a crown doesn't make a king and nor does peace! Haven't you learned that the weight of the crown must remind you to be cautious, enquiring, sometimes aggressive? My illusion beguiled him – he did not yet realise that mirages should be doubted, not pursued.

Arthur was proving to be a peacetime king. He followed the maidens with his men, into a room, richly decorated with brocades and tapestries from the distant East without asking once whose hospitality he was accepting. He shared delicious foods, created to titillate the tastebuds of gods, without once wondering if they might be poisoned. He was entertained by the most glorious musicians and storytellers without suspecting magic or listening for lures. Then he went to sleep in a private chamber without taking precautions to protect himself or his weapons.

I had to try him further – there was no doubt about that.

So the next morning, though my husband Urien awoke safely in Camelot where we had gone to stay, Arthur found himself in the dungeon of a castle belonging to the brothers Damas and Ontzlake. Beside him languished twenty knights none of them strong enough to fight. They told Arthur they were there because they had opposed Sir Damas who refused his brother Sir Ontzlake his rightful share of their inheritance. Arthur promised the men he would ensure their release.

Spoken like a king but conceived like a groom! When my woman went into the dungeon later that morning and offered Arthur the opportunity for release he ran bullishly into a fight without stopping to use his head. Wisdom, I thought, wins more battles than the sword. Wisdom and wit. Arthur had made a grave mistake. He should have known by now that something was amiss. That nothing short of sorcery could have brought him here. But he had not even paused to check if he had Excalibur. I had taken the sword. The first part of this ruse had been intended to ascertain caution and alertness. The king had failed miserably. Now he also failed the test of awareness.

Arthur, Arthur, how will you save England when you can't even save yourself? Years of peace had lulled Arthur's senses, dulled his wit. He revelled in his success and the prosperity of his country. Well, I would have to shake him awake harder than I had expected. Peace was preserved through constant vigilance, not torpor and smugness.

My woman told Arthur she would release him and arm him if he defended Damas in a fight. With no thought for right or wrong, or for his status as sovereign, Arthur agreed on one condition. Damas must release the twenty knights.

'I will duel for you,' he promised the villain. And not a question did he ask about this mysterious knight who waited by the well. What was his name? Why was he obliged to challenge Damas? And, most importantly, was the stranger aware that he was duelling the king and would he like to consider settling his differences without a skirmish? But no, Arthur said nothing. Confident in his past triumphs, he did not cast his mind back over the events of the past hours.

Along with the armour my woman took for Arthur was a sword that looked like Excalibur. But did Arthur inspect it or test it? No, he hung it in his belt and headed off to fight.

It was to Accolon that I sent the real Excalibur, charging him to defend my honour against an armoured knight who would meet him near the well by noon of that day. Later he would have to kill the king himself. Accolon did not balk. Why should he? With Excalibur in his hands, he would be invincible.

There, Arthur! You see what loyalty you engender? Have your knights pledged allegiance to you, or to your magical accoutrement? Watch them, Arthur and watch yourself. This contest may cost your life.

Now Arthur approached Accolon, his visor covering his face. In the distance, Accolon stood up, sword drawn. Excalibur glinted and flashed. Viviane was nearby, trying to signal both knights that trouble was brewing. But neither man was using his mind. Battle lust raged in each, casting the other as a demon to slaughter. Each was possessed with the determination to survive – the fear that makes men so brave that they risk the life they want to protect. Like possessed men, they faced each other, visors down so that neither recognised the other by his face or his armour. Though Accolon had Excalibur, the fight was always Arthur's – that was why Excalibur had come to the king and not to anyone else. But for the first time Arthur tasted its steel. Severely wounded, hardly able to rise, he suspected at last that Accolon had Excalibur.

Then as Arthur paused to recover himself, Accolon made his first mistake.

'I won't be kept waiting,' he growled. 'Get up and fight.'

'You call yourself a knight?' retorted Arthur. 'Do you know the code of honour?'

But Accolon didn't bother to answer. Instead, he dropped his head, held his sword out like a tusk from his chest and rushed for the reclining man.

The king was outraged. Come on, Arthur. Act like a king.

Arthur picked up his false sword, ready for Accolon and as he drew near, he struck him again and again and again in the thigh. Excalibur flew from Accolon's grasp and landed beside Arthur. Arthur struck Accolon again, higher up this time, crushing his helmet to his skull. Then as Accolon's body came to rest beside him, he laid down his sword.

At last, as both lay wounded, Arthur demanded to know Accolon's identity and uncovered my plot.

'Morgan Le Fay,' confessed the dying knight. 'She asked me to do this. She gave me Excalibur. I agreed to kill you because I love her. She promised to kill Urien in his bed and come to me when he is dead.'

'But why does she want me dead?'

The knight could not answer. I had never told him. But he had done his job well. Now my husband Urien would be cleared of treason and regicide. Arthur would think he too was to be my victim.

Bt the trial of kingship was not yet over. Arthur had shown bravery and the ability to protect his person without his magical sword. That augured well for the safety of his kingdom. But would he survive without the scabbard? Because it was said that no one could kill Arthur as long as he wore his scabbard.

I waited for Arthur at Camelot and while I waited, I kept an eye on Guinevere and an ear in Arthur's court. Unease was rife. Guinevere and Lancelot met and spoke and laughed at every excuse. The queen was becoming careless. Her passion for Lancelot was showing. And though lesser queens like myself and all the others were at liberty to entertain men so long as they were discreet, Guinevere as wife of the sovereign overlord could not, because her betrayal would have consequences for the land. She knew this when she married Arthur.

Guinevere knew instinctively that I was watching. Nor did I attempt to conceal my dark glances in her direction. She was a spring creature: her love came and went, gorgeous and fragrant like the little season. She was full of blossom and fanfare, then gone at the prime of youth. As soon as I heard Arthur was returning, I told her I was leaving Camelot. She was relieved.

But I hid myself until Arthur arrived after dark and when he had gone to sleep, I crept into his room. Thankfully, he lay in bed with his sword in his hand. Bravo, Arthur! You are following your instincts. You know danger lurks. But it was not the sword I was after. Swiftly, I released his scabbard from his belt, hid it under my black mantle and sped from the castle. Once again, bravo Arthur. The king was up in a flash and pursuing me nimbly as I fled. Outside, my forty riders were ready with my horse.

By the time Arthur had mustered his men, we were miles ahead. I thrilled and exulted as the horses caught us up. Never had I enjoyed a chase so much. The hooves of the king's horse thundered in my heart as I spurred my steed on, further, faster, fleeter. *And then the transcendent moment. The Dark Woman of Knowledge recognises that she cannot outrun the king. Sooner, rather than later, he will catch her up.*

I rode on, listening for the sound of water. When I found it, still and silent, I hurled the scabbard in as far as I could. If Arthur deserved it, Viviane would return it to him. Meanwhile, the loss would force him to examine his ways, to use his mind, to improve his alertness. Arthur was not yet the perfect sovereign. He had much to learn. And I would make the path of learning as stringent as necessary.

A million sparkling droplets rose from the centre of the lake like a shower of gold as the jewelled scabbard struck the surface of the water. I heard Arthur and his men thunder on to the scene. With a glance, I petrified my men and then turned myself to stone, too.

Arthur watched the transformation and drew the sign of the cross, large, from crown to belly and across his shoulders.

'God have mercy!' he breathed. 'Her treachery has been punished.'

Then, without enquiry or investigation, he ordered his men around and returned home. If only he had ridden forward, looked into my face, he would have seen the contempt on my lips, the conquest in my eyes.

When they had gone, my men and I returned to life. I disbanded them and rode on alone until I found a knight with whom to send Arthur a message.

'Tell Arthur, that as long as I can transform myself and others into stone, I have the upper hand.'

I left some time for Arthur to soak up the message and let its weight show in this thoughts, its measure in his deeds. When his courtiers heard about my magic, they swore I was a witch. Ignorant louts! Some of them even demanded I should be captured and burned at the stake. But Arthur made no attempt to follow their advice. He found it hard to accept that he was in continual danger from me, his own sister. I suspect that his inertia in this direction also came from his conviction that as king, protected by divinity, he was more than a match for any woman – even the Dark Woman of Knowledge. Did he know he was pitting himself against her?

Soon afterwards, my woman walked into his court as bold and bright as day and handed him a gift.

'Morgan Le Fay sends her greetings,' she said. 'She offers you her deepest apologies and would like to make amends in any way you ask. As a first sign of her remorse, she sends you this mantle.'

She lifted the folds of cloth which concealed the magnificent cloak. Its gold and jewels glittered magnificently on the kingly blue ground. Arthur's eyes lit up. How he loved beauty. He stepped down from his throne, arms outstretched, and would have taken it, if he had not been interrupted.

Viviane, the Lady of the Lake, walked in and demanded a private audience with Arthur.

'Don't wear that cloak,' she warned. 'It is lined with acid.' And then she vanished.

Arthur returned to his throne. 'Let me see the mantle.'

My woman held it up.

'Now,' said Arthur, 'put it on.'

'Put it on, my lord?' my woman asked. 'But it is for the king.'

'And I, as king, order you to put it on.'

Without further hesitation, my woman swirled the cloak of jewels around her shoulders and fastened its clasp at her breast. Arthur's eyes glinted. The woman began to turn blue, then fell to the ground. In the shape of her body glowed coals and embers. The cloak and its wearer were immolated.

Finally, Arthur's guard went up. He sent immediate word to Urien telling him that he knew how evil I had become, adding that he knew I was plotting my husband's death along with his own. He knew, therefore, that Urien was no part of my treason. But he expelled Owein from the Round Table because he believed that a knight who bore his mother's raven on his shield must be her defender. I was not anxious for Owein. He had many faithful friends and it would not be long before he was reinstated. All the same, to ensure the safety of my husband and my son, I enacted a brief assassination attempt in which Owein saved Urien from my dagger and I cut myself loose from them both.

Morgan Le Fay became the king's primary enemy. They accused me of the Black Arts though my magic was of the natural kind. They called me a troublemaker and accused me of costing the lives of good knights, and even my own people. But I had my duties as Arthur had his and both required the sacrifice of lives. Neither kings nor the managers of their sovereignty can afford to regret the loss of lives when a greater good is at stake.

Arthur was more vigilant now in matters regarding his person. But how prudent was he in judging those around him? Had the treachery of his own sister alerted him to the possibility of other traitors in his close circle? Was he more attentive to the growing passion of Lancelot for Guinevere? Far from it. Now that I had revealed my hand to him, Arthur was content to charge me with all the evil around him. For Arthur as for Uther, Morgan was the holder of all darkness. But Arthur had to be made aware that he would face havoc if Lancelot and Guinevere could not contain their growing love.

Look around you, Arthur. There are secrets at the Round Table. No one speaks openly any more. Your knights fight each other in the woods and the plains. They agree like Accolon to take up arms against you, like Damas, they deceive their own blood for the sake of possessions. Is this the honour that you promised Viviane? Is this the chivalry for which your court and company became famous? But who knows what blows Arthur had suffered in his life that made him close his mind to discord. My job was to ensure that as king he had the ability to embrace the ugly with the beautiful, hold his country together during the sordid spells as well as the glorious ones. But Arthur could not bear to look at ugliness. He left that to his other knights.

Now those knights were turning renegade. And among them was one called Sir Meliagaunt who had lusted after Guinevere for a very long time. He gazed at her from secret places, stalked her in the wood, crept up behind her in the castle corridors. But Arthur did not notice, while Guinevere, wrapped up in Lancelot, saw no one any more, not even her husband.

May came and with it the lushness of the land, the bursting of blossom, the rush in the rivers as mountain caps thawed and flowed down to the valleys and plains. Guinevere, spring flower, bloomed and blushed and one day woke up and dressed herself all in green. Today she would go out and pick flowers. She would fill up her basket and bring spring to the castle. But Guinevere did not fulfil that morning's dream. For as she reached up her hands to bring the blossom-laden branches lower, buried her face in their scent, breathed in their freshness, she was being watched by Meliagaunt.

Seeing her absorbed, he took his chance, swooped down on her from his horse and carried her to his castle. When Lancelot heard, he set off immediately to rescue his beloved. I observed them. If Lancelot and Guinevere survived this trial of their love, if they managed to remain chaste in this situation, Arthur need never fear damage from them. But in my innermost heart I knew that the goal was an impossible one.

And I was right. When Lancelot took over Meliagaunt's castle, Dolorous Tower, and renamed it the Joyous Guard, I had no doubt which joy he had named it after. Arthur was betrayed by the two people closest to him.

Well, when the days began to shorten and the nights to lengthen, I knew it was time to act once again. If Arthur had failed to take account of what went on now under his very nose at Camelot, then I would have to tell him.

As it happened, his own knights did the deed. Morgawse's stepsons, Sir Agravaine and Sir Mordred of the Orkney clan, could no longer contain themselves. While out on a hunting expedition, they told the king of their suspicions. As always Arthur's first reaction was to protest.

'Lancelot defends us both with his life. He would not disgrace us.'

But Mordred's eyes were fixed on the throne. With Guinevere gone, Arthur would only be half the man he was now. Then Mordred would step in. He insisted that Arthur lay a trap for the lovers and establish the truth for once and all. For himself and for England. So, Arthur told Guinevere he would be out the following night. Guinevere, delighted with the unexpected opportunity, suspected nothing, invited Lancelot to her bed.

How Lancelot's nephew begged him to stay away from Guinevere that night. How he pleaded! But would Lancelot listen? No, he must see Guinevere. He could not let down his lady. He was, after all, a knight. He would go, even if it was simply to tell her he could not stay.

But what lover can bear to cut short his stolen chances? Once Lancelot was in Guinevere's chamber, he stayed. That was when Agravaine and Mordred surrounded them with twelve other knights. Lancelot came out fighting. He killed or wounded most of the knights and Mordred himself was badly hurt. Then he escaped to the Joyous Guard where he kept Guinevere under his protection.

See now Arthur? Do you see how you revelled in false glory? Why have all these knights left you to side with Lancelot? Where is the solidarity and safety which made you so smug? Not only have they gone, bag and baggage, to the Joyous Guard to support Lancelot; they beg and entreat you to receive him again.

Arthur let Lancelot come with Guinevere and with pretty, impassioned speeches. He reminded Arthur how he had served him and swore to defend Guinevere's honour. But Arthur still sent her to the stake. And that was when Lancelot attacked again – this time with the passion not of honour or glory, but of love. He would not let Guinevere die.

The place was chaos. Everyone's arm was a sword, every sword in action. Attacks took place from behind and before. I watched from afar. All this bloodshed, all this disaster. All this to make a king out of a king. Arthur would go like gold through the purging process. But when he came out with all the impurities burned away, would it be too late? Perhaps not. Already there was a wisdom about him that poured like blood from the marriage wound. And he smelt of kingship, of justice and of duty – and most of all, of the awareness that, in the end, a king is always alone. No one shares the sphere of the crown though they may come near the king's person and his throne. Arthur had always dreaded this position but now he accepted it and the glory that shone around him was so clear and bright even I lost my doubts. I infused him with strength. I stood behind him in spirit. I sent him clarity.

The battle continued across the seas where Lancelot sped. Scores of knights were wounded and Viviane was kept hard at work. Then came news of Mordred's treachery. He had announced Arthur's death, and taken over the throne of England.

Immediately, Arthur returned to England.

'If Mordred will return the throne willingly,' he offered, 'I will give him Kent and Cornwall.'

'On condition that Arthur appoints me his heir,' returned Mordred.

A meeting was arranged. Each leader would attend with a few men.

'But,' insisted Mordred, 'at the first sign of an unsheathed sword, there will be trouble.'

As they marched to the meeting point, one of Arthur's men was stung by an adder. The next moment, his sword flashed in the sun, cutting the creature in half. A few yards away Mordred's eye caught the flash. Though he knew that the sword had not been drawn against him, he used the chance to attack. Arthur moved forward, determined to bear the brunt of the fight. Both Arthur and Mordred were mortally wounded. Death did not frighten Arthur but he feared leaving his country in the hands of such a foul man. Die he might, but he would dispense with Mordred first.

He heaved himself up and lunged at Mordred just as he came rushing like a wild boar. The impact of the collision brought them both crashing to the ground. Mordred was dead.

Arthur looked around at his dying men and saw his friend Bedivere.

'Take Excalibur to the lake,' he commanded, 'and throw it in.'

But Bedivere could not make himself obey Arthur until his third command. Then at last I had the chance to go to my brother's side. But some opportunities come too late. If Bevidere had obeyed Arthur at once, the Pendragon might have stayed to rule Britain. As it was, the only way I could save him was to take him away to Avalon. The Isle of Apples, the Fortunate Island. The place of healing. My true home.

I raised my hand and a coracle came towards us. My eight sisters in trade stood in it, hooded in black, wailing and lamenting. My tears flowed and I used them to wipe Arthur's wounds. Tenderly, I carried him over and laid him in the barge. Then I stepped in after him. Away in Avalon, he would be healed and safe, waiting for the call for help. True to his word, he would always fight with the warriors who defended Britain.

My job was done. I had made a king.

How did I find Avalon? You remember that ford where I washed the corpses? Well, if I had stepped into it when Viviane invited me I would have been there then. But I had an earthly life to live. And without me where would Britain have been?

Eve

The trouble with Eve was that she asked too many questions. But they just kept coming, those questions, flooding into her head from a great silvery ocean of chaos, which made her think there must have been something before.

'No,' said Adam, 'this is it. We are the first of God's living creations. He made Eden for us.'

'But then what are these pictures I keep seeing? And these feelings I feel? And these urges which come over me and shake me?'

'Urges.' Adam's eyes shone with lust. 'I feel those too.'

He leaned over and kissed Eve, full on the mouth, and gently stroked her breasts. 'It is quite right that you should feel urges. That was why you were made. Flesh of my flesh, bone of my bones.

Eve pushed him away. Somehow it didn't feel right. Particularly lately, since she kept having flashes of Adam bounding around trying to mate with animals – even plants. And he felt somehow so *new* – as if he had been born out of her rather than the other way round.

'Are you sure,' she demanded, 'are you absolutely sure that it wasn't you who was created from me?'

'Oh not that again,' groaned Adam. 'Wouldn't I have known if you had come first? I remember how I suffered, looking for a mate, here, there and everywhere. It was lonely. I begged God for a mate. So he made you. From my rib, for me and me alone.'

He put his arm around her but she pushed it away and stood up.

'Then why do I feel as if I was here before you? And,' she paused, trying to find the words to express her turmoil '. . . as if I have things to do that I can't get on with?'

'Things to do?' Adam was bemused. 'Things like what? We eat, we wander around Eden, we make love. What else is there?'

'That's the whole point.' Eve was listless. 'I feel as if there are worlds out there waiting to be sampled. And here I am, wasting time, frolicking in the jungle.'

But Adam's eyes glazed over, fearful and dull. Eve longed to discover what Adam's life had been like before she was sent to him. But none of her probing and questioning ever got her anywhere. It was as if he had forgotten everything – everything that was, except the Expulsion. Sometimes Eve suspected that there'd been another woman in his life. But when she raised the subject, Adam got into such a state, flushed, eyes popping and – worst of all – completely mute. So she'd stopped asking him.

Now she pushed away his persistent arm. There must be more to existence than – well – just *existing*.

That night Eve was woken by one of her many dreams. They had been coming to her of late, like memories of another consciousness. She looked at Adam, sleeping deeply beside her. He didn't even know what memories were. Well, not properly, any how. She got up and strolled to the stream. It was her favourite part of Eden. The grass and foliage grew thicker around it and the stream itself made sweet music, changing its rhythm and tone to reflect every movement, every variation in its surroundings. From the morning breeze in which Yahweh the Creator travelled, to the falling of a blade of grass on its surface, to the removal of a palm full of water. Eve loved to play with it. She liked to make a different kind of music; she blew gently, strumming with her fingers on its surface, put her lips to it, braided strands of grass to tickle its surface.

And all the while she did these things, she could see the two trees in the near distance. She could see them clearly as she made water music. What made those two trees different? she wondered. Why were they, of all the plants in Eden, forbidden to her and Adam? The Tree of Life was tall and its foliage was all shades of green from almost black to almost yellow. All manner of life nested in it. And its fruits were manifold. Yet Adam said if they ate any of that fruit, they would die. The other was the Tree of Knowledge. It was quite a small tree with strange leaves which looked as if a great giant hand had come and crushed them all in one squeeze so that they were able to spring back, a little, to their normal state but never quite to perfection. Its fruit was beautiful. It emerged from delicate white blossom and grew round, luscious and crisp as it ripened and blushed a deep, vibrant red. Eve often imagined herself holding an apple. Somehow, she felt it was her fruit. She had fantasies in which she was a leader of people – of worlds, even – and her symbol was the apple. And she carried a sceptre around which was twined a serpent.

Serpent – serpent – serpent. A sibilant resonating sound rustled around her. The stream sang and simmered, its surface sparkling. Serpent.

Eve was entranced. From the top of the Tree of Life she saw a trembling and a shaking, and down slid the movement, down, down, to the lowest branch. Eve was magnetised even before the serpent put out its head and called to her. Its eyes glistened and sparked like a hundred fireworks and she let herself be drawn to it.

'You summoned me, sweet one,' hissed the serpent. 'Now ask me what you want to know.'

'Whatever you can tell me.'

The serpent's laughter was soft but so commanding that Eden seemed to undulate to its rhythm.

'I can tell you about worlds before the first world. I can tell you about a time before time. I can carry you on the twists of my words into prisons of pain so great that they could drown – and have drowned – many worlds. And I can carry you on the stream of story, into pasts, presents and futures that you once knew as your own. But you must be the one to choose.'

'What is a story?' Eve asked, intrigued.

The serpent laughed again. 'An invented memory, a piece of imagination, a fantasised future. The words you speak, the answers you seek. They're all stories.'

'Tell me why I'm so restless? Am I made of Adam or is Adam made of me?'

'Adam is the first of a new race of humankind. The first of a new order of existence. His stories will destroy your stories. But you are right. He is of your *prima materia*. You are the blood that flows in his veins. Yahweh knows but for reasons of his own, he won't say so.'

'Why does Eden weigh on me so?'

'To be oppressed by the oppressive is not surprising.'

'But Adam is happy enough. Why not me?'

'Adam is new. He knows nothing about memory. He has no prior existence.'

'But I sense another presence – a female in Adam's past. I feel her in parts of Eden. Am I wrong?'

'She is Lilith of the beginnings of Sumer. Wiped from Adam's mind. For him you are the first.'

'Tell me about myself.'

'In the past, present or future?'

'The present I know and long to be released from. The future I will discover when I'm free. Tell me about my past.'

'And can you bear the grief that has torn apart worlds?'

'I think I can bear it.'

'Then, Woman, listen to my story. Once there was Tiamat, salt water. She was dark and fluid and she danced and rolled and heaved and swelled, for all of potential was in Tiamat. Her mate was the still, calm Apsu, sweet water. Perhaps lazy, a little selfish, very self-content. For he was the only entity that engaged the full attention of surging, vital Tiamat.

'"I must create," said Tiamat as she gushed ashore, her salt spray mingling with Apsu's sweetness. "I must create," she said as she gushed back, away, into her own depths. "There is too much life in me, too much energy. I must share it. I must pass it on. Apsu, we must procreate."

'So, Tiamat swelled with Apsu's progeny. Her wild surges turned to rhythmic, soporific rolling. Her song of longing became the song of creation. She felt herself filling, expanding, glowing. And she brought forth the elements, the winds, the open spaces. The sky, in turn, fathered Ea who brought the light of wisdom into creation.

'Apsu looked at her contentment and felt the first stirrings of jealousy. Calmness had always been his preserve. Tiamat was the wild one, the unruly one – it was his job to contain her. Without him she would long have dashed her waves into spray, been reduced to a million droplets and laid herself waste. He knew he had made a mistake to give in to her. Apsu felt threatened.

'He hardly spoke to Tiamat any more except to complain how noisy their offspring were. They fell out with each other, fought and clamoured and raised bedlam. Apsu, the father, withdrew completely, cutting himself off from them, swearing to stifle them.

'Silence.

'He wanted silence.

'He brooded and fretted and pondered.

'How could he find a plan to get rid of them and regain his tranquillity?

'He grew so obsessed with recollections of his childless days that he decided to kill his children. The great sky, the throbbing earth, the horizons which separated them.

'"I will kill them all, then sleep in silence and waken in the peace of stillness. I will destroy the noise and the clamour that disrupt my peace. Once again we will be just you and I, Tiamat, sweet water above, salt water below."

'But Tiamat's waters turned dark. Great whirling pools appeared on her surface, sucking from her very core to fill the gaping abyss of fear that Apsu's words opened up inside her.

'"You can't kill them," she dissented, and her command echoed and re-echoed, forcing Apsu to cover his ears.

'"Silence!" he thundered. "The word is spoken, the deed is done."

'Apsu commanded Ea to bring his wisdom to bear on the problem. But Ea knew what Apsu did not, that once created, new beings cannot be controlled even by their Creator. Desire and wilfulness are conditions of life and if the Creator withholds those natural rights, the creatures turn renegade and battle for them. The tales of patricide and regicide are interminable, they are a repeating pattern in the process of creation.'

Eve spoke in a hushed voice. 'So that's what alarms Yahweh. That's why he scares Adam into obedience.'

The serpent nodded sagely. 'But unless he rebels, Adam will never be anything but Yahweh's plaything. Rebellion is his only password to new worlds full of experience and fulfilment.'

'And strife?'

'Strife? Strife completes existence. It offers something to motivate and conquer. Without strife there's neither victory nor glory. But let me continue my story.

'Ea, the essence of wisdom, spoke to Apsu. Words so sweet that he fell asleep, lulled by their music, rocked by their charm, into a deep, deep slumber. He sank beneath the waters of his own substance, merging, dissolving, never to awaken, eternally peaceful. And thus in the same act, Ea granted Apsu his dearest desire and also saved his kin.

'But Tiamat was distraught. She had lost her twin half. Her male element. Her grounding soul. Without Apsu she knew no boundaries, she was cut loose, turned wild, left to her own resources. She battered against her shores, rose in great breakers, grieving, heaving almost to the sky, dashed herself against herself, then, in sheer exhaustion, fell still.

'Above, from Apsu's space, dressed in royal regalia – the cloak of glory, the crown of splendour snatched from his father's corpse – Ea watched and bided his time. He built himself a sacred palace, married, reared magnificent Marduk – God, Hero and Divine Saviour of Babylon. He would one day defend Ea's people against Tiamat.

'Ea was wisdom and he knew that as Tiamat lay stilled by her grief, her potency grew. If she rose in revenge against him, he and his supporters would have no quarter. So he created the mighty tornado and the four winds of power and sent them to torment Tiamat.

'"Invade the Oldest One," he commanded. "Goad her and bait her into a frenzy. We will be ready to beat her back and subdue her for ever. Mighty Marduk has been reared to defeat her."

'So the tornado entered Tiamat's belly and whirled and burrowed until the world was filled with a wild moaning and groaning as she rolled and thrashed about in agony. When the storm winds tortured the rest of her children too, Tiamat knew it was time to retaliate. But to rise as the massive salt ocean would be unfair. Not even Marduk could withstand the force of the flooding ocean in all its grandeur. Instead, Tiamat created eleven ferocious battle monsters. Poison ran through their veins instead of blood and they stood facing the skies, created to fight, unable to turn back until either they or their foe were dead. And Tiamat, the Primeval Mother, stayed in her bed.

'Up in the skies, the ruling gods heard news of the activity on the ground. The consellor supreme of the synod bowed his head, slapped his thigh, bit his lip in distress. A powerful groan welled up from deep within him and he covered his mouth with both hands to stifle it. He knew his mother. He knew she would never harm her children unless driven. He knew there was not a god who could defeat her in single combat. He summoned Ea.

'"Not one of us can defeat the tempest power of Tiamat. Go to her, use your wisdom and the power of reason. She is a mother, she will be persuaded. Offer her words of comfort, offer her plans of peace, offer her your apology. Placate her, Ea. That is our only hope."

'"I trapped Apsu with the melodious air of my knowledge. I will enmesh Tiamat's fury in the sweet nets of the principles of peace and harmony. I will calm her. Trust me."

'So Ea set off, full of confidence. But when he saw Tiamat in the distance, a dark, writhing mass behind her troops, he retreated, cowering.

'"I am no match for Tiamat, the tempestuous crone. I can't confront her."

'One after another, Ea's warriors refused to face Tiamat. But Marduk came to his father Ea, his four eyes glaring in different directions. Lightning played around his head and sparks flashed from his tongue as he spoke. He was a being to defeat all monsters. The most powerful hero of all. Reared to destroy Tiamat. Marduk's time had come. And in return for the kingship, he agreed to fight Tiamat.

'Seven winds helped Marduk to mount his chariot drawn by the four steeds – Slayer, Ruthless, Crusher and Speed. The hurricane was his lieutenant. At last he was ready to face unarmed Tiamat. Surrounded by the gods, he terrorised Tiamat's monster hordes and godly troops until at last he stood face to face with the raging goddess herself.

'"So it's you they hide behind now," she bellowed, churning and crashing. "The fruits of my womb and Ea, the killer of my husband. They send you to fight me, cloaked in their collective powers, armed with wind and storm and metal."

'"You chose war, witch, not I," thundered Marduk.

'"No," snarled Tiamat. "It was you who chose war. I merely accepted the challenge."

'Marduk's people bowed their heads. They knew they had provoked war. They knew they had ratified it.'

Eve interrupted. 'Who was right?'

'There's no right and no wrong,' hissed the serpent. 'Just a cause to effect action. Marduk was more heroic than wise. He challenged Tiamat, charging her to fight him alone, one to one, in single combat. Tiamat arose, reduced herself to a tangible shape, and faced Marduk, ready for a fair fight.

'But Marduk – he unleashed the hurricane and his team of four ferocious horses. He rallied the seven winds and commanded them to infiltrate Tiamat's body and awaken the tornado inside, to confuse and distract her. And as they entered her Tiamat gasped.

'Immediately Marduk commanded: "Enter her gasp!" As the hurricane blustered into her open mouth, holding it agape with his body, Marduk shot an arrow into her stomach. The arrow tore Tiamat's bowel; her womb, the birth place of Marduk's ancestors, was split apart. As she began to lose consciousness, Marduk, the hero, battered her head with his mace. He gashed her veins with his daggers, so that the blood gushed like maddened breakers from Tiamat, the source of all creation, to the four corners of the universe. It collected in places that were hidden even from the gods.

'Then Marduk looked down at his trophy, the corpse of Tiamat's dragon-like incarnation, and he swelled with pride. He had brought the source of creation to his feet. He was the bravest, strongest man. He reflected how he might use it to glorify himself even further. Then he remembered – he was a god now, supreme king of the skies – he had the power to create.

'"I will create a world," he announced. "And it will be the centre of the cosmos. I will call it Babylonia."

'So he broke the corpse of Tiamat in two. He hurled the top half up where it filled the empty Heaven and formed the huge sky-arch. He flung the nether half below, making a basin to hold and sustain the ocean, bind it for ever so that the newly created earth could contain its waters. Then he built himself a palace and placed his male relatives in the most powerful positions.

'And now, they all told themselves, they were the creators of the world and Tiamat the principle of evil and destruction. Thus were born the notions of Good and Evil. And these were attached, in turn, creation to the first and destruction to

the last. Tiamat is remembered to this day as the poison
dragon slain by a mighty hero to deliver the world.'

Eve was so deep in thought, she hardly realised when the
story ended on the serpent's tongue to continue in her mind. It
pulsated like small shocks in her body, as if events like it had
occurred many times in her own life. She felt the hot sensation
of rage, of being violated.

'But how is destruction measured?' she wondered, oblivious
of the serpent's gaze. 'Is Tiamat evil because she tried to save
her children? Tiamat was the power of Good, her enemies
were the killers, the destroyers.'

'Is that how you see it?' the serpent was cryptic.

'That is how I see it.' Eve was unequivocal. 'Am I right?'

'I don't know right or wrong,' said the serpent, 'I merely tell
stories.'

'But don't forget, it was from Tiamat's *prima materia* that
the world was made,' the serpent reminded her quietly. 'She
was creation. She remained creation. But how often words
alter realities.'

Eve could not bring herself to talk to Adam about her
encounter with the serpent. She knew he was not capable of
listening as she had listened. And he would condemn her and
call her blasphemous for saying that the cosmos was created
before Yahweh's Seven Days. Adam was not the son who could
kill his father. He was not the creation that could challenge his
Creator. He quaked with fear at the mention of Yahweh – and
yet he professed to love him. So Eve rummaged around,
instead, to find out about this strange spell he seemed to be
under.

'What is the first thing you remember properly about
Yahweh?'

'I remember when he lifted me, a handful of clay, and fashioned me into the perfect creature I am now,' exclaimed Adam,
his face shining.

'Then you existed before he formed you from the clay!'

Adam blanched. 'I did not! Yahweh formed me from the clay,
blew life into me. That was how I came to be. That is when I

began to breathe. Thought and knowledge came afterwards.'

'But you said you remember when he lifted you.'

Adam was bemused. 'I made a mistake,' he said. 'I simply meant his touch made me feel alive.'

'Before you were formed?'

'Eve, Eve,' protested Adam, holding her by the shoulder. 'You were not made to think. You were made to mate.'

Eve covered his hands with hers, stilled them. 'He frightens you, doesn't he?'

'I love him.'

'He frightens you, Adam. You don't even dare to look at the two trees, much less touch them.'

Adam cringed.

'What can he do to you, Adam? What will he do, that could be so bad?'

'We won't be immortal any more, Eve. We'll die if we eat the fruit of those trees.'

'Die? Is dying any worse than living in a celestial game where we are the toys?'

'Eve! Be quiet! Yahweh will hear.' He covered her mouth with his hand.

Eve shook it off, walked a little way, turned and looked at him. Their eyes met and she held his. Adam could not bear the pity in hers.

'Adam, what did he do to you? What did you see that has frightened you so much?'

'You haven't seen his wrath,' whispered Adam, his tears beginning to flow, 'when Satan disobeyed him.'

'Tell me.'

Adam was shaking now. He slumped to the ground and Eve put her arms around him, soothing him, stroking his hair.

'Tell me.'

'When he had finished creating me, he gathered all the angels around him and asked them to admire his handiwork. This marvel I was, this man, formed to perfection in every limb. Then he turned to them, his first created beings, and commanded them to bow to me.'

Adam stopped, trembling. Great, racking sobs came from his body. But Eve's fingers soothed him, raking his hair, trailing over his skin, working soft soothing magic that lulled him.

'The angels were startled at first, but they did not hesitate to obey Yahweh. They bowed – each one of them – except Satan.' He paused, his eyes staring, insane with the images of the moment. 'For an instant, a single pulse, the world held still in the resounding drumbeat of Yahweh's anger. It was as if the reverberation would consume us in its still, infinite sound. That fear! I hope I never have to experience that fear again. But worse followed. Yahweh commanded Satan again "Bow to the Man!" But Satan didn't move.'

Eve tensed, riveted.

'And there was that still drumbeat again. We were deafened with its crashing, feeling we would all explode inside. Then a frenzied wind seemed to rip the world apart. And Yahweh said those terrible words. "Cast him out. Let him fend for himself." He drove Satan away from him for ever,' Adam ended on a sob. 'He's out there, somewhere, away from the grace of Yahweh, wandering lonely, no friends, no companions – but worse, dispossessed for ever of Yahweh's love.'

'Does anyone know where he is?'

'That would be unbearable,' gasped Adam.

'How do you know that?' demanded Eve. But she knew what Adam's answer would be and mouthed it with him.

'Yahweh said so.'

'He may be separated from Yahweh, but he can do what he likes now. He can create his own game, like Yahweh. He is the player, like Yahweh himself, not a pawn like you or I.'

'Shut up, Woman!' commanded Adam, shaking with terror. 'Or we, too, will lose the protection of Yahweh.'

'But don't you see, Adam, if we lose Yahweh's protection, we gain our own world?'

This was too much for Adam. His arm flashed out and he struck Eve. She fell back against a rock. A tremor ran through her, another memory. A curly beard, yellow-gold. A man chasing her, striking her. That same fury she had felt before . . . then nothing.

She raised herself from the ground, wiped the blood from her forehead, rubbed it on the foliage as she passed. She made her way, resolute, to the stream. She had to find the serpent. It was the only one she could speak to. She felt it had always been her companion and she was not surprised to find it waiting. It saw her coming and writhed down from its perch on the Tree of Life. And before her eyes, it enacted its miracle. Slowly, patiently, it twisted and turned until it sloughed off its skin and emerged from it, shiny and new.

'How do you do that?' breathed Eve, fascinated.

'It is part of the mystery of renewal.'

The mystery of renewal? From the distant past, images flashed through Eve's mind. Grains of corn and wheat. Human bodies. All being buried, mourned, then falling into a great earthly cauldron, rotting, splitting, decaying, reintegrating with the soil, then as the sun warmed the earth and their substance in it, reforming and growing again. The mystery of the cycle of life. The serpent was a visible symbol of that, sloughing its dead skin and renewing itself, just as the harvested or dead plant went to seed and grew again. That was life's mystery. But where was the room for this miracle in Eden?

'I see things sometimes . . . do they come from the past or the future? Did they happen? Am I inventing them? Can you tell me?'

The serpent smiled, encouraging. 'Tell me.'

'I sometimes see a beautiful woman. Numinous, larger than life. Goddess of life, Goddess of crops. Her people are conquered by a golden-haired race with war in their eyes and their limbs. They are ruled by a god called Zeus – rescued from his mother's womb to kill his own father. I see this god chasing the Goddess, grabbing her. His penis is hard against her even before he throws her to the ground. He bears down on her.'

Eve clenched her eyes and hugged herself tightly as if

pushing away an assailant. 'I'll not be defeated by him. I'll not submit to him.'

She pulled her knees up close to her womb and kicked out with all her strength. 'He recoiled for an instant and I dragged myself out from under him. But he won't give up. His penis is still erect. My resistance excites him. I turn myself into a stone. But before the metamorphosis is complete, he ejaculates on my leg.'

Eve was shaking when she opened her eyes. 'I felt as if it was happening to me.'

'I heard.'

'Did I imagine it?'

'The place is Phrygia, the woman is Cybele, Magna Mater, Goddess of Anatolia. It was Zeus' way to subdue women through rape. When a mother is conquered, her children, too become slaves. When a male child is born he is believed to perpetuate his father's nation. And so the old nation is muffled in the blood of the new.'

'But I did not give in. I wasn't conquered.'

'You didn't. Great religions revolved around Cybele and she was worshipped in many names. The Weeping Mother, she who married her son only to sacrifice him to be born again and again as the Child of Grain – to bring light and food to her people.'

Eve was curled into a ball now, shivering and sobbing as if she would never stop.

'Remember!' commanded the serpent. 'Try to remember.'

Eve shook her head violently. 'No! I can't.'

'You can. This is your present. If you can remember the essential truth, you will have the answers to the questions that plague you.'

After several moments, Eve looked up, blinded by her surroundings by what she could see in her memory. Occasionally, as she remembered something, her body would convulse.

'That was me! And I came back to be a mother again. I knew it. I knew I had a function other than to splay my legs for Adam. I knew that he came from me and not I from him.'

The serpent chuckled. 'And it was not so long ago that you felt you knew the present.'

Eve stood up, swaying a little from the weight of the memories she had released. There were questions still to be answered. Questions her dreams kept asking. She meandered back to Adam, choosing the route which kept her close to the stream the longest. She thought carefully: what could she tell him, what must she keep from him?

Adam was still asleep when Eve returned. She looked at him affectionately. New man, fashioned from clay, you don't have the profound and ancient wisdom of the past. And probably, you never will. I will love you and support you but until you recognise my worth, accept the shades and contrasts in me, you'll never be worthy of me.

As she lay by Adam's side, Eve floated in and out of dreams. She saw a wounded man, dragging himself along until he reached a temple shaped like a tower, tall, narrow and built on a hill.

'Ninhursag!' he called, 'Goddess. Come heal me, I beg you. I am wounded and you are the only one who can help.'

A woman came down from the highest tower, answered the door.

'It is you, Ea. You say you're hurt? Show me your wound.'

Ea, wisdom, pointed to his wound. Ninhursag inclined her head, scanning it with her all-seeing gaze, examining it carefully.

'I see now. You are badly wounded. Only one person can mend this wound. Nin-Ti.'

Ninhursag raised her arms high above her head and chanted the words to summon Nin-Ti, Lady of Life, nicknamed the Lady of the Rib – for wasn't it she who amused herself by entering the wombs of women to fashion babies from the bone of their ribs?

Nin-Ti came, swaying and coquettish. 'Let me see you, Ea. Let me see how I can help you.'

Eve knew her form, she recognised her voice but her face was obscured. She strained her eyes trying to see beyond the shadow of the veil.

Then Eve sat bolt upright remembering. Nin-Ti had pulled a rib from Ea and used it to fashion a new leg for him! She prodded Adam to wake him.

'It wasn't his idea, you know. Yahweh wasn't the first to think of using a rib to fashion mankind. Nin-Ti did it centuries before you were ever thought of. Yahweh stole her idea!'

She chewed her lip, thinking hard. Beyond the shadow – the face. She screwed up her eyes. It was! It was her own face.

'He probably wasn't even invented then,' she announced. 'I was there and we had never even heard of him. Unless, of course, he's one of the others come back as Yahweh just as I am the primeval essence . . .'

'Blasphemous woman, you'll bring disaster on both of us with your profane talk. Yahweh was the first, the pre-eminent soul. There was no one before him, none equal to him. He is the supreme life-source. Offend him and we both die.'

'And what is this terror you have of dying? Do you know what death is? Have you experienced it? Just because Yahweh tells you it's terrible, you shiver at the mention of it. The terrors of death are just myths, spread to frighten people into obedience. Death is the gateway to another existence. At worst it is oblivion. Surely, that is better than this oppressive place, this life of fear that we live in Eden.'

Adam put his hand over Eve's mouth. How she hated the gesture: it muzzled her, tyrannised her. She struggled and bit, scratched and clawed until Adam stepped back. Eve began to run. Adam ran after her.

'Come back here, Woman,' he called. 'Where are you going?'

The animals and birds heard them shouting, saw them coming.

'All is not well in Eden,' they said, shaking their heads. 'Eve has fallen under an evil influence. Adam had better watch out.'

Adam caught up with her and seized her elbow.

'Where are you going?'

'To see my friend.'

'I am your friend.'

'You?' Eve spat the word as if she was declining some hideous-tasting poison. 'What do you know about me? You are a prisoner – a puppet who dances to Yahweh's twitches. You have no will, no goal – you're not my friend.'

'Who is this friend?'

'The serpent.'

'I don't think I know him.'

'You don't. The serpent is an ancient creature who has seen many worlds created and destroyed. In its coils is the complete record of all creation. There are words in its minds which give shape to chaos. It has spoken some of those words to me and I am beginning to understand.'

'It is a bad influence on you,' Adam said, picking up the whispering of the animals and birds. 'It is an agent of Satan. Don't you see it wants to corrupt you in its battle against Yahweh?'

Eve shook her head impatiently. 'The serpent has no battle with Yahweh. Come with me, Adam. Listen to it speak. It doesn't judge, it doesn't lay down the law. It merely tells stories. This is your chance to break Yahweh's spell.'

But Adam pulled away from Eve. Horror-struck by her words, mortified that Yahweh's wrath would be visited upon her, he let her go. He would sit by the sunflowers and reason with her – if she returned.

The serpent was waiting when Eve arrived, alerted by the commotion of her disagreement with Adam.

'I knew you'd come,' it said. 'A pity you couldn't persuade Adam. It could have done him good. Who knows, if he has any potential left for memory, it might have been helped by listening.'

'He said you were an agent of Satan.'

'Am I an agent of Satan?'

'What if you are? You've returned some of my past to me. You've reassured me that I am not insane, that my memories are real.'

'Some would define these as Satanic acts. In some of the worlds yet to be created, the dissemination of knowledge will be forbidden, as it is here in Eden. For knowledge brings power. And the ambition and capabilities of humankind are boundless.'

'And is that a bad thing?'

'I've told you before. I do not differentiate between good and bad, I merely record events. And I know that it is easier to retain control when people lack knowledge.'

'Why is Yahweh so afraid? Why can't he protect us from the deathly fruit?'

'Deathly?' hissed the serpent and it laughed so much its silvery coils slithered beneath it, falling this way and that. 'Apples won't kill you. Yahweh might.'

Eve was troubled.

'You might see things more clearly if I tell you a tale of the future – a tale of destruction that will change Yahweh's dealings with his creatures.

'Imagine Yahweh a thousand years from now – looking down on the word. Far, far from Eden in a world peopled with a race of creatures born of you and Adam. And this world is filled with people who lie and cheat and lack respect for each other. They are violent and kill each other at the least provocation. Life is cheap. Now, Yahweh is sickened by their behaviour and decides to destroy the entire race and the earth with it. He looks down to see if anyone can redeem them – and he remembers Noah, a good man compared to the rest. So he instructs Noah to build an ark and enter it with his entire family. They are to take with them a pair of every species of animal, bird, reptile, insect and other life form. When it is all done and Noah and his family are safely inside, along with all the animals and others, Yahweh opens the windows of the sky and the downpour begins. Now he moves the portal that closes the yawning maw of the Great Abyss and lets the waters flow with such torrents and wild gushing, that the earth is soon submerged.

'But as the waters pour and swell the ark rises too, always on the surface, bobbing rakishly as the waters lash around it. And everyone and everything inside is safe and dry. Believe me, it is all that is dry in the world for a year and a day. When the rain eases, Noah sends out a raven to check if the downpour has stopped, but it does not return. So he sends out a dove and she returns to say the earth is beginning to dry.

'Then Noah tells his family to release the animals and come out of the ark. "Mate together and fill the earth with your kind," Noah instructs them as he says goodbye. And Yahweh speaks to Noah and his family.

'"Go forth and multiply," he says, "and people the earth again."'

'Then God looks at the earth, fresh and new and sweet and instead of rejoicing, he is filled with grief for the destruction he has wreaked. He vows that he will never again exterminate humankind *en masse*, like this, nor will he devastate the earth.

'I suppose now that you will ask if Yahweh is good or evil and I will have to answer yet again that I do not distinguish good and bad for I have learned never to judge. But Eve, has this story brought you any closer to what you are seeking?'

'I know now that destruction and evil are sometimes a necessary part of life. Evil is as empty a word as good. Still, Yahweh uses it to his advantage. Perhaps, like Tiamat, I must for now accept the mantle of evil. But later I'll be accepted for who I am.'

Eve knew now she wanted knowledge more than anything else in her life. She stood up and walked resolutely to the Tree of Knowledge. She reached above her head, closed her eyes and clasped both palms firmly around the apple that hung over it. She pulled it off with a jerk that made the branches and leaves shudder.

She ran up and down the stream, looking for Adam, calling to him until she found him lying in a terrified heap, beneath a bush.

'Don't leave me ever again, Eve,' he begged, sobbing like a child. 'I can't bear to be alone again. I thought you'd gone.'

'Gone? Where?'

'I don't know, away. With your friend the serpent.'

Eve crouched on her haunches and gripped Adam's shoulder. 'Look, Adam, I've decided to eat an apple.'

Adam gawped, recoiling. 'The Forbidden Fruit.'

Eve nodded. 'Yes. I've got one here. I'm going to eat it, now. And you can too, if you like.'

Adam hesitated.

'I think it would do you a great deal of good,' Eve insisted. 'You'd get to know so much more than you do now.'

'But,' gibbered Adam, afraid, 'I don't want to die.'

'You won't die. Well, not for a very long time, anyway. You'll just find out about things. Without knowledge there's nothing.'

Adam's eyes lit up with the first spark of rebellion. 'Do you think I should?'

'Yes, I do.' Eve bit into the apple. It was crunchy and sweet and it made all of her tingle. Adam saw drops of its juice glisten on her chin.

'It didn't kill you.' He held out his hand.

'It didn't.' She held out hers.

The apple passed from her hand to his.

He bit.

Suddenly, he knew what Eve had been talking about.

Then Adam and Eve noticed their bodies and felt the urge to cover bits of them. They reached up and pulled the leaves of a fig tree nearby.

There was a huge lightning clap, followed by a thunderous bellow from Yahweh.

'Here it comes,' said Adam, holding on to Eve. 'The Fall.'

'We'll have a world of our own,' exulted Eve. 'And we'll fill it with the human race.'

'What's that?'

'Your children.'

Adam thought a moment. Then he looked at Eve. She was so beautiful and wonderful and exciting.

'You know what?' he said. 'He's not going to be angry long. Right at this very moment, he's stitching some animal hides together to clothe our bodies. They'll keep out the weather and they're far more effective than these silly fig leaves.'

Notes

Lilith

I found Barbara Black Koltuv's *The Book of Lilith* (Nicolas-Hayes, New York, 1991) invaluable during my research for this story.

Lilith is one of the most powerful archetypes of evil to be found – chthonic, terrifying and ever-present. She represents death for children, sex-slavery and sexual abuse for men. In fact she is the ultimate threat and taunt to men and everything manly. For women she is presented as the ultimate, invincible rival. The creature they never want to be – or in Jungian terminology, the Shadow.

Melusine

Katharine Briggs' *A Dictionary of Fairies* (Penguin Books, Harmondsworth, Middlesex, 1997) contains the blueprint for my version here. Melusine's whole life was a punishment for ousting her father. But Melusine suffered at the hands of her own mother. Women in a patriarchal set-up often internalise oppression and the men in this tale prove to be unequal to the challenge of living with an unusual woman.

Sheba

I owe a great deal to both Barbara Black Koltuv's *Solomon and Sheba: Inner Marriage and Individuation* (Nicolas-Hayes, New York, 1993) and Jacob Lassner's *Demonising the Queen of Sheba: Boundaries of Gender and Culture in Postbiblical Judaism and Medieval Islam* (University of Chicago Press, London, 1993). Both contain stories of the Queen of Sheba garnered from legend, and various religious sources including, of course, the Bible and the Koran, but also the lesser known *Kebra Negest* (The Ethiopic Book of Kings) and the Aramaic interpretation of the Bible, known as *Targum Sheni*.

Medea

The story here is substantially based on Euripides' eponymous play. Today when women find out about their husbands' affairs, they shred their men's most expensive shirts or give away their vintage wine. Medea's revenge was somewhat more lethal – but she was no worse than the many kings in history and legend who killed and tortured for their own gain. Incidentally, the only source for Medea's killing of her brother is a one-liner from Cicero to the Senate. He offers no evidence, simply allegations. The charge that she killed her sons is also a bit dubious. There is a theory that in order to shift blame away from themselves, the Corinthians paid Euripides to concoct a charge of child-killing against Medea herself.

Medea went on to marry and abandon Aegeus, win back her father's favour and eventually rule Colchos. After that she decided to pass on to the Elysian fields where she became a deity called Angitia.

Granya

My story is based on Lady Gregory's magnificent telling in *Gods and Fighting Men* (Colin Smythe, Gerrards Cross, 1970)

first published in 1904. Granya is sometimes called the Celtic
Eve.

Lamia

Lamia's myth is fragmentary in Greek sources. We know little
beyond the fact that Zeus impregnated her several times and
Hera killed her children out of jealousy, then drove her mad
and chased her out of Greece into Libya. Some myths say
Scylla the sea monster is her daughter.

Katharine Briggs' *Dictionary of Fairies* gives intriguing
information about her existence beyond the Greek myth. In
Europe, she is accused of killing children and therefore
becomes a 'nursery-bogey'. But she is also described as a suc-
cubus who tempts men in the guise of a young an beautiful
woman.

Morgan Le Fay

Morgan Le Fay, Fata Morgan, was of course a goddess. I have
reconstructed her story from sources including the standard
Arthurian texts, Geoffrey of Monmouth's *Vita Merlini*,
Thomas Malory's *Le Morte D'Arthur* and various fragments.
Legend treated Morgan badly – but that has not stopped her
being an intriguing character.

Eve

Eve is the first mother of the Christian world but there were
many others before her and she shares some of their qualities.
The gender battle resounds through all their stories and so
does the process of demonisation. Tiamat, the Creator goddess of the Akkadian *Enuma Elish*, changes from loving
progenetrix to a hideous, poison-spitting dragon while Cybele
provides the blueprint for the 'devouring/castrating mother'.